2855

✓

MAY    2001

D0992017

# A STAR TO SAIL BY

G·K
Hall
&Co.

This Large Print Book carries the
Seal of Approval of N.A.V.H.

# A STAR TO SAIL BY

## SUSAN DELANEY

**G.K. Hall & Co. • Thorndike, Maine**

Published in 2000 by arrangement with Signet, a division of Penguin Putnam, Inc.

G.K. Hall Large Print Core Series.

The text of this Large Print edition is unabridged. Other aspects of the book may vary from the original edition.

Set in 16 pt. Plantin by Minnie B. Raven.

Printed in the United States on permanent paper.

**Library of Congress Cataloging-in-Publication Data**

Delaney, Susan.
  A star to sail by / Susan Delaney.
    p.  cm.
  ISBN 0-7838-9011-7 (lg. print : hc : alk. paper)
    1. Time travel — Fiction.  2. New Jersey — Fiction.  3. Sailors — Fiction.  4. Widows — Fiction.  5. Large type books.  I. Title.
  PS3554.E114137 S83   2000
   813'.6—dc21                                             00-025702

For Sammy

*I must go down to the seas again, to the lonely*
   *sea and the sky,*
*And all I ask is a tall ship and a star*
   *to steer her by,*
*And the wheel's kick and the wind's song*
   *and the white sail's shaking,*
*And a grey mist on the sea's face and*
   *a grey dawn breaking.*

   — John Edward Masefield (1878–1967)
   "Sea Fever," 1902

# CHAPTER 1

I once daydreamed of being at my husband's funeral, elegant in a stylish black dress and stockings, and a hat with a veil whose mesh hid my tear-filled eyes. Maybe at one time or another all the women of my generation, influenced by the grace of Jackie Kennedy, have had this same vision come to mind. I certainly never expected to be a widow while still in my twenties, and the guilt at remembering this forethought was only one more drop of water in my ocean of emotional pain. You see, I loved my husband beyond words, and, in an instant, he was gone.

Peter and I had been married four years, and now he'd been gone nearly two. I had yet to really pick up my life. I'd discouraged contact with nearly everyone with whom I'd daily associated, so that, where I'd once had a comforting circle of friends and colleagues, I was now intentionally alone most of the time. One by one, my friends had given me up as a lost cause, tired perhaps of being repeatedly rebuffed or ignored. I'd consistently declined enough invitations since Peter's death that they'd eventually, much to my relief, petered out pretty much altogether. This lack of personal communication seemed like a mercy to me, as no one knew what to say anyway. It had been painful listening to these generally confident people trying unsuccessfully to sound up-beat, avoiding mention of the one name that was never far from my thoughts.

I'd stopped, too, doing many of the things I'd once loved — planning and tending my little terraced garden, adding to my various collections of old textiles, books, and literary-related knick-knacks, reading for the pure pleasure of it. I'd dropped all but the most necessary correspondence, though I'd formerly been a great one for writing long eclectic letters, something that Peter had teased me about good-naturedly from time to time. Even the activities that I'd maintained — swimming, running on the beach — had become solitary pursuits now that Peter was gone.

I had, over time, packed or given away most of Peter's personal things; I had finally even stopped sleeping with his Yankees cap under my pillow. But I lived in fear of forgetting little things — the sound of his voice, a certain expression he would make when he was puzzled, the way he absentmindedly brushed his hair off his forehead with his hand. My mother, and my sister, Marjorie, urged various therapies on me — work, shopping, evening classes — but part of my soul seemed to have gone missing.

After you've heard a poignant song a hundred times, it loses its power to move you. I thought Peter's death would be like that, that each tear spent would diminish the ache. I found, to my dismay, that this was not so. Daily I felt like shouting at the world, "Don't you understand? My husband is dead!" I wanted to cram my pain down someone's throat; but, rant at the world as I may, I more and more sought no one's company but my own.

With Peter I had come to expect happiness, not through having earned it, but as one expects at each breath to find sufficient air. Sleep I had also taken for granted, and now I often found that respite a difficult commodity to come by. And though I often wished for the end of a particularly long night, still I had to force myself to get up morning after morning, to face yet another day without Peter.

On one such hopeless morning, as the insensitive sun rose in all its glory out of the sea, I made myself go through the motions of starting the day and found myself clean and dressed at the kitchen table with a cup of coffee in my hand. It was hard to believe that I had once greeted the day with a spring in my step and a million things on my agenda, most of them worth looking forward to. It might have been easier, I thought as I took a drink of coffee without really tasting it, if I hadn't been so keenly aware at the time of just exactly how good I'd had it.

I don't know how long I'd been sitting there, unfocused and numb, when a knock was immediately followed by the opening of the door. It could only be my sister; everyone else knocked and waited, or simply entered. For some reason she always did both.

I had often thought my sister pretty, but I hardly took notice of her face. I was vaguely aware that she wore a jacket and skirt that looked both stylish and professional.

"New suit?" I asked in what I know was the dull apathetic voice that had appeared just as the crying phase had ended and had been my trademark ever since.

"I've only had it close to a year. You must have seen me wear it a dozen times."

"Sorry," I said, but I wasn't. It was just a meaningless word. I certainly felt nothing.

My sister fixed herself a cup of coffee and sat down. I could feel her looking at me, so I reluctantly took my eyes off the dregs in my cup.

"Bill and I are going to try a new restaurant Friday night. Why don't you come with us?" she asked.

"Marjorie, you know I just don't feel up to it."

"Peggy, it's been almost two years. All the experts say that the mourning process takes about two years. You should be about ready to get your life together again. You're young! You should be out having fun — going places with your friends, having new experiences."

"Peter's still dead."

"And he always will be, Peggy. But you're not."

"Really? How can you tell?" I said as I picked up my cup and carried it to the sink.

"Friday night. How about it?" Marjorie repeated.

When I ignored her, she changed her tack.

"Have you written anything lately?"

I shook my head. For the first year after Peter died, I didn't work at all. In the second I produced a manuscript that was uncharacteristically dark and savage, and my agent begged me to hold off for six months before deciding to release it. It would probably sell as well as any of my other books, but since they're all part of a series, and in this latest one I killed off one of my main characters . . . well, I guess I could understand why she wanted to wait. It wasn't exactly what she'd had in mind when she'd repeatedly urged me to get back to work. I knew, intellectually, that I should be worrying whether or not my career as a writer of fiction wasn't, in effect, over now, but the nagging feeling that used to hang at the periphery of my consciousness whenever I let too much time pass without writing, or at least jotting down notes about my characters' next adventure, was now dormant.

"Peggy," Marjorie began, interrupting my thoughts. I could tell by the hesitation in her voice that I wasn't going to like what followed. "There's a new attorney at the office. I think you might like him."

"No, thank you."

"It's time you started thinking about seeing people."

"You mean men."

"Yes, I mean men! I don't think it's too early for you to start dating." I shook my head, and she continued before I could cut her off. "I know it's a bit of a jungle out there. But there *are* some nice guys, and you won't find them sitting around here."

"Listen, I appreciate your interest and your concern. It's not a question of being ready. What I had with Peter was once-in-a-lifetime stuff. No one finds *two* perfect matches in her life. Hell, most people never come close to finding *one*."

"Peggy, you're my sister, and I love you. I hate to think of you alone in this house for the rest of your life. It always was like a museum in here with all your old flea market junk, but now it's like a mausoleum. I'm not expecting you to find Prince Charming, just a nice guy to take you to the movies and out to dinner. Someone to sleep with, for God's sake. You must be lonely. And now that it's September, there'll be hardly anyone around. . . . Even that wouldn't be so bad if you weren't intentionally isolating yourself the way you are."

I could see how much she wanted to fix up the loose end that I'd become, and I felt bad that I couldn't help her. I shrugged my shoulders and agreed to think about it so she'd go away.

"OK, kid," she said. "I'm off to the station. Do you need anything in the city?"

The city, of course, to residents of Slea Head, meant New York, where my sister and her husband worked in the high-priced law firm where they'd met. The train station was only a couple of towns inland, on a direct line to Newark where commuters can easily change for New York.

I gave Marjorie a hug, an empty gesture on my part, and watched her through the window until she was gone. I was relieved to be alone, but conscious now of all the time I'd have to get through to be able to mentally cross another day off the calendar. It was still early, I knew, because Marjorie liked to get into the office around eight, and she still had almost an hour's commute. She and her husband Bill led such "full" lives, they rarely even drove to the station together as they often had to work different schedules or needed to go their separate ways after getting back to New Jersey.

Like Peter and me, they'd never had children, but with them it had been a conscious choice. With us it had been a different story. I'd been pregnant twice with babies that hadn't "formed" properly (whatever that meant), and we'd had to realize the futility of trying, and give up. Such a small defect — my inability to produce a child — had lain in wait, unknown, since puberty, only coming to light when it would have mattered. Peter had had a defect, too. *Intracranial Aneurysm* was the term so scientifically applied, but by then it was all over.

In those days I was on a roll professionally. My books were selling well. My two sleuths, sort of updated versions of Nick and Nora Charles (sans Asta), were very popular, and the words "movie rights" were bandied about on more than one occasion. I often wrote ten pages in a day, sometimes more.

When I got stuck, I used to walk, sometimes for hours, around town, along the beach, to the old lighthouse — whatever it took to get the creative juices flowing again — but I was home when the call came.

It had happened right there in his own office, on a sunny Monday, amid the usual worries of daily life — did I mail the car insurance bill? can I get out this laundry stain? should I renew this magazine subscription? His last word was another woman's name. "Beth," he said to his hygienist, in a calm businesslike voice, and then dropped dead on the floor.

"Peter Millwright, Slea Head Dentist," the obituary heading had read, accompanied by a photograph I don't remember choosing. The black-and-white face that looked out at me was handsome, almost dashing, with dark hair and soft, kind eyes that I knew to be brown. And all I kept thinking was that there must be some mistake. The phrase repeated itself in my mind whenever my thoughtful sister hadn't come up with some little chore for me to do. She'd certainly been a lifesaver in those earliest days.

But now I was sitting at the kitchen table, a pathetic widow without a plan. I decided that a project was in order. My library had gradually gotten into a terrible state, with dozens of books strewn about the house. Part of my "flea market junk," as Marjorie calls it, includes a vast collection of books on all sorts of subjects written by myriad authors. For Christmas one year Peter and I had converted a spare bedroom into a library as our gift to ourselves, though I knew it was mainly for me. He had had to squeeze his baseball books into half of one of the sixteen floor-to-ceiling bookcases. The rest he had ceded to me.

Well, one way or another a lot of my collection had ranged about the house, appearing on tables, mantels, steps — anything horizontal, really. It was time to put them in order.

I busied myself for over an hour, collecting the escapees, stopping to browse now and then. I spent quite a while perusing a book of baby names that I use to dub minor characters and murder victims. It used to hurt to see its title and remember there'd never be a baby to name, not in this family, but it no longer held the power to wound. Alone as I was, being childless was no longer a regret.

I thumbed through an atlas, then a thesaurus, then a copy of *Kidnapped*, illustrated by N. C. Wyeth. God knows why I'd had that out. The color plates, though, were as enchanting as ever and looking at them killed some more time.

When I grew bored but not finished with the whole thing, I stopped to have lunch. I decided to go for a run on the beach afterward. Maybe I'd pick up some smooth sea glass, which, by habit, we'd always deposited in a jar on the windowsill.

It was in this desultory way I'd been passing my days, the motivation for my activities based on nothing stronger than a whim. Sometimes the time passed quickly, usually not. Once the evening news ended, though, I knew I was almost home free.

I picked up a novel sent to me by its author, a fellow mystery writer, and began to read. It felt like an assignment, an obligation, to be engaging in this small act that once gave me so much pleasure. After all, I'd enjoyed the genre enough to make writing mysteries my own vocation. I'd met a lot of interesting and fun-loving people through it, too, at regional and national conventions. All in all, it had been very satisfying work on many levels, and Peter had gotten a kick out of even the most dramatic of my acquaintances who wrote tales of murder and detection. Now, reading mysteries sent to me out of courtesy by my colleagues only served to pass the time and, with this latest one, I painlessly got through the intervening hours until it could be called a reasonable time to go to bed.

I slept well and deeply for a change until I was awakened by a storm. I didn't know what time it was, but I lay still and listened to the thunder and rain, remembering with a smile a similar storm, not so long ago, during which Peter and I had awakened, come together, and made love without a word spoken between us.

I never fell back to sleep after that, and in the morning I rose early. Feeling the warmth and moisture of the air, I decided I might go for a swim. I pulled on a modest black tank suit, grabbed a towel, and let myself out.

The air was balmy and still, without a breeze to dissipate the gentle fog that blurred my view of the beach. I tested the water with my feet and found it typically comfortable for the time of year. A number of days had passed since Labor Day, and the tourists were gone, just as the water was at its warmest. Not that Slea Head ever gets the carnival atmosphere of a lot of other Jersey Shore towns; it's just not that kind of place. Primarily residential and without a boardwalk, it attracts mostly older and quieter folks. It's also pricier than the glitzy teen haunts and family-oriented vacation spots farther down the coast.

I stood for a few moments in the blending of pale color that was both the sea and the sky, washed over as they were with mist. Physically I felt very little; I was neither hot nor cold, hungry nor thirsty. No strong aromas assaulted my senses; no intrusive noise disturbed my world. And yet, inside, I suddenly felt as though I could go on no longer. What was to make tomorrow more meaningful than today? The next year better than the last? What could ever match what I had once had? It seemed hopeless, yet I had only days to reach that magical two-year point at which I was supposed to emerge healed and whole. I knew I had become tedious even to my own family in my grief, but I felt no more distant from its pain than I had the day Peter was buried.

I didn't have it in me to drown myself, and I had no desire to run away from the physical surroundings that remained of the life I'd held so dear, but I was exhausted at the very prospect of trying to go on existing within this shell I'd managed to create. Sleep was the only thing I could think of to look forward to; it couldn't bring happiness, but it could for a short time break the chain of regret.

Standing at the edge of the water, I felt as though I had hit bottom, that from this heartbreak and distance from the world, there could be no lower state of consciousness. I needed a reason to continue, but without Peter I felt lost.

I looked up at the sky, though it was like looking into a cloud, and hoped my voice would carry to where I aimed it.

"Peter, I can't do this anymore," I called softly, tears coming unbidden to my eyes.

There was no response that I could discern. It wasn't the first time I'd tried vainly to communicate with Peter, but it had been some time since I'd felt a need to speak aloud to him. I still lit candles and sent messages in my mind, but this desperation made me want to hear my own voice, to be sure I'd done my all to get my words through to him.

"I need a reason to go on, Peter. Otherwise, I'm ready to be with you wherever you are. Can you hear me? Peter?"

My voice at the end was little more than a whisper. It wasn't out of a feeling of foolishness that I stopped. I just found it hard to believe that any amount of pleading would change my plight. I had once been quite an independent person, but after Peter and I had fallen head over heels for each other, I no longer felt complete on my own. He had been my only lover, and I couldn't see myself ever trusting another man with my whole body and soul. I know I was a bit old-fashioned in this, but I'd always taken the physical aspect of a relationship as seriously as the emotional, and felt convinced neither would ever be fulfilled again because the two sides, for me, must be interconnected.

Forget it, I thought. Get back to the apathy that keeps you going and doesn't allow the world to see you've never healed at all.

My attempt to thicken my skin didn't seem to be working. I still wanted to cry out to Peter for help, but I would put on a stronger facade, I told myself, and prepared to take a literal plunge to steel myself to the job at hand — that of continuing on after all joy in life had gone. What would a few pathetic drops more of salt water mean to the mighty ocean anyway?

I dropped my towel and threw myself into the water. Although warm for the Atlantic, it was still brisk, and I felt physically invigorated and a bit more alive than usual when I emerged. I was back in control of my outward emotions, though no closer to making peace with my loss. As I wrung out my hair, I could see that I had the beach to myself. Fog still clung to the shore, although I could see it beginning to rise in smokelike tendrils off the sand. I knew I had drifted a bit from my point of entry to the beach as I recognized the nearest house as one about a block from my own. Its yellow and white awning was just distinguishable from the high tide mark where I stood. I began my way back toward my own little patch of sand at a gentle jog to warm myself up, but stopped short when I realized I was *not* alone. In an almost direct line from my house to the sea, I could see through the fog that someone was lying, facedown, on the beach.

I had dealt for years with dead bodies, at least in my mind, on an almost daily basis. It is an absolute necessity in my work. But I found myself praying for all I was worth that this body should be a live one. I was consumed by an almost superstitious fear of the prone form on the sand, but for purely humanitarian reasons I couldn't just walk away. What I really wanted to do was run and keep running until death would tire of chasing me, but I advanced to the pounding beat of my heart and of the surf until I looked down upon what I fervently hoped was not a corpse but a man.

# CHAPTER 2

It was with extremely mixed emotions, to say the least, that I had crossed that small expanse of beach to do what I felt to be my duty as a human being. In that short space of time, the many sides of me had warred, most urging me to fly or pretend I had seen nothing. During my internal debate, I had first argued to myself that the man must surely be dead and, therefore, be beyond my power to help. I wanted to avoid, at all costs, the ugliness of a bloated, battered corpse, to escape imprinting on my mind a picture of horror that would surely never be erased, but the waves seemed to repeat, "Go on, go on," over and over as they tumbled the sand across my feet.

I knew I should hurry, that I would never forgive myself if my fear and loathing led to my delaying or preventing the administration of prompt medical care and cost someone the ultimate price. But why did *I* have to be the one here this lonely morning? I felt resentment for this intrusion on *my* solitude, on *my* beach. Then I thought, conversely, that if there were other people here — happy holiday-goers with their noisy children or teens in search of the perfect tan — I would be absolved from responsibility, and I felt angry at being abandoned by these imaginary companions.

"Why aren't you here, Peter?" I cried aloud. "Help me!"

A pair of gulls answered me, their raucous calls contrasting sharply with the regularity of the endlessly pounding surf. The water massaged my ankles and, looking through the dissipating fog at the vulnerable body, dead or alive, I felt a strength enter me and I knew what must be done.

I silently thanked Peter for urging me on and, with some purpose at last in my step, I neared the figure from which I'd been unable to take my eyes. I grabbed my towel from the sand and wrapped it around my waist, as though that could ward off the chill I was feeling, and prepared myself for the worst.

On closer inspection, I could see a small rivulet of blood flowing from a cut at the man's hairline that, although clotted with sand, was not entirely stemmed. Since the wounds of a dead man can be expected to cease bleeding with the stoppage of his heart, I inwardly sighed with relief and went on to try to assess the damage.

In passing, I noted that the man was young, but nearer thirty than twenty. His hair was long by most standards, at least by mine, and hung in sand-encrusted clumps to his shoulders. It might have been blond, but with the water, the sand, and the seaweed, it was difficult to tell. I could see a fair number of bruises on his face, arms, and legs, and through the rents in his clothes. There were curious scars on his back as well, but there was nothing so obvious as an unnaturally bent limb to make me think he had any broken bones. I prodded his shoulder cautiously with my hand, afraid to roll him over in case he had serious neck or back injuries — a precaution that had come back to me clearly from a first-aid segment of high school health class. To my surprise, he rolled himself onto his back without further incentive and opened his eyes wide to the vague white sky. Staring at nothing, he looked more dead now than he had before.

It was eerie to look on his seemingly sightless eyes. I found it odder still when it finally registered in my mind that they didn't match. The right was a surprisingly bright blue, the left an equally vivid green. I had once seen a white cat with eyes like that, but never a man. When he finally blinked, I saw that his lashes were light, quite long, and very straight.

"Hello," I called softly, and he glanced at me before dropping his eyes and breaking into a long resounding cough. This finally over, he looked at me again — only for an instant — and blushed to the roots of his filthy hair.

"Have you come off a ship as well, miss?" he asked without raising his eyes. "Let me give you my shirt."

At any rate he spoke English. Due to the odd cut of his tattered clothes, I'd assumed he was probably foreign.

"Is that what happened? You fell off a ship?"

"Aye, miss," he replied, and began to remove

his shirt, presumably to give to me in some sort of act of chivalry. I wasn't so sure now that he wasn't foreign, as I thought I detected something of an accent in his speech — like a Scottish burr, only softer, more subtle to my American ears.

I told him I didn't need his shirt, but he replied, "Please, miss," and handed it over. This revealed a few more bruises on his lean torso and sinewy arms, but it seemed natural that he might have been knocked around a bit before being washed ashore. He was sitting up now, and, taking his ragged shirt from him, I asked him if he thought he could stand.

In my observation, few things are as good or as bad as we expect them to be. Such was the case with this Jersey Shore castaway who seemed to be all in one piece but was decidedly a bit unsteady on his feet. He was in a state of being *not quite* good as new, but this sufficed for walking up the sand toward my house, which directly faced the beach. Slender though he was, I certainly would have been unable to carry him.

As a lone gull screamed and the waves performed their unending dance, he leaned on my shoulder, but only when he would otherwise have fallen. At first I thought him distant and aloof. In my parents' circle of friends, I'd certainly known my share of snobs but, remembering his flushed cheeks (I had never before seen a grown man blush), I realized that what I had taken for conceit or reserve was merely shyness.

It wasn't until we had almost reached the house that my natural curiosity snapped out of the spell it seemed to have been under. For a moment I'd taken his appearance on the beach for an everyday occurrence, as though men washing up with the tide was as common as shells or jellyfish.

"Do you want me to call someone? The Coast Guard? Or the police?" I asked.

"The police?" He looked at me questioningly, as though I'd made a very puzzling suggestion.

"There must be *someone* looking for you."

"No," he answered, without self-pity, as a statement of fact.

"What about the ship's captain, or your family?"

"I've no family but a stepfather, and it's certain *he* won't be looking for me."

"Were you a passenger or part of the crew?"

"The crew, miss."

"What are you? A waiter on a cruise ship or something?"

By his blank look I could see that I'd addled him again. "I'm only a common sailor," he answered.

"You're in the navy, then?"

"No, miss. In the merchant service."

I guess it was my turn to look confused. I figured I'd get back to a more basic line of questioning.

"Where are you from?" I asked.

"Nova Scotia."

"What's your name?"

"Owen."

"Owen what?"

"Sorry, miss. Sinclair, Owen Sinclair."

"Well, come on. Let's get the sand off you. Then maybe you'd like something to eat."

"Aye, that I would. Thank you, miss."

"My name's Peggy."

My house, bought by Peter and myself with so much hope for the future, was a Dutch Colonial that showed its barnlike roofline to the sea. Years of sun and salt had leeched the color from its cedar shingles, but still it looked welcoming with the light I'd left on in the kitchen, keeping the fog at bay.

I opened the gate to my property and walked Owen to the wood-enclosed outdoor shower at the back of the house. It felt cruel not allowing him in without first rinsing off, but sand clung to just about all of him except what had been covered by his shirt. Keeping the gritty stuff under control in a shore house is hard enough without asking for trouble. Luckily, we had had hot water run to the shower.

Owen looked kind of bleary, so I showed him how the thing worked and told him to get rid of his torn clothes. That wasn't asking much. He'd already been barefoot when I found him; his wide-legged, once-white trousers were beyond repair, and, due to a strategic tear in the seat, I knew he wasn't wearing anything else.

I promised to give him a towel in exchange

until I could find something of my husband's that he could wear.

I went in, quickly got out of my wet bathing suit and into dry jeans and a T-shirt, and grabbed a beach towel on the way out.

Owen was still under running water when I returned.

"How do I make it stop?" he called to me.

I was starting to think he was only rowing with one oar, or maybe he'd hit his head on something when he was in the water. The sailor talk — at least the "aye" for "yes" — had struck me as kind of funny, too. Colloquially, the guy was a trip, and if he hadn't been so banged up, I think I would have laughed.

Then, for the first time, it occurred to me that maybe I was being had. I hadn't considered before that point the possibility that this could all be an elaborate joke or a scam. Still, the bruises looked real. I decided to start exercising a little caution. I hadn't even locked the door to my bedroom when I'd gone in to change. I didn't know this guy from Adam, and he *was* decidedly strange.

I explained how to turn off the water, and Owen eventually figured out my instructions and complied. I handed him the large gaily colored towel over the wall of the shower stall.

He emerged, dripping, with the towel around his waist.

"Is the sand all out of your hair?"

He felt his scalp and shook his head. "I don't

know if it ever will be."

"Come on," I said, and led the way to the door.

I guess he hadn't noticed my car in the driveway on the way to the shower, because now he stopped and stared as though it were an exotic beast and not a three-year-old sedan. He seemed so transfixed I was afraid he'd drop his towel.

"What is it?" he asked.

"A Honda."

He continued to stand and gape.

"Come on," I repeated, and led him to the Bar Harbor wicker settee on the glass-enclosed sunporch. I asked him to wait there while I got him some clothes.

I still had a couple of boxes of Peter's clothes — things that I hadn't had the heart to give up. I dug out Peter's favorite pair of button-fly Levis and an oversized blue T-shirt of mine. The jeans, I had no doubt, would be a bit big for Owen, but he certainly wouldn't fit into a pair of mine. Tube socks are pretty unisex, but I had nothing he could use for shoes. He'd have to get by with what I could offer. Later he could wire somebody for money to buy the rest of the stuff he needed.

I showed him to the downstairs powder room, where he could change. When he came out, he didn't look much worse than the average teenager, but it was clear that, long-term, he'd need something closer to his own size to wear.

"What place is this?" he finally asked. I guess his curiosity was a little less assertive than mine.

28

"Slea Head," I answered, then added, "New Jersey" in case he really had no clue.

"You have a lighthouse here, at Slea Head Point?"

"Yes," I confirmed, and he smiled as though he were pleased that he could place where he was on some mental map of the world.

"I was looking for it when I got washed overboard. Later, I thought I saw its light, but I was pretty busy just trying to keep my head above water."

"Did you get washed over in the storm?"

"Aye, a huge wave came out of nowhere, and all at once I was in the sea. I don't remember a whole lot after that, but I'm not a very good swimmer so I'm really very surprised to be here."

I had heard of sailors who couldn't swim, but it still seemed sort of stupid to me.

"Well, would you like to get the rest of the sand out of your hair?" I asked and he nodded.

Peter and I had had a new laundry room installed upstairs, where the dirty laundry generally is, and that's where I now led Owen. I grabbed a clean towel, and, throwing it over his shoulders, I asked him to bend down over the utility sink next to the washing machine. He kept glancing over at the washer and dryer curiously until I had to tell him firmly to keep his head down or we'd have water all over the floor.

I wet his hair again and liberally applied shampoo.

"That smells wonderful. What is it?"

"What do you think it is? It's shampoo, of course. Now, hold still," I replied, and massaged his scalp, feeling the particles of sand still there with the tips of my fingers. It suddenly dawned on me that this was such an intimate thing for me to be doing with a complete stranger, but he was docile as a child until I heard him take a sharp intake of breath and say "ouch," quietly, as though he didn't want to be a bother.

"Sorry." I'd forgotten about the cut on his head. "I'll put something on that as soon as we're done here. OK?"

"OK?" he asked, as though to clarify the question.

"Yes. Is that all right?"

He nodded and said "aye" again, which, to me, was either going to become his endearing trademark or a very annoying affectation.

Finished, I turned off the water. He thanked me and vigorously towel-dried his hair. I could see that the wound at his hairline was bleeding again. In the bathroom I got out some gauze, tape, and a bottle of rubbing alcohol. In a short time, and with only a wince on his part, I had everything under control.

"Do you want to dry your hair?" I asked, motioning to the hair dryer that hung on a brass hook next to the mirror.

He narrowed his eyes like people do when they're not comprehending something, then answered, "It's a warm day; it'll be dry soon. I *would* like to shave, if your husband has a razor I could use."

I gave him a disposable shaver, kind of a cute bright pink affair. It wasn't too manly-looking, but at least it was new and undulled by my legs. He couldn't seem to make head or tails of it. I guess I shouldn't have been surprised, considering his generally odd behavior. Maybe he just wasn't very bright. I showed him how to squirt out the shaving cream and then how to use the razor. Once he could see that it did the job, he went about his business. I had started out the door when he asked me a question that, coming from him, shouldn't have seemed so very strange, I suppose.

"Do all the women in New Jersey wear trousers?"

I think the only reason he had the nerve to ask was that his eyes were glued to the mirror as he shaved and he wouldn't have to look at me.

"Yes, at one time or another just about every woman in New Jersey wears 'trousers.' "

This was getting pretty weird. I hoped he had a plan of where to go. His earlier denial of having any family surely couldn't mean he thought he was staying here for any length of time.

At any rate, aside from the stark-white bandage on his forehead, he looked pretty presentable now that he had dry clothes on and was clean-shaven. I decided I'd at least see that he had something to eat before trying to send him on his way.

I have never been much of a cook, and now, with Peter gone, I rarely put together anything more complicated than a sandwich. The sympathy casseroles had long ago stopped coming, and I just didn't have the inclination to make elaborate meals for one, or in this case, two. Therefore, I whipped up grilled ham and cheese sandwiches, microwaved some canned split pea soup, and felt that a "common sailor" should be grateful.

Owen was that and more. He ate as though he hadn't in weeks.

"This is delicious. Thank you," he said with his mouth full and then plowed on through the rest of it.

I poured him a cup of decaf, which soon went the way of the sandwich and soup.

"Do you mind if I sleep now?" he asked.

When I said no, he curled up on the wicker settee where he was sitting and closed his eyes.

"You might be more comfortable up in the guest room. You can't really stretch out on this."

"No, thank you. This is fine," he replied and, in a very few minutes I could swear he was fast asleep. I covered him with an afghan and let him be. Maybe falling off a ship was harder work than I'd thought.

# CHAPTER 3

He slept for hours. It was just after noon when he awoke — lunchtime, as opposed to the ridiculously early time we'd eaten our midday meal. I'd spent the time meandering — washing the dishes, hanging up wet towels, browsing magazines. At twelve I'd come back out to the sunporch and put on the television with the volume low to watch the news. I guess it woke him. I was sorry to disturb him but more than a little relieved to find that he would be waking up at all. The more I'd thought about his strange behavior the more I figured he might have a concussion and need to see a doctor.

"Hi," I said as I saw him sit up and take in his surroundings, darting his eyes from one thing in the room to another. He looked scared or skittish, like an animal — a kitten, maybe, or a colt. The afghan I'd thrown over him fell unnoticed to the floor.

"I'm still *here*," he said, and ran his fingers through his hair in a gesture of panic. His hair was now dry and more than a little disheveled. It was striped in half a dozen shades, all of them blond.

"I thought I had dreamed this place and all of these . . . *things*," he explained. He was breathing hard and fast, and he blinked repeatedly, as though holding back tears. His eyes fixed at last on the TV, and I could see he was now hyper-ventilating in earnest.

"Calm down," I said in what I hoped was a soothing, nonthreatening voice. "You'd better put your head down between your knees before you make yourself pass out."

He complied, and with his hands raking through his hair, he began to cry. When he sat up, he covered his face with his hands.

"What did I do?" he asked, but he obviously wasn't addressing me.

"Maybe you'd better explain to me what's wrong. It might not be as bad as it seems right now."

He calmed himself enough to speak, and I braced myself to hear the worst. I hoped he hadn't killed someone. It's one thing to write flippantly about murder, but I had no desire to be in any way involved with the actual crime.

"Everything here is so strange. I was sure it was a dream. But you're still here, and I'm still in this place. Please, just answer one question."

"All right."

"The year — it's not '53 anymore, is it?" he asked, and held his breath for my response.

"I wasn't even born in 1953," I answered, un-sure what he was getting at. Did he really believe that to be the year?

"1953," he repeated dully, and tears fell list-lessly from both his eyes. "When I was washed overboard, the date was September the 19th, 1853."

"What? You're joking." I told him that it was September 20th, all right, the day after the night he'd gone overboard, but when I told him the year and that I was sure he knew it as well as I did, he just kept repeating, "Oh, God, what did I do?"

"I think you need to see a doctor. You probably hit your head when you fell in or on something floating in the water."

He answered me in a monotone, the way one numbly reads off facts. I wasn't sure whom he was trying to convince, me or himself.

"I was born in 1825 in Yarmouth, Nova Scotia. When I was fifteen, I left home to become a sailor. Since then I've served aboard a number of ships, beginning with the schooner *Glen Rover* and ending just now with the clipper *Elizabeth York*."

Well, that explains everything, I thought. I've got the freaking Ancient Mariner staying at my house. But he was crying now to break my heart, and I found the sarcastic laugh that had been building up in me replaced with compassion and a willingness to at least listen to his bizarre tale.

I couldn't place any credibility in his words, of course, but his face showed such honesty and lostness that I was determined to keep any expression of judgment for the time being from mine. He looked so sincere, so distraught, that I had to keep reminding myself that his story was clearly not possible.

I had dismissed the premise of his narration,

but not the feelings behind it. It was obvious that he'd been through something traumatic and, though I couldn't give credence to his words, there was something so out of the common way about him that I hoped he'd go on talking. His clothes, his hair, something in his speech, all marked him as out of place, and I could see no profit to be gained from such an outrageous lie on his part. He couldn't have planned our meeting; there was no regularity to my ocean swims. His coughing up water on the beach had not been faked and neither was the cut on his head. He hadn't asked for anything, not even the basics for survival. I was the one who had offered him a meal and a place to lie down for a while.

"I don't know how I came to be here," he said with real despair in his voice. "I'm sure I must sound mad to you, and maybe I am, but I know who I am, and I know what the year was when I went overboard. Oh, God, my stepfather must have been right."

"What does your stepfather have to do with anything?"

"He told me I would never come to any good because I was marked by the Devil."

I could tell that he felt ashamed, that he had taken to heart what he had been told, as incomprehensible to me as that seemed.

"What did he mean by that?"

"Haven't you noticed? My eyes are two different colors, and I'm left-handed, too," he said as if that proved something.

"Just because your eyes don't match doesn't mean you're possessed by the Devil, and plenty of people are left-handed. I think your stepfather must have been an ignorant, superstitious man."

"Then, why am I here, and not in heaven . . . or in hell? I must have done something very wrong. I know I have, and now I'm being punished," he said, and hung his head.

"What? What have you done to make you think you deserve whatever the hell you think has happened to you?" I wondered if I was making any more sense than he was, but he seemed to know what I meant.

"When I ran away to sea . . . I couldn't even leave a note to my mother. I was gone three years before I ever got back home. I went to my stepfather. He wasn't very pleased to see me, and when I asked to see my mother he told me she'd been dead almost a year. She was going to have a child, *his* child, and she and the baby both died. And my mother never knew where I had gone, that I was well and able to take care of myself. I only left not to be a burden to her. If only I'd stayed, or somehow let her know I was all right. . . ."

"She would have died just the same. It doesn't make any difference, Owen. The people we love die in spite of us. There's nothing you could have done."

"Then, why has God forgotten me? What did I do? Why am I still here? *Here,* in the wrong time — wrong for me at least?"

"I honestly don't know what to think. I don't even know if I believe you. I do believe that you really think you came here from the year 1853. If I take you to a doctor friend of mine, will you let her have a look at you?"

"Her? A woman physician?"

"Yes," I said, and he nodded dumbly.

I wanted so much to believe him. At first, I think it was only mere politeness, but as he'd gone on I'd wanted to show him at least one person would have faith in him. The head injury theory would probably prove correct, but within the confines of his own reality he'd sounded coherent and reasonable, and his eyes beseeched me out of fear and aloneness and not guile. He needed a friend. It was plainly evident that he keenly felt how solitary he was, and *that*, at least, I could understand. Logic told me not to get involved, not in this impossible past of his, but I had known real emotional pain of my own, and I was moved for the moment from my deadness of spirit. Hadn't I only that morning been praying for a reason to go on? Perhaps protecting this one misplaced soul for a time was my penance for that selfish plea. Be careful what you wish for, I always say.

If I decided to take on the responsibility, Owen Sinclair was going to be quite a project indeed. I didn't know if I felt up to it; I honestly didn't know if I wanted daily human contact. If I did decide to help him, it would be like offering a home to a stray dog or cat — seeing that it had all its shots, the right things to eat, and somewhere to sleep. But perhaps a day or two of companionship would be a welcome change.

He seemed to sense my concerns because he said, "I have no money. If you could help me find work. . . . I don't know where to go. Maybe, if I could get to New York, I could find a ship ready to sail. . . ."

"Let's not worry about that just yet," I said.

Owen nodded, then asked, "Will your husband be home soon?"

I'd forgotten that I'd let him believe Peter was alive. In giving him Peter's jeans and complying when he'd asked if he could use "my husband's razor," I had felt safer with a reassuring, if imaginary, other male presence just out of range. I don't know why, but I knew now that there was no harm in Owen. Confused though he might be, he was no threat to me or anyone else. His helplessness made him childlike, and I was the childless widow come to his rescue.

"My husband is dead. In three days it will be two years since he died," I explained, and the explanation made me weary. "Come with me. I'll call my friend the doctor."

I felt like a fool as I explained what I was doing while I dialed, or rather pushed, the Touch-Tone numbers of the phone. Boy, did I hope I wasn't being scammed. My sense of humor since Peter died wasn't what it used to be.

I let him hear the number ringing, then took the receiver to talk to Arlene's nurse. When I gave her my name, she immediately offered to let me speak to Arlene herself, who, as good luck would have it, was standing right there at the reception desk.

Slea Head is a small town, and a good many of the year-rounders know each other. I'd known Arlene Graber for years. She and her husband were older than Peter and I, and I think I remember hearing they'd been hippies, instead of the children of parents who bitched about hippies, as Peter and I were. Still, we'd become pretty good friends and had, up until two years ago, socialized fairly often.

"Arlene, it's Peggy. . . . I know it's been too long . . . I've got a favor to ask of you. . . . I need you to squeeze an appointment in for me if you can. . . . No, I'm fine . . . A friend?" I looked over at Owen. "Well, not exactly . . . Actually I found a man on the beach this morning. He said he fell off a ship. . . . Yeah, well, he may have hit his head; there's kind of a gap in his memory. Quite a big gap, really, especially if you believe everything he's told me. . . . Now? Are you sure? . . . Thanks, Arlene, I knew I could count on you. . . . We'll be right over."

The whole experience of driving to Arlene's office was ludicrous. I had to explain even the most basic functions to Owen, starting with how to open the car door. I could tell that he was more than a little frightened but, his white-knuckled hands gripping the sides of his seat, he kept his peace, only asking me once in moderately heavy traffic whether or not everyone had his own "Honda." Of course, I tried to explain that a Honda was only one make of car, but I wasn't sure whether I got through to him or not. He was pretty busy just being terrified. I have to admit that I may have driven a little faster than usual just to see the look on his face. I guess I was expecting that my little attempt at sadism would force him to confess that he'd been kidding all along. If so, it didn't work, and I slowed down. For a writer, I guess I'm not very good at suspending reality but, then again, I asked myself, who *would* believe such a crazy story?

I looked over at his face, noting the wide eyes and rapid breathing that manifested both wonder and fear on his part as the car negotiated Slea Head's main thoroughfare. He sure didn't look like he was having me on then. He kept his eyes fixed to the rapidly changing vista visible through the windshield, and I took the opportunity to steal stray glances at this man who would have me believe he'd come from another time. His coloring gave him the look of a Norseman, but I'd noted that he was, perhaps, a bit less than average height for a man, only a few inches taller than myself. I'd heard that people were getting taller with each generation, but warned myself not to start taking his story seriously. It certainly made him an interesting character, but I had enough problems grounding myself in the here and now without the possibility of a time traveler sitting with me in my car. If only his manner

41

weren't so very sincere, I'd have had an easier time dismissing him as either insane or merely conniving.

His eyes behind the long lashes I'd noted earlier were equally light, the green one being the only one I could readily observe from the driver's seat. In his nose, his cheeks, and his chin, I could discern nothing particularly notable or unusual, but together with his eyes the impression was rather pleasing and generally marked by kindness. His flesh was tanned and weathered by the elements, but I knew rather than suspected from seeing him earlier in nothing but a towel that he was naturally fair-skinned. Then I'd seen, too, that he was leanly muscled, but whether his tan and state of fitness were from work aboard a ship had yet to be proven.

At the office I introduced Owen and Arlene to each other. Arlene hadn't changed a bit that I could see. Her long, very curly salt-and-pepper hair was pulled back loosely in a ponytail that threatened to come undone at any time, and her eyes behind her large owlish glasses were as probing and warm as ever. I didn't realize until then how much I'd missed seeing the people I'd once cared so much about.

I think Arlene's nurse was appalled, but Arlene let us into an examination room without first having our completed forms and insurance information. I briefly repeated to Arlene what Owen had told me after I'd found him. Then, not being family, I excused myself so she could examine and speak with him privately. I was a little touched when Owen asked me to please stay. As a stranger in a strange land, he looked to me as a kind of lifeline, I guess.

"How old are you, Mr. Sinclair?" Arlene began.

"Twenty-eight," he replied. He was either a year younger than I or more than one-hundred-forty-years older. All a matter of perspective, I guess.

"Do you remember hitting your head?"

"No, ma'am."

"Are you experiencing any dizziness?"

Owen shook his head.

"Headaches?"

"No."

I've never really understood doctors and the mysteries of their art. Arlene seemed to do all the usual stuff, gleaning information with her stethoscope, her blood pressure cuff, and that cute little penlight doctors are so fond of shining into our eyes and ears.

Owen was both passive and brave as he sat per-fectly still and did as he was told. He didn't even make the slightest fuss when Arlene checked and redressed the cut on his face. She then had him remove his shirt (actually *my* shirt) to listen to his breathing and heartbeat and generally assess his physical condition more thoroughly. The hair on his chest that ran down to his waistband was golden — there was no other word for it — and it was plain to see that he'd spent a lot of time outdoors stripped to the waist. This was quite a contrast from Peter, with his rich dark brown hair and smooth bare chest. Peter was taller, too, and so much more confident and easy. He would have been talking away, I'm sure, in a similar situation, but then I would probably have been sitting outside reading some mindless drivel in a stale waiting room magazine until the examination was over. I began to wonder if I still shouldn't excuse myself to allow Owen some privacy when Arlene took notice of the scars that I'd seen earlier on Owen's back.

"What happened here?" she asked, tracing one of the pale lines with her finger until it intersected another.

"That happened on the *Aurora Borealis*. She was a cursed ship, the worst ship I ever sailed on."

"Go on," Arlene said. She wasn't the only one curious to hear the end of the story.

"One night in Baltimore, my friend Frenchy and I — we had just finished serving two years on board the *Topaz* — and we were, well, we were drunk, Dr. Graber," he said with a look of contrition, "and coming back to our boardinghouse from the grogshop when we were waylaid — that is, we got hit on the head from behind and came to on board the *Aurora Borealis*, already at sea bound for Singapore. The owner of the boardinghouse must have been in on it, because our belongings had already been brought on board. We were forced to sign on, and so, like it or not, we became part of her crew. The mate took a terrible dislike to me, and that's how it happened."

"How what happened?" Arlene asked and, believe me, I was sharing her frustration with Owen's roundabout way of answering her questions.

"Well, Wilkins, the mate, was a terrible man, a real bucco. I'd heard plenty of times from other sailors about cruel or drunken captains and mates, but I'd been really lucky, I guess, starting with my first captain, Captain Arniston, the best man that ever lived. But this Wilkins, he was terrible mean and used to kick and hit me whenever he got the chance. I don't know why he decided to haze me so in particular. He beat and cursed all the men, not the captain or the other mates, you understand, just those of us before the mast, eh? — the crew — those of us that are quartered in the fo'c'sle." I could tell he was treating us like simple uncomprehending landlubbers, and it didn't help that he was right.

"In the what, Mr. Sinclair?" Arlene asked, and shot me a glance that showed she was both bemused and concerned.

" 'Forecastle' is how they tell me it looks on paper, ma'am," he said, enunciating the word carefully.

"Please, go on."

"Well, Wilkins used to put me on bread and water for days for no reason or he'd have me put in irons below decks or keep me walking the deck for hours, sometimes when I'd just gotten off my watch and gone to sleep, and still he wasn't satisfied. Finally, he broke my wrist with a belaying pin, and I guess he didn't know I was left-handed, because that's the one he broke, and when I couldn't do my work, he flogged me in front of the entire crew for being a slacker."

"What did you do?"

"At Singapore Frenchy and I went to the consulate, and I was able to get discharged and to have my wrist splinted. The consul got me the pay I was entitled to and a little more to tide me over until I was fit to work."

This was the most I had ever heard Owen speak. His voice, as ever, was soft in volume but gravelly in texture. He had related his tale of cruelty and criminal behavior without anger, as though it were not unbelievable, but something that probably happened, somewhere in the world, every day.

Arlene took hold of Owen's arm at the wrist and felt along the bones with her fingers.

"Hmm," she muttered. "Here . . . I see."

"See what?" I asked.

"The fracture was never set properly," she said as though she were speaking to herself more than to Owen and myself. "I can feel quite a bump at the point of the break."

"I can use it the same as before," Owen assured her, bringing Arlene back from her musings.

"That's quite a story you have to tell, Mr. Sinclair," she said, and I could tell that he'd taken her by surprise, probably the first time that had happened in her office in a good long while. "I don't see any sign that you have a concussion. Do you have insurance?"

Owen looked to me to answer.

"I don't think so," I said.

"Well, I can send you over to the hospital for a CAT scan, but it's quite expensive and, I believe, unnecessary. I might not be the right kind of health professional for your problem, Mr. Sinclair," Arlene said and, looking at me, added, "if you know what I mean."

I mouthed the word "shrink" and she shrugged with a tilt of her head and a lifting of her eyebrows.

"I do have a couple of medical concerns, however," she said, and turned to Owen. "I see signs that may point to malnutrition and vitamin deficiencies. I also think a tetanus shot would be in order, considering we don't know how you got that cut on your head."

"I don't know what any of that means," Owen answered.

"What have you been eating lately?"

"Salt pork, mostly, but sometimes beef, sea biscuit, peas, and beans."

"I'd suggest a lot of fresh fruits and vegetables in addition to the rest of a balanced diet."

"All right, until I sail again. Then I'll have to wait until we're in port for the fruits and vegetables."

Arlene shook her head at her poor deluded patient. "Do you remember having a tetanus booster in the recent past?"

"I don't think that's something I've ever had," he said, and looked to me for confirmation.

"Let's go on the assumption he's never had a tetanus shot," I said.

"All right?" Arlene asked Owen. I nodded, and he took it on trust that I wouldn't steer him wrong.

"All right," he answered.

I could swear he had no idea what was coming as Dr. Graber swabbed his arm with an alcohol-soaked pad and prepared the syringe. He watched her with curiosity until the prick of the needle when he tried to pull away. Arlene was no novice, though, and there was no need for a second attempt.

"It's medicine, Owen. It can keep you from getting really sick," I explained, feeling a bit silly, as Owen silently watched Dr. Graber put an adhesive bandage on his arm.

"Well, thank you, Arlene," I said, turning to Dr. Graber. "Just send me a bill."

"Forget it, Peggy. Just come around a bit more often, OK? I've missed you."

"OK." I nodded and hoped my face adequately showed my gratitude. Then she pulled me a bit aside.

"I honestly don't know what to think, Peggy. On the surface his story sounds completely crazy, but it's apparent that he hasn't had much benefit of modern medicine. That wrist, for one thing, was never x-rayed, or else it was seen to by an incompetent doctor. And that diet of his — I know it sounds fantastic, but it's consistent with his physical condition. Where on earth did he come from and, perhaps more relevant right now, where will he stay, Peggy?"

"I hadn't really thought about it. Not past today anyway."

"You know Marv and I have all that room now that the girls are in college. . . ." she offered, her eyes searching mine from behind her glasses, giving me a chance to wash my hands of this strange man through her own unusual generosity and kindness.

To just walk away and go back to my aimless wallowing existence was tempting, as hard to believe as that may sound, but I turned her down and thanked her all the same. Her openness and caring were reassuring, though, and I gave her a big hug before turning to go.

I guess I had decided for the time being that if anyone was going to give this young man a helping hand, it was going to be me. I had no doubt that Arlene had meant her offer to give Owen a place to stay. He had a certain trustworthiness about him, coupled with a need for guidance, that was nearly irresistible to anyone with an ounce of compassion. But it was going to be strange, even if this was only to be for a short time, to have a man around the house again. It wasn't really until this checkup with Arlene that I'd paid much notice of Owen as anything other than a lost waif in need of help. I could see now that, given different circumstances in which he felt at home (nineteenth-century or otherwise), he was probably a strong, competent individual with normal expectations and desires. But here, now, he was anything but this confident person I imagined him as being before he'd washed up here in Slea Head. I left Arlene's office no further along in deciphering Owen's story, but I was, at least, relieved that there was physically no serious damage.

Back in the car Owen was silent, probably pondering his fate now that the immediate need for medical assistance was dismissed. I looked over at his concerned face and started thinking about all he'd said at Arlene's office.

"Are you OK?" I asked as I started the engine.

"Aye, I'm 'OK,' " he answered, using the term for the first time.

"All those things you said . . . that man Wilkins . . . all that really happened to you?"

"It did."

"What a horrible life you must have had . . . before." Was I starting to believe him or was I only humoring a madman?

"It wasn't all like that. On a good ship it's a decent life. It's hard work, but a man needs to work hard, and you don't go hungry. We even had a bit of fun at times."

"You said your first ship was a good one," I reminded, hoping to hear more of whatever he had to tell me, real or make-believe.

"Aye. Captain Arniston was like a father to me, and Mrs. Arniston was always very kind."

"But she wasn't on the ship with you?"

"Aye, she made the voyage, too. I wasn't much more than a boy, really, and they took good care of me. Captain Arniston didn't allow the men to swear or drink, and the food was the best I've had aboard a ship. He even read to us from the Bible on Sundays. He had the most wonderful voice. He was born and educated in Edinburgh, and he spoke like a true Scotsman. I used to imagine my father as being very like him."

"What happened to your father?" I asked, wondering why he'd only his imagination to go on.

"I never knew him, really. He died when I was very young. My mother said he'd come from the top of the world, and I used to think he was a Viking or something, but really he came from the far north of Scotland. I guess that's why I pictured him later as being like Captain Arniston, though I'd always been told my father looked much as I do and not like Captain Arniston at all."

"And your mother?" I asked, fascinated by the intricacy of this past life that I wanted to believe belonged to this man of about my own age who sat beside me.

"She was a good woman," he said simply. "She used to work six days a week doing heavy cleaning, mending, and laundry for people — whatever work she could find. She might have done better as a domestic, but she had me to see to and couldn't very well live in someone else's home with a child of her own. I earned what I could, but times were very hard before she married Mr. Campbell, my stepfather. I should have been grateful to him, but I never liked him. For one thing, he told my mother she couldn't be a Catholic anymore, that she'd have to join his church, and I know that was terrible for her. But he could provide for us, and on our own it was getting harder and harder to pay for our lodgings. I brought home a little money, but when I overheard my stepfather say that I wasn't clever enough to ever earn my keep, I decided to go to sea."

"Weren't you still in school?" I asked, remembering that he'd said he'd only been fifteen when he'd left home.

"No. I worked all day cleaning stables and grooming horses."

I was intrigued, in spite of my reservations as to the veracity of these related experiences.

"You can't have been very old," I said. "Weren't you required to be in school?"

"No."

"There are laws now regarding child labor, you know. A kid can't work around here until he's well into his teens, and only then with parental permission, and he has to stay in school until he's at least sixteen. Most stay until they graduate, usually at eighteen."

"I don't understand. How can industry and

commerce prosper if a man's wages need to be paid for work that children can do?"

"We manage just fine without exploiting children. They have the rest of their lives to earn a living."

"At least I didn't work in the mines like my mother's family did back in Scotland, and work in the stables was far better than that in the factories."

"But you did go to school before that?"

"I have almost no schooling; I only went for a couple of years."

"Well, you don't sound like it," I conceded, fearing that I had come close to badgering in my defense of our system versus the one he described. It seemed to me, though, that he felt he had no inalienable rights, and I wanted to reach out to him, to show him that he was wrong. I reminded myself that this must be only some crazy act or unexplainable delusion of his. Probably he'd had a normal modern suburban upbringing that he just couldn't recall. Yet the more I heard, the more real his words became to me.

He thanked me for my compliment on his speech and went on to explain. "Captain and Mrs. Arniston used to help me, to correct me when I'd say the wrong thing. I'll always be grateful for the interest they took in me. I was only a cabin boy, and a green one, too. I'd get seasick and homesick," he said, and laughed. "I probably wasn't much use at first, but they were always very good to me."

"They sound wonderful, but isn't it unusual for a captain's wife to travel with her husband?"

"Aye. It's generally believed that women are bad luck on a voyage."

"Oh, yeah? So what else is bad luck?"

"Well, you never want to start a voyage on a Friday. Or have a minister on board, or furry things."

"Furry things?"

"Aye, rabbits. You don't even mention them by name when you're on board."

"Is anything good luck?"

"An albatross is a sign you'll have good fortune and fair winds."

"An albatross?"

"It's a great big white bird."

"Yes, I know," I said, amused at the oddity of the common ground we sometimes came across.

Our conversation had carried us back to the house. A bee, one of the few annoyances of early autumn, chased me from the car to the door.

"At least at sea you probably didn't have to deal with insects," I said as I batted it away.

"Only the ones in the bunks and in the food," Owen replied with a grin as he dashed into the house after me.

# CHAPTER 4

"We need to go shopping tomorrow," I said as we sat, once again, on the sunporch. "Can you think of anything you need other than some new clothes?"

"No, please, you've done too much for me already," Owen replied.

"Listen to me. I've decided to help you, and I'm not used to doing things halfway. Now, is there anything you left behind that maybe we could replace?"

"Would it be too much trouble to get a new pair of spectacles, then?"

This was a surprise. "No," I answered. "We can probably take care of that tomorrow. I'll just call in a minute to be sure you can get an appointment for an eye exam. Is there anything else?"

"The only other things I miss are my knife and my pipe, but I can live without them."

"I don't know anything about knives, but there's a tobacco shop right here in Slea Head, where I'm sure we can get you a pipe."

"Peggy," Owen began, and I realized it was the first time he'd called me by name, "I can't believe how kind you are. You're like an angel."

I laughed, but thought how hard his life must have been for so little to elicit such a response. I felt my throat tighten with the denial of tears. Like it or not, I had found myself back among the living, as though I were shedding a shell or breaking a sheath of ice that had shut me in and the world out.

"I'm no angel, Owen. Now, let me go call and make you an appointment to get your eyes checked." I excused myself to use the phone in the kitchen.

I got everything set up for the next day with an optometrist at the giant eyeglasses-in-an-hour place located about twenty minutes away. I even threw in a dental appointment for the following week. We'd see if he thought I was an angel after that.

I decided it was time to introduce my guest to the everyday world of the late twentieth century. I collected him from the sunporch and showed him everything I could think of that he might not be familiar with, starting with the light switch.

"It's a far cry from tallow candles, rushlights, and whale-oil lamps, I'll give you that. But how is it done?" he asked with predictable amazement when I'd turned on all the lights in my kitchen.

"Well," I began, unsure of the actual mechanics of the thing, figuring I could fake it if he really did only have basic knowledge from over a century before. "Electricity — you know, like what lightning's made of — comes into the house from wires on poles outside. The energy comes from some kind of power plant — hydro-electric or nuclear or coal-burning or something.

I honestly don't even know what kind."

Owen gave me a weak smile as if to say, you might as well go on since you've lost me and I may pick up something later that will actually make sense.

"Anyway, the electricity travels through wires behind the walls, and you can tap into it wherever you need it through one of these outlets," I said, pointing to where I had the coffeemaker plugged in on the kitchen counter.

"Is it quite safe?" he asked skeptically, gingerly touching the wall with his outstretched fingers as though he expected a shock.

"Of course, it's perfectly safe," I assured him. "Let's see, what else? The telephone you've already seen," I said, picking up the receiver and then putting it down, "and the TV," I added.

"The TV?"

"The television," I said and, feeling as corny as something from a bad Tarzan takeoff, I elaborated. "You know, the box with the moving pictures in it, out on the sunporch."

"What is its purpose?"

"You can get information, like from a newspaper, but for most people, it's how they get their entertainment."

"It seems a lonely way to pass the time. Usually amusement means the company of other people."

"You're right, I suppose, but people don't always have a lot of free time to go out with friends or family, and this comes right into your living room. There are programs on just about everything — travel, cooking, sports. . . .”

"It sounds like watching people live instead of doing it yourself."

I looked at his face to see if he'd meant this as a biting criticism, but he only seemed puzzled, and perhaps a little sad. "I guess so, from a certain point of view," I conceded, "but that's the way it is. What do you like doing for fun?"

He shrugged. "Playing at cards or drinking," he said with some embarrassment as though keenly aware that I would not think these pursuits appropriate to one of my class.

"Anything else?"

He looked like he was trying hard to think of something.

"Do you like to dance?" I prompted.

"Oh, no, I'm no dancer," he answered promptly, as though afraid I was going to ask him to demonstrate. "Are you . . . fond of dancing?" he asked.

"Hate it, actually," I said, and he looked relieved. We both smiled to find that we agreed on this at least.

"Well, there's more to show you if you're ready," I said.

"I am, thank you."

"This is the refrigerator. It keeps things cold," I said, and opened the door to show him.

"Look at all this food! You've got fruits and vegetables, and I don't know what else in this chest!"

"It's called a refrigerator. There's more to eat in the cupboards. You can help yourself once I've showed you the can opener and so on. And this is the freezer."

"You mean you can put something frozen in here, and it will stay frozen?"

"Yes."

"It's a marvel, this is. How is it done? Where is all the ice?"

"It uses Freon or some other refrigerant — it's a chemical of some kind. Technical stuff isn't really my strong suit. All I know is it works."

"And the food stays fresh?"

"Sure, that's the whole point."

"So you don't have to send someone to do the marketing every day? And you don't have to bake all the time?"

"Bake? Get real. Now, you aren't just having me on, are you?"

"What do you mean?"

"If this whole thing is a big joke, you can tell me. I can take it."

"What whole thing?"

"You know, you being a sailor and all."

He looked hurt. "You think I'm lying? God in heaven, I half wish I was."

"I'm sorry," I said, and I meant it. "Come on and I'll give you the rest of the tour."

I showed him the microwave, which he seemed to view with distrust. To him it must have been like something from a science fiction story. I introduced him to the stove, the can opener, the coffeemaker, the dishwasher, even the kitchen sink. It was actually kind of fun. Then I took him into the bathroom.

"This is the . . ." I began.

"The necessary?"

I had to laugh. "Yeah, the 'necessary.' Men usually use it standing up and put the seat up when they use it. And they *always* remember to put the seat back down."

I think Owen was embarrassed almost to the point of death. The appalled expression on his face mocked me, though, breaking the silliness for me of this whole bizarre experience.

"Sometimes, the things you say and do . . ." he began with a false start. "A proper lady would never . . ." he began again, but with no more success.

"I suppose I'm not an angel anymore then? I assure you that my behavior is perfectly 'proper,' " I said, getting angry at being accused in my own home of lacking class or a decent sense of decorum. "You've got a lot to learn about women in the twentieth century, Owen. We do a whole lot more than wear trousers. We can be surgeons and judges and anything else we want. Why, we even have the vote now!" I was really annoyed, but I shouldn't have been, considering his old-fashioned ways, and I guess knowing I was wrong made me act all the more self-righteous. I walked back to the kitchen in steaming silence. Owen followed.

"Please don't be angry with me," he said, and

took one of my hands in both of his. In the classic juvenile way, I wouldn't look at him. "I'm only ignorant, but I'll try to learn. I don't mean to offend. Your ways are just so different. Peggy, please, I haven't got anyone else."

I felt like a jerk. His hands were warm but calloused; they made me think of his voice that was at once both soft and rasping. He was a gentle man who had lived a rough life, and they suited him. I looked him in the face and noticed that a lock of almost white hair had fallen into his eyes. I brushed it back where it belonged with my free hand.

"I'm sorry, Owen," I said. "This has been the strangest day of my life, and yours, too, I imagine. I can't believe it's still the same day as when I found you on the beach. I guess I'm just a little overwhelmed. Come on, let's go for a walk."

We went to the beach, of course. The blue of the sky was unusually vivid where it glowed between the scattered drifting clouds, and the march of the waves and cries of the seabirds were soothing. We walked in silence for some time, watching the silly antics of the gulls.

"You know," I began, "I was in Nova Scotia once, with Peter. Yarmouth is still a lovely town. Actually, all of it was beautiful."

"Did you know Donald MacKay was Nova Scotian?" he asked with pride.

"Donald MacKay? Who's he?"

Owen looked at me with frank disbelief. "He's

the greatest ship designer in the world. Have you never heard of the *Flying Cloud*, then?"

Owen had the peculiar Canadian pronunciation that turned "out and about" into "oat and a boat," and so "Cloud" came out as something close to "Cload."

I smiled, "Yes, I've heard of the *Flying Cloud*."

"Well, that's one of his ships. I've only seen pictures of her, but I saw the *Stag Hound* once. She's one of his, too."

We were silent again for some time and then, gazing at the horizon, where one could never be sure of the border between sea and sky, he said, "You must come out here sometimes just to watch the ships." It was more statement than question. "The sails, when the wind catches them . . . there's no grander sight in the world."

"Owen," I said softly, "there are no sailing ships anymore, not like you knew."

He looked down at the sand, then far out to sea. "I was afraid of that. I'd heard it said that steam would mean the end of the great sailing ships."

He squinted up at the painful blueness of the sky. "It'll rain by morning," he said.

"What makes you say that?" I asked. The clouds that floated across their cerulean sea were few and, besides, after a very dry summer I'd grown used to false alarms.

"Experience, I guess. I got very good at telling when it would rain and when it would really storm. But it may be that that's changed, too."

I had no answer to that.

"Let's go home." Just like that I'd said it, "home," as if it was the place where we both belonged.

That night I cried myself to sleep. I don't know why. Of late I'd been too numb to do so, I guess, but I hadn't forgotten how. I awoke in darkness. It might have been four or five o'clock in the morning. I got out of bed and softly padded down the hall past the guest room where Owen had gone to sleep. The door was open, and I could see that the bed, which I had earlier turned down, was once again neatly made.

In my half-awakened state I told myself that Owen had been a dream, that I'd only imagined a poor wayfarer that needed my guidance and gave me a reason to feel alive again, but I wasn't very good at self-delusion, and so I decided to go downstairs to look for him. For a moment, while I slowly descended the steps, I felt as though the weight of the world was on me when I thought of the responsibility I'd taken on. Yet, when I pictured Owen and his warm sincerity, a man who had not deserved to end up as so much flotsam on the Jersey Shore, the onus lifted and was replaced by a serene feeling of appreciation at the good fortune that had brought him into my life.

Thoughts of his naïveté and general sweetness of temperament again put his actual existence into doubt in my sleep-addled brain, but as my mind cleared, I recalled that he was generally more earthy than otherworldly and that he'd never claimed to be an angel or supernatural being, only a man out of place in time. Perhaps, I thought, he had disappeared back into the breach of time through which he'd come, leaving me alone with my old unending sorrow and loneliness. The idea gave me a moment of panic, as I had not yet seen or heard any sign of him. Then, my mind at last came into a more alert state, and I was reasonably sure I knew where I would find him — on the sunporch, where he could hear the sea.

When I entered the room, the only brightness came from a neighbor's porch light, not enough for me to do much more than sense Owen's presence. I didn't speak, but lowered myself silently into the wicker chair across from where he sat.

"Everyone I ever met is dead," he said in a voice so low that it seemed as though the stillness had never been disturbed when he was done.

I listened for the sound of the waves outside. Tempered by glass, wood, and plaster, they ceased to really roar, but still the slow-measured tread of life on the coast was marked by their tireless motion. Rush and recede, rush and recede, they kept the time as we sat without speaking, and I waited for him to go on. I tried to see his face, but only barely picked out his fair hair in the darkened room. Behind him, through the windows, I thought I could just discern the phosphorescence of the foam against the deepest black of the night as successive waves hit the beach. I imagined the saltiness of the air outside, but the only scent in the room was the faint one of an unlit vanilla candle that sat on the small wicker table beside me. The silence of our own making went on for some time, and, when he was finally ready, I just let him talk.

"I've been used to being on my own, having lost both my parents," he said, and I waited patiently for him to continue. "No one I've even so much as laid eyes on before yesterday is still alive. I can't seem to grasp the idea of that. My friend Frenchy . . . he's been dead over a hundred years, yet, for me, it's only been a day or two since I last saw him. And Captain Arniston. I hadn't seen him in a couple of years; his sailing days were over, but I knew he was still alive, back in Yarmouth, and I'd planned to call on him the next time I got back. They're all gone," he said, more in amazement than disbelief.

The waves outside sounded unnaturally loud when he stopped talking. I have always had to work hard at being more patient, especially when my curiosity is aroused, but minutes passed with grace as I waited again for him to let me in. I think some of my doubts passed with the time. I knew I was faced with a man who'd all but lost everything he ever knew, not a charlatan out to make a fool of me. The horror of the situation was at least real to him. I hungered for his next words because I knew they meant that he trusted me, that whatever he was going through, he would share it with me. I expected him to be angry, and I was prepared to let him express his sense of being cheated out of a familiar existence and thrown willy-nilly into my life.

The only sounds came from beyond the windows, and it began to seem to me after several minutes more as though the ocean's persistent washing of the beach would be the only sound I would ever know again. I became mesmerized by its regular rhythm that drew enough visual associations in my mind to never become merely white noise. Over and over I waited for the crashing surf to tell me something, to give me a reason for the situation in which we now found ourselves. I almost forgot that I wasn't alone here in the dark, that Owen wasn't some fond imagining or pleasant memory from some half-remembered dream. Then I heard him begin to cry.

When the tears had run their course, he spoke. "I'm sorry," he said.

"I can only imagine what you're going through," I answered. "It must be truly awful. But from what I've heard, it sounds like the life you had was pretty dreary, if not downright horrible. I don't know anyone who's had any experience as bad as the one you described at Dr. Graber's office. Maybe you're only remembering the good things. Think about what happened on the *Aurora Borealis*. You have to admit that's pretty terrible."

"It was. But that only happened once. It wasn't all as 'dreary' as you'd have it. I think you expect too much. Why do you think you can have paradise on earth? I was taught that we would find it only later, and then only if we were deserving. And I don't seem to have earned it."

"Maybe this is a second chance for you. Maybe there's a reason you were in limbo, or whatever, all this time," I said. "I can't promise you'll never have regrets about ending up here, but I think you could be happy."

"I will try to be patient. It may be that a reason will show itself. I do want to thank you, Peggy, for everything."

At that moment, like a release, the rain Owen had predicted began to fall.

"Why don't we try going back to sleep," I said.

"You go. Please. I always have trouble sleeping the first couple of nights back on dry land. Everything's so still, and I miss the sound of her."

"Her?"

"Aye. The ship. She's like a living thing. Frenchy used to say you've got to love her, and never cross her, and treat whatever ship you're on like she was the only one you'd ever known. He was always a bit of a loon," he said with a soft laugh, "but I knew what he meant. A ship's a beautiful, powerful thing, and when you're out at sea, she's the only thing between you and certain death. You respect her, and I guess you love her, too. It's hard to think my sailing days are gone for good." He paused a moment. "Now, I've kept you awake for far too long as it is. Please, I'll be fine in a bit. Go on up to bed."

I did, and slept well until the percussion of

gently falling rain brought me into the new day. The light in my bedroom was diffuse from filtering through raindrops and lace curtains. I took my time stretching and yawning, luxuriating in the thought that I had nowhere to go and yet would not be spending the day in meaningless solitude. I finally rose. I wasn't tired, merely relaxed and content. It had been a long time since I'd felt that way, and perhaps, I thought, I was on the way to being fully alive to the possibilities in life again. It was a pleasant, though somewhat frightening, idea, in light of how rusty I'd become at the whole thing.

When I finally left my room and got halfway down the stairs, I heard voices. I recognized them both — Owen, of course, and Marjorie.

"Good morning, Peggy," Marjorie said. Owen had risen from his seat when I'd entered the room and murmured his "good morning" as well. I could see, or rather smell, that Marjorie had made herself comfortable in my kitchen, but the scent of the fresh pot of coffee was more than welcome. I poured myself a large mugful.

"I've just been talking to your new friend," Marjorie began, her voice and expression investing the term with a slew of connotations. "He said you met on the beach."

"I'm sure he must have told you that I *found* him on the beach, washed up with the tide."

"Yes, very charming. Almost romantic, I'd say."

"Don't you have to get to work?"

"Oh, I've got plenty of time. Mr. Sinclair, was it?"

Owen nodded.

"Tell me all about yourself."

I could tell that Owen was embarrassed. "What do you want to know?" he asked, and smiled uncomfortably.

"Well, what do you do? Where did you go to school? All the usual stuff."

Oh, God, I could see it coming. I guess it was inevitable that they would meet, but I should have somehow prepared Owen for my sister and her legal mind. It's not that I would have asked him to lie or to pretend to be something that he wasn't, but I think I got all the imagination in the family, and in meeting Owen, I think a little might have been helpful.

"I was a sailor until recently."

"A navy boy, eh?" Marjorie asked, shooting me a suggestive glance. I figured it was time for damage control, but Owen was already explaining.

"No, ma'am. I was a sailor on a clipper ship before I was washed overboard."

"Uh-huh," Marjorie said, and I quickly changed the subject.

"We've got a busy day ahead. Owen lost his glasses, and we're off to get him another pair. First, we've got some shopping to do, then his eye exam. . . ." I was talking quickly, trying to give Marjorie the impression that I didn't have time to chat with her, but she was being intentionally obtuse.

"I always love getting my eyes examined," she said. "I'm always so good at reading all that fine print — no legal joke intended — and my optometrist is always so jealous."

"Peggy," Owen began, but couldn't seem to continue. Even Marjorie stopped talking as I waited for him to go on.

"Can we cancel the appointment?" he asked.

"Why?"

"I can't read." He said it softly, looking me in the eye, but still with something downcast about his face.

"What do you mean? I thought you said you went to school for a couple of years. Surely, . . ."

"I couldn't learn it," he said miserably. "I tried, but I just couldn't." He was clearly mortified. I didn't know what to say.

"Do you even have a job, Mr. Sinclair?" Marjorie asked, not missing a single beat, as always. I had forgotten for a moment she was in the room with us. When Owen didn't respond, she went on to make matters worse. "What's your angle? Money? Sex?"

Owen blushed furiously, but didn't answer. This wasn't going well at all.

"Marjorie, stop it!" I said, but she was on a roll.

"If you think I'm going to stand by while you try to take advantage of my sister, you've got another thing coming. You try anything funny, and I'll have your ass in court so fast it'll make your head spin." At any other time I might have stopped to wonder if this wasn't a case of mixing metaphors.

"Marjorie," I yelled. "If I need your help, I'll ask for it."

"Please," Owen said quietly. "I think I should go. I don't want to come between you. But I want you to know," he said as he turned to Marjorie, "I would never do anything to hurt your sister. She's one of the kindest people I've ever met." His crazy mismatched eyes met mine. "I want to thank you, Peggy. I won't ever forget all you did for me." In spite of his recent admission of ignorance and his ill-fitting clothes, I think he was the only one of us with his dignity intact.

"You apologize now, or I'll never speak to you again," I hissed at Marjorie as I watched Owen walk out the door.

"What's the deal with this guy, Peggy? Two days ago when I stopped by, you were in an emotional coma. Now you've got this strange man staying with you, and he can't even read? What's wrong with him, and what makes you think he's your problem?"

"*Now,* Marjorie," I said, ignoring her questions, as I headed for the beach, where I hoped to find Owen. Marjorie followed.

I reached him easily. He was standing in the surf in his bare feet, throwing shells as far out as he could into the water. The rain had almost stopped, but the air was cool and what precipitation there was acted like a mist, coating our skin and hair with fine droplets of water.

"Listen, Mr. Sinclair, I'm very sorry," Marjorie said. "I'm only looking out for Peggy. Surely you can understand that."

"Aye," he said, but didn't turn to look at either of us.

"Will you say you forgive me, then, so Peggy won't be angry with me, and we can get in out of this rain?"

I held my breath and my peace as I waited to hear his response.

"I'm no one to be forgiving anyone."

"Will you come back, Owen? Please?" I asked, and I think he saw the futility of pretending he had anywhere else to go. He nodded his head and dropped the last of the shells from his hand.

"Will you at least shake hands?" Marjorie asked him, and he complied with the look of a chastened man.

Marjorie and I followed him back to the house. Her usually perfect hair was limp and damp.

"I *am* sorry, Peggy, but you've got to admit there's something really different about this guy. It was only natural I'd be suspicious. Don't be mad, OK?"

"Yeah, OK," I said. I was tired of arguing. I wanted to get back inside.

"Will he be staying long?" she asked tentatively, obviously afraid of starting anything again.

"I don't know, Marjorie. I hope so."

In so saying I had surprised myself and finally

committed to adopting Owen's problems, long term, as my own.

After Marjorie left, it took a lot of banter and smiles to restore some semblance of good humor to the house. I tried to excuse her behavior but could not.

"She cares a great deal about you. You're lucky for that," Owen said, more forgiving than I would have been.

"She thinks like a lawyer, Owen. She can't help that, I suppose."

"I guess I haven't gotten off to a very good start with your family."

"Families can be a real liability sometimes," I said, "but, please, let's forget about Marjorie for now. All right?"

He agreed with a smile.

Together we made breakfast — bacon, eggs, the whole nine yards. Something of the sourness of the morning still hung in the air for a while, but by the time I'd showered and dressed and Owen had done the same, albeit in the same hodgepodge of hand-me-downs, my spirits had risen with the prospect of our day on the town.

Slea Head, New Jersey, is predominantly Irish, definitely lace curtain. In fact, it takes its name from a point near the end of the Dingle Peninsula, not far from Tralee. It's not unusual to see the flags of Eire and Notre Dame fluttering in the wind outside some of Slea Head's grander homes and the main street boasts not one, but two, shops that sell Irish imports. There are also two chocolate shops for sweet tooths and tourists, three or four realtors, and a number of upscale clothing, toy, book, and antique stores. Beneath the variegated rooflines and among the quaint mix of facades can be found the usual jumble of small-town establishments, too, but with a charming seaside air. Most of the display windows paid homage to Halloween now, the last hurrah of autumn before the retail push for Christmas. Elsewhere in town stood large elegant homes on manicured lawns, an enormous Victorian hotel, and several tastefully maintained bed-and-breakfasts.

My family had lived here for many generations, having come from County Kerry in the dim and distant past. By the time Marjorie, my brother Ryan, and I had been born, the Celtic stock was still pure, but only my grandmother had raised an eyebrow when I'd married a blue-blooded WASP instead of an O'Grady or a Flynn.

Normally I would have walked downtown, but for several reasons I elected to drive. For one thing, the rain had stopped, but its continued abeyance was by no means guaranteed. I also planned to buy more than we could probably carry home comfortably. Lastly, there was the matter of Owen's shoes, or rather, lack of them. Taking care of that problem would be the first order of business.

I found a parking place along the curb on the main shopping street, not too difficult a feat at this time of the year, and Owen and I got out. I could tell that he was self-conscious in his bare feet, but it wasn't so very far past the height of the summer season and the weather was still generally mild enough that I didn't think people would take much notice. Luckily, we didn't have far to walk to reach Gilpin's Shoes, one of the shops that had been serving the locals of Slea Head since before I was born.

On entering the store, which had kept up with the times and looked no more out-of-date than any other store at the local mall, Owen commented first on, not the new carpeting or jazzy acrylic display stands, but on something more fundamental.

"It sure is bright in here," he said under his breath to me, and I automatically looked up.

"Oh, they're fluorescents. It's just a different kind of electric lighting. And, yes, they're very bright," I said, validating his remark to let him know that his comment wasn't so very far out of line.

In a couple of minutes we were joined by the store's only employee at the moment, a young man of about twenty, who looked as though he'd taken a bad turn somewhere and had ended up on the wrong coast. His hair was short and spiky and bleached a remarkable platinum blond, but with dark roots all the same. He wore several earrings in each ear, a choker of shiny chrome beads, and a tattoo of a stylized sun was clearly visible below one short sleeve of his blue dress shirt. The shirt and neatly pressed khaki slacks were no doubt a concession to the requests of the store's management, but his hair, jewelry, deep tan, and way of speaking once he'd addressed us were like a caricature of a California surfer boy.

"What happened to that boy's hair?" Owen asked under his breath.

"Never mind, I'll explain later," I confided before facing the young salesman with an open smile. His words to Owen served to widen it into a broad grin.

"Hey, man, you sure came to the right place. I mean, like, you're not wearing any shoes!" he said, clearly amused at Owen's plight, but his half smile was nothing if not good-natured. Owen seemed a bit ill at ease to be out in public in such a state. I think the age of the clerk gave him some confidence, though, and he made a visible effort to hold up his head and get through with this very necessary errand.

I let the young man know we'd need a few minutes to look around, and he shrugged with a smile and went back to whatever he'd been doing in the back room before we'd entered. I could faintly hear an electric guitar wailing on a radio in the general area of where he'd gone.

"How about these?" I suggested, holding up a pair of white-soled moccasins commonly worn at dockside and on sailboats.

Owen only gave me a quizzical look in reply and continued straining his eyes for something more in keeping with what he was used to.

"All these are already made?" he asked. "The mates to these, too?" he added, picking up a sample shoe that was set out to showcase that particular model.

"Yes, you'll be able to get whatever you need today."

He studied a very high-heeled black woman's shoe that mainly consisted of a series of thin satiny straps and held it up for my inspection. He raised his eyebrows in an unspoken question.

"What?" I asked. "They're impractical, sure, but with the right outfit, I don't know. . . ."

"You would wear this?"

"Probably not, but it's *acceptable,* culturally for me to wear those if I want to."

He nodded silently, storing another bit of information for his future in the modern world.

He then selected a sturdy-looking work boot and held the sample next to his own bare foot.

"Too small," he said, and I laughed spontaneously when I figured out what he'd meant.

"That's just an example to show you what it looks like. I'm sure they'll have a pair in your size in the back."

"Already made up?"

"Already made up," I assured him.

"Then, that's what I'll have, if you'll promise that I can pay you for them later. Can you tell me how much money that will be?"

"Don't worry about it. I just want to know if you're sure that's what you want."

"The number of choices *is* baffling, and

they're all a bit strange to me. Is this something appropriate for me? It seems . . . sensible." He seemed to be choosing his words with some care, and I assured him that his choice was both "appropriate" and "sensible."

"You'll need a pair of dress shoes as well, and I'd like you to get a pair of sneakers, too."

"No, Peggy, enough is enough. I can't even repay you for these boots now, and I've no need of another pair."

"Well, what did you used to wear on board your ship?"

"Nothing if it was warm enough, seaboots otherwise."

"And before you were a sailor?"

"Short boots with laces. Not like these, really, but near enough. As close as I can find here."

"Well, you'll probably find that sneakers are the best thing for everyday. They're very comfortable, and you'll need dress shoes eventually, so you may as well get them now."

"I must insist, Peggy, that you don't spend any more money than is absolutely necessary. I've never owned three pairs of boots at one time in my life. Such a thing is clearly excessive in my case."

His stubbornness surprised me, but I had ammunition against his arguments.

"Owen, I don't have any money problems, OK? My grandparents have left enough money in trust for me to keep me comfortably all the days of my life. My husband was obscenely well insured when he died. My writing makes enough that I could live on it if I had to, and I've been living like a monk the last two years. So just let me enjoy myself, will you?" I asked, ending my verbal onslaught, knowing I had worn him down with my arguments.

"When I'm able, you *will* let me pay you back?" he asked in return, and there was a demanding note to his words and mien.

"All right, if it makes you happy."

He nodded that it did and then asked rather bashfully, "What are sneakers?"

"Come on," I said, motioning with my head for him to follow me to the back wall of the store, which displayed one of each of perhaps fifty different styles of athletic shoes.

"Some of these are very odd indeed," he said, picking up a pair of basketball shoes with acid-green trimming and a clear plastic cutout in the heel.

"They're for playing sports, or at least that was the original idea. They're very comfortable and acceptable for all but the dressiest occasions these days."

"Most of them are terribly . . . *white,*" Owen replied, "or worse."

"You just look around when we leave here. You'll see, everybody's wearing them, men and women of all ages, children. Look, even I am, OK?"

The clerk chose that moment to make his reappearance, and Owen checked out *his* footwear and murmured "sneakers" under his breath, as-sured now that they were appropriate at least for both males and females.

"Can we have one of those things for mea-suring your shoe size?" I asked the kid.

"You mean, like, you don't know your own shoe size?"

"We just want to be sure, OK?"

"Fine with me. I'll just have to find the thing. I think it's in the back someplace. Hang on while I go look, OK?"

"No problem. Hey, have you been working here long?" I asked, curious at his lack of knowl-edge and incongruity with what had always been a rather stodgy family-run business serving the discriminating well-to-do patrons of Slea Head.

"Only since June. It's my uncle's business, you know, and he and my dad decided if I wasn't going to go to college right away, I had to work here. Bummer, huh?"

"Yeah," I agreed, "but it could be worse. The family business could have been meatpacking or landfills or something worse."

"Oh yeah," he grinned, "or a funeral parlor, huh? And this is right near the beach, and any-place with babes in bikinis can't be all bad!" he added, and left on his search.

"Bikinis?" Owen asked.

"Never mind. Let's just take this one culture shock at a time," I said, remembering his embar-rassment at seeing me in my very undaring swimsuit.

We eventually settled on an appropriate pair of sneakers, the work boots, and a somber pair of black dress shoes that I was sure would come in handy before too long. We also picked out a pair of socks so that Owen would be able to leave the store wearing his new sneakers. As I paid at the register, Owen fingered the packaging on a pair of shoelaces, obviously taken by the transparent plastic that he kept testing for flexibility and durability with his thumbnail. Seeing him study the most mundane things was good for my soul as I became more alert to the subtleties in life than I had been in a very long time, perhaps in some ways more than I had ever been before.

As we left the store, Owen's gait showed that he was clearly enjoying his new purchase. There was a bounce in his stride as he explored the never-before felt comfort of a good pair of sneakers.

"They're very light," he said, "and soft inside. It's like walking on clouds!" he added, and then looked down, apparently embarrassed at such a flowery remark.

"I'm glad you like them," I said with a smile I couldn't stop from coming to my face. "We've only just started, though, so we'd better keep moving."

The next stop was a gentleman's clothing store, also on the main street, where my father had shopped since he'd come of age many years before. When we entered, we were greeted by Mr. Murray, a fixture at the store for as long as I could remember. I really didn't know if he was part owner in the business or just a salesclerk of the old school. In any case, he spoke smoothly, as though he had only seen me the week before, as though my young husband of four years had not dropped dead in his dental office not five doors down from where we stood. Neither did he bat an eye at Owen's presence.

"Mrs. Millwright, how are you? You look well. How can I help you today?"

Owen had wandered off somewhere in the maze of shelves and racks.

"Well, Mr. Murray, I've got my cousin Owen with me. Owen Sinclair, of the Yarmouth Sinclairs," I said and thought, there's nothing quite so predictable or useful, really, as snobbery. "He hasn't been quite the same since a boating accident," I said quietly, as though this were just our little secret. Mr. Murray nodded his grey head sagely. This was really getting to be fun. "I need you to help him pick out just about everything — starting with socks and underwear. Assume he has nothing."

"Very well."

"He'll need jeans, some other casual clothes, some in-between stuff, and a nice suit," I said, thinking, sooner or later, he was going to have to meet the rest of the clan, and I wasn't going to have him at a disadvantage when he met my grandmother. "Oh, and an overcoat."

In deference to my family, Mr. Murray saw to Owen himself. He didn't show a sign that he was

82

ruffled in any way, even when Owen asked him to explain what a zipper was for. I hung in the background, pretending to browse, waiting to hear the next challenge to Mr. Murray's straight face.

I could tell Owen was groping for anything familiar, so I wasn't surprised to see him pick out a peacoat, a navy blue oiled-wool crew neck, and a traditional Aran knit sweater. I think the rest of the stuff was more or less foisted on him by Mr. Murray, who knew as well as anyone what a young man needs and, moreover, had excellent taste.

This was the first time I'd ever seen Owen not at a sartorial disadvantage. In his properly fitted jeans and sweater, he was more than presentable, and the blue of the wool complemented his eyes. He was not as handsome as Peter had been, but there was something about the curve of his upper lip and his Devil's eyes, as his stepfather would have it, that held my fascination. I had to admit that his shyness, too, had a charm of its own.

Mr. Murray carried Owen's new clothes to the counter, where an ambitious young man carefully packaged them.

"You still have an account with us, Mrs. Millwright," Mr. Murray suggested, and I knew that he meant he'd honor the tab he'd set up for Peter.

"Thank you, Mr. Murray, but I'll be using my credit card today."

"Of course."

Owen carried the bulk of our purchases, but when he headed in the direction of the car, I told him we had one more quick stop to make.

He followed me a few doors down to the tobacco shop. We passed by Peter's old office, sold with all his dental equipment and practice to an older, but healthier man. I wondered briefly if Beth, his hygienist, was happy there. Sweet Beth, with her short dark hair, pastel uniforms, and reassuring smile — I hadn't seen her face in months, though we once had had almost daily contact. To me, she was as much a part of that office as the familiar waiting room furniture, and it was hard to picture her carrying on in the same capacity that she had for Peter for the new man who'd taken over. I forced my thoughts back to the present, realizing that I'd slowed my pace without quite stopping outside the door.

"Is something wrong?" Owen asked me. I guess he was more perceptive than I'd given him credit for.

"This used to be my husband's office. I haven't been by here in a while, that's all."

Owen took the few packages I had from my arms as if that could ease the other, invisible load I carried inside.

"Come on," I said, determined for a change not to wallow.

We were welcomed warmly, if not as personally, in the next shop. The proprietor could tell from our bags that we were no mere window-shoppers, and the treatment we rated was in accordance with that. Or maybe I was just being cynical, and the old pipe smoker behind the counter was just as genuinely nice as he seemed.

"Hello, hello! Has the rain kept off?" he boomed in a rich resonant baritone.

"Aye, it has," Owen answered.

"You sound like a sailor, young man," our retail host observed enthusiastically.

"Aye, I was, until not long ago."

As far as I was concerned, the purchasing of a pipe was a manly domain, and so I left them to it.

"What can I get for you today, sir?" The man's round-faced good humor was infectious. I found myself liking him — thundering voice and all.

"I need a new pipe," Owen said. "I lost my last one going headfirst in the drink," he added, and they both laughed.

"I haven't done that yet, but I dropped my house keys over the side of my boat last summer," the store owner said, and laughed again. He actually guffawed, and I watched the wrinkles form around his eyes and on his perfectly bald head.

"A clay pipe will do."

"A clay pipe?" the man asked, unsure, I guess, of whether or not Owen was pulling his leg. I decided to step in.

"How about this one, Owen," I said, pointing to a simple, but probably expensive, meerschaum in the display case under the counter.

"It's very nice," Owen began politely as the

still-jolly owner took it out and handed it to him, "but, really, all I need . . ."

"We'll take it," I interrupted. "Now, how about picking out some tobacco."

There was apparently more to this process than I would have imagined, and it was a full twenty minutes later before they'd argued the merits of various blends and had settled on one. The scents were a heady mix of spicy, herbal, and fruit-like perfumes, unspoiled by the smell of the tobacco itself.

"We've got to get going, Owen," I said, and paid for the pipe, tobacco, and a lighter, which I looked forward to demonstrating for him.

On the way back to the car, he expressed his concerns again about the upcoming eye exam.

"Do you know your letters?" I asked, careful not to sound condescending. After all, I was hardly qualified to judge him, coming from a completely different world as I did.

"Most of them. I always get a couple of them mixed up."

"Well, if they can test children too young to read and get them the right prescription, I guess they won't have any trouble with you."

Owen seemed reassured, and when he was finally settled in the car, smoking his pipe, he looked downright content. He'd done pretty well with the lighter, too, after I'd shown him how it worked, only once coming close to setting his hair on fire.

The exam itself went smoothly after I explained to the optometrist that Owen was unable to read. He raised an eyebrow in question but competently steered Owen in the right direction to get an accurate rating of his vision. After the exam, I expected to spend a good deal of time watching Owen choose frames. This he did in about five minutes, selecting a pair of round gold wire rims that he said were the closest the store had to the pair he'd lost. With an hour to kill, there was nothing to do then but to go out for lunch. It wasn't exactly what the doctor ordered, but I had my heart set on taking him out for burgers at a fast-food joint.

"Well, what do you think?" I asked when we'd sat down with our order at one of the restaurant's bright red and yellow booths.

Owen scanned the dining room with its vibrant hues and cartoon characters on the walls. "Don't they make anything out of wood anymore? Things at your house look *real*, well, mostly anyway, but what is this stuff?" he asked, knocking on the molded seat of the booth.

"Plastic. It's just cheaper to use than wood, I guess, and you don't have to cut down trees to make it."

"Oh. It's a shame it's so cold and ugly, though, eh?"

I laughed. I think he was really starting to trust me as an unconditional friend. I then explained to him that my house was definitely not the norm, that I collected what were to me "antiques," but that in most homes, unlike public places such as restaurants, stores, and offices, the furniture was still mostly made of wood. He looked relieved, as though he'd feared we'd become creatures that preferred impersonal, sterile environments, and was gratified to find we hadn't — at least not entirely.

"Well, eat up," I said. "It's not every day you try your first cheeseburger."

Owen picked up the burger, smelled it, and, eyeing me over the top of it, took a healthy bite.

"Oh, it's beef," he said with his mouth full. "I expected something exotic. It's good."

He seemed to like the root beer well enough, too, although he'd made a face after the first sip.

"Why is everything so fast now?" he asked. "This 'fast food' as you call it, the spectacles in only an hour. . . . Why is everyone in such a hurry?"

"That's a good question, but you're not a good one to ask it," I answered.

"Why not?"

"Just look at you. You're already done eating," I said, and it was true that, although he didn't really eat a lot, he bolted his food.

He looked sheepish. "Sorry," he said, "I'm used to food so bad there's no reason to stop and enjoy it. Some of it you'd just as soon eat in the dark, if you know what I mean. Sometimes, too, you've got to get to your watch, so you haven't got a lot of time to lollygag over your dinner."

"Well, feel free to 'lollygag' next time, OK?"

He grinned but then turned serious. "Peggy, I need to find work. It's not right for a man to be living off a woman like this."

"Owen, you've only just been fished out of the Atlantic. Consider yourself on vacation."

"Vacation?" he asked, as though such a thing was not for the likes of him.

"Like when you're between voyages, then. We'll find a place for you, don't worry. For now, why don't you just try to have fun. Come on, it's about time we got going."

Back at the store, Owen was thrilled with his new glasses.

"They're fantastic!" he enthused. "Things have never looked so clear. They're much better than my old spectacles ever were," he added, and gave me a big bear hug. "Thank you, Peggy."

"Let me look at you," I said, pulling back. I think we were both a little embarrassed by his ardor. "They make you look smart."

"I've never been accused of that before." He smiled, but I didn't doubt the sincerity of his remark. He wasn't prone to self-pity, but he certainly had a sense of his lack of significance in the big scheme of things. A school of hard knocks sort of lesson, I imagined.

Back home, the comment wasn't far from my mind when I picked up the phone that had begun ringing as soon as I shoved my key into the lock of the side door of my house.

"Hello," I said, relieved to have won my race against the answering machine, which would have picked up after the fourth ring. Out of the corner of my eye, I could see Owen bringing in the bags from our day's shopping. I covered the mouthpiece of the phone.

"Just put them anywhere. We'll sort out where everything goes later," I told him. He wandered off, I assumed to allow me some privacy.

"Peggy, it's Bill." Wry, tall, elegant Bill, my brother-in-law. "I heard all about your flaxen-haired sailor boy, Peggy. I guess if a man can have a bimbo, why not . . ."

I cut him off. "What do you want, Bill?"

"Sorry. Couldn't resist. Listen, Marjorie and I really want to get together with you. With both of you, if that's the case."

"It is. For the time being Owen is my house-guest, and you might as well know it."

I guess I sounded defensive because he said, "OK, OK, it's not a problem. We just want to see you, Peg."

Bill was the only one I let get away with calling me that. Bill and I had always shared a sarcastic sense of humor and good-natured cynicism that Marjorie and Peter had not always appreciated. He'd also been a good husband to Marjorie and a true and worthy friend to Peter. I owed him enough not to shut him out anymore. There was also a part of me that wanted to share Owen with the people who had been important in my life before I'd hidden myself in my sorrow. Sooner or later I'd have to trust that my family would accept him as he was. Come what may, I was finished with my life as an emotional cripple sequestered in the eternal winter that had existed in the private garden of my mind.

# CHAPTER 5

Two days later, on the second anniversary of Peter's death, my heartache forgot to wake me, and I slept later than I had in years. Perhaps it was knowing subconsciously through the night that there was another heart beating under my roof, or perhaps time had finally begun to heal. I don't know. I only realized that this day would be hard, but that tomorrow would be better, and the next better still. My feelings of guilt as I suffered my mourning to slip from me were few, but there nonetheless. I wondered briefly if it wasn't selfish of me to want to go on living. Before, I had survived because my grief was only capable of wounding, not of delivering the mortal blow I would have welcomed like a lover. Now, I no longer feared my life. My time with Peter had been nearly perfect, a precious jewel I could treasure in my memory if not hold in my hands. If something as good would never come my way again, so be it, but it was time to breathe the fresh air outside my sepulchral existence, even if it turned out to be bitter and cold.

I wandered the house like a phantom in honor of the day. Owen stayed in the background, like the hearth that is both the soul of a house and its most tangible source of warmth. He left me to myself but not alone. I appreciated his tact and the companionship I knew I had only to reach out to find.

At the appropriate times he would seek me out and bring me something to eat or drink, but very few words passed between us, and when the day ended, I felt as though I had survived a rite of passage, that my catharsis was at last complete.

I suppose that elsewhere in the Garden State, the last of the crops were being harvested — the pumpkins, the gourds, the shocks of corn sold for autumn decoration. But, as September gave way to October, the autumn for me now held a springtime of the soul. I agreed gladly to see Marjorie and Bill, to share my good fortune. I was coming to life again, rediscovering the pleasures of the world. The oddity of Owen's being here was like a wonderful game of make-believe, which I willingly played, to hell with the rules of logic. Almost nothing was immediately familiar to him, and so not invested with the contempt that generally rendered mundane things all but invisible in my daily life. I had always taken technology for granted and never wondered how things worked, but Owen was curious as a child and I played along as he explored my world. When knowledge could be gained without the written word, he learned quickly. We watched a lot of public television, at my insistence, to get him up to speed on everything from the history of space travel to the glorious past of baseball. It was a time of constant discovery, and he absorbed his education like a sponge.

He still surprised me daily with some anecdote from his earlier life or belief that had long since been discounted. He was seldom without his pipe in his mouth, lit or unlit, and this weighed against his overall boyishness to make me take him more seriously as a man. Still, I had to keep myself from laughing as I'd listen to some particularly outrageous piece of superstition or misinformation of his, and it never failed to make me smile when I caught him crossing himself at the sight of an airplane or helicopter.

At the end of the first week of October, after two days of warm winds and rain carried north from a tropical storm in the Gulf of Mexico, Marjorie, Bill, Owen, and I finally got together for a late lunch at Chick's, a popular local pizzeria.

The air had turned crisp or "bracing," as the English put it, but I insisted that we walk. We had pizza, of course, which is the only thing served at Chick's. Owen hadn't yet tried it, but I think he enjoyed it well enough after he saw the rest of us eating without ill effects and decided to give it a try. He even slowed down enough to taste it.

The decor inside Chick's had probably remained the same since the 1950s. Neat, but worn, Formica-topped booths line one knotty pine wall of the narrow premises, with one long table for larger parties of customers and the work area for food preparation and pizza ovens lining the other. Patrons can't get salads, sandwiches, or side orders, and they must bring their own wine or beer, but the pizza is legendary in the area. Pepperoni and other toppings are grudgingly supplied, but anyone who is any kind of a regular there or considers himself an aficionado of "tomato pie," as the locals call it, gets one of Chick's specials with extra tomato, that is, heaping with chunky, homemade, miraculously delicious tomato sauce. There are times when people are lined out the door and down the sidewalk waiting for one of the dozen or so tables inside, but we were lucky to find a place to sit at once as it was still afternoon and not yet time for the dinner rush.

Marjorie and I had been patrons of the place since we were girls. Even my often-stodgy parents had had to admit that it was worth braving the humble decor to have a taste of a Chick's special, arguably the best tomato pie in the state. I fondly remembered our tradition of pizza after dance lessons with the Hurley family, whose son and daughter were both in our Irish stepdancing troupe. Darren Hurley, I well remember, was the only boy in the class who had participated willingly. At the time, Marjorie and I had predicted a lot of girlfriends in his future because of this willingness of his, little realizing at the time that he identified himself more as one of us than as one of our male counterparts. He'd grown up, though, to be quite successful in the art business, owning galleries both at the Shore and in Manhattan.

Other memories of the place surfaced as we

waited: of dinners with high school friends, stop-overs after the movies with Peter and, some-times, Marjorie and Bill as well. I felt a warmth sitting there from more than just the proximity of the big ovens.

The pizza, when it arrived, was as good as I had remembered it. In fact, it was so good that, until we had all satisfied our hunger with a couple of slices, hardly a word was spoken. At last I had had enough and sat back to enjoy the last of my birch beer from the plastic cup in which it was served.

In spite of the last meeting between Marjorie and Owen, the atmosphere over the meal was lighthearted. I was proud of her and Bill for being so accepting. I realized they hadn't had time to get used to Owen as I had, and at least they had the grace to pretend they believed him.

"So, Owen, Peggy tells me you're from Canada," Bill began, the light twinkling in his bright blue eyes and highlighting his black curly hair and pugnacious chin.

"No, Nova Scotia," Owen said.

"Same thing," Bill said in his own defense.

"Well, Nova Scotia, New Brunswick, Prince Edward Island, Newfoundland, and Canada East and West — they're all British North America, but they're not all one united nation."

"They are now," Bill said.

"Oh. I didn't know that," Owen said.

I could see that Bill, in spite of his doubts of Owen's sanity or intelligence, was willing to be cordial, no doubt for my benefit. He tried again to start the conversation rolling.

"It must have been pretty exciting sailing on a clipper ship," he said.

"Aye, sometimes it was."

"Did you ever lose a man overboard? I mean, besides yourself."

"Aye, some good men, the last on our way back around the Cape."

"Did you sail on American ships, or what?"

"My first ship, the *Glen Rover,* was a Bluenose. That means she was from Nova Scotia," he explained. "After that I always served on Downeasters."

"Downeasters?" Marjorie asked.

"Yankees . . . American ships."

"Oh. Were the rest of the sailors American?" she asked.

"No, mostly not," he answered.

"Why not, if the ships were American?" Bill asked.

"Most Americans won't, that is *wouldn't,*" he corrected himself, "work for the wages we got."

Bill raised an eyebrow and nodded, taking another swallow from his glass.

"Where were some of your shipmates from, then?" I asked.

"Well, the doctor was a Dutchman . . ."

"Doctor?" Bill asked. "You had a doctor on board?"

"That's what we call the cook," Owen explained.

"Oh."

"My friend Frenchy was a Quebecker, although he'd moved his family to Boston."

"What was he like?" I asked. I was curious since I'd heard Owen speak of him several times before.

"Frenchy? He was a good man. The worst singer you'll ever hear, but a fine scrimshander."

"What's that?" Marjorie asked.

"Putting pictures on whales' teeth."

"Oh, scrimshaw."

"Aye, he taught me, too," he said, not without a touch of pride.

"Did you ever sail on a whaling ship?" Bill asked.

"No, hunting spermaceti's not for me. Never wanted to work on a slaver, either. Guess I'm just too softhearted."

"Well, the days of whaling and slavery are both over, thank God," I said.

Owen nodded as though this piece of information had suddenly put a lot of other observations into order. He'd held up very well under this impromptu and informal interrogation, but I figured enough was enough.

"What do you say we go back to my house for a while?" I asked.

Everyone agreed.

On the walk back I felt mellow. My appetite was sated; I was surrounded by people I cared for. It had been a long time since Marjorie and Bill had slowed down their lives enough for a lazy Saturday like this one. It hadn't been so unusual in the past for them to join Peter and me for a leisurely night out, but then even Peter and I had eventually let the pressures of work get in the way. If only we'd known how precious each hour was to be, we wouldn't have put off sharing times like these. As small compensation, at least there was this present serene moment to enjoy.

Bill and Owen had gotten half a block ahead of Marjorie and myself as we meandered along past the glorious homes of Slea Head toward the ocean and home. They looked comfortable together — not like the longtime friends Bill and Peter had been, but like the way two guys will hit it off once they start talking sports. I smiled.

I turned to Marjorie to comment on the luxuriousness of the indolent afternoon when I was interrupted by the screeching of brakes. I looked up the block to see a Cadillac stopped in the street, and Owen sitting on the pavement in front of it. I ran to catch up.

"What happened?" I asked in panic. "Owen, are you all right?"

The driver wanted to know the same thing.

Owen got up, rubbing the grit off his hands. "I'm fine," he said. "Please go," he added to the owner of the Cadillac.

The driver didn't wait to be told twice and, muttering to himself about crazy tourists, got behind the wheel and drove away.

"You bastard," Owen seethed to Bill. "Are you trying to get me killed?"

"I'm sorry," Bill said lamely.

"What the hell happened?" I demanded.

"Bill?" Marjorie asked her husband, giving him a chance to explain, but clearly not expecting blamelessness on his part.

"It was just a joke, really. I didn't think he'd really do it."

"Do what?" I asked. Owen's fists were clenched at his sides as he waited for Bill to explain.

"I told him that cars had built-in sensors so they couldn't hit objects in their path, and if he jumped out in front of a car, it would automatically stop in time."

"Why the hell did you tell him that?"

"Listen, Peggy, I don't want anybody taking advantage of you. I just thought it was time somebody called his bluff."

"Jesus," Marjorie said under her breath.

Owen took a step toward Bill. Bill had a good three inches on Owen and years of better nutrition, but Owen was resilient and used to hard labor. I was afraid they would come to blows. Half of me was hoping they would and that Owen would clean Bill's clock for the dirty trick he'd just pulled.

"I'm sorry," Bill said to Owen, clearly sincere. "I was totally out of line. I just thought you were bullshitting us and you'd know I was lying about the sensor thing. I never thought for a minute you'd really jump out in traffic." He held his hand out for Owen to shake.

In the frozen moment while we waited to see

what Owen would do, I thought of how he was forced to accept that everything there was in the world was changed for him forever. We had only to accept the anachronism of his existence among us. But while he believed he was where and when he was, we had done nothing but treat him as a liar and a fake.

"I can't prove to you anything about myself," Owen began. "You'll believe me or you won't. But I am a man, not a raving lunatic, nor a child, and I expect to be treated in keeping with that. It's true I don't know your ways, but neither do you know mine. I daresay I could make an ass of you at sea, but where's the challenge in that? I may have been a common sailor, but that doesn't mean I can't behave like a gentleman. I expect no less from you who are one." He spoke quietly, but with dignity and strength.

"You're right. I'm sorry. I know I can't really make it up to you, but will you at least let me buy you a drink? Please?" Even at a disadvantage, Bill's charm could work miracles. Owen took his hand and then apologized to Marjorie and me for his language. We followed Bill to the nearest bar.

On the way I suddenly realized that Owen had been willing to put his life on the line, not to prove that he was who he said he was, but out of trust for all of us. If I had been contemplating that he might be nothing more than a talented actor, I think the last of my doubts were fading fast. I smiled at the secret that Owen was, that only we chosen few were in on, as we walked through the somewhat battered oak door of what was once a local hangout of ours in the summers between college semesters.

McGuinn's. I hadn't seen the inside of the place in years. Not much had changed, though. The exposed brick walls still sported their photos of hurling teams and boxers. I think I even recognized some of the graffiti carved into the table where we sat.

Much of the rest of the world maintained a smoke-free atmosphere; much of the rest of the world, in that respect, had passed McGuinn's by. Not only was smoking tolerated, it was actively encouraged by the owner, who was never to be seen without a cigar in his mouth that seemed to hang on the edge of his lip while he talked as if by a conjuring trick or super glue. I looked around for him to see if he'd changed in the years that had elapsed since my last visit and was rewarded with a glimpse of his stocky figure, his customary tweed cap on his head, a natural half snarl on his face, giving him the appearance of an overaged dead-end kid. Despite having the looks of a bully, though, I remembered him as being full of humor with his cronies and tolerant of us students as long as we kept the worst of the rowdiness to a minimum.

And we had been decidedly boisterous at times, with even Peter chiming in on one notable occasion. Though generally a moderate drinker, on the night in question, Peter had undoubtedly kept up with the rest of our group, and by the end of the evening, every last one of us was smoking a cigar and singing along to a rollicking rendition of "The Wild Colonial Boy" that was being played on guitars by the proprietor and one of his mates. It felt like a bad remake of a scene from *The Quiet Man*. After the set ended, I remember Peter giving me his best Groucho Marx imitation just before he turned rather green around the gills and had to give up on his one and only attempt at cigar smoking. I smiled at the thought of that remarkable evening, giving one last affectionate glance at the burly owner as he played darts in the back room, remembering the part he had played in the fun. But now it was time that we decided what to order.

"Why don't you just get a pitcher?" Marjorie suggested, and Bill walked over to the bar to comply as we had all agreed with her that that would probably be easiest. I was surprised when Owen went with him, and together they carried back the pale amber beer and four glasses. Bill poured, and we drank to "no hard feelings."

"This is terrible," Owen said, making a face after he had swallowed. "Sorry," he amended. "It's just different than what I'm accustomed to. I expect I'll get used to it."

"No, you're right, it's pretty bad," Bill said.

"I'll drink it," I volunteered, like a martyr, and Marjorie offered to help.

"Be right back," Bill said, and he headed back over to the bartender, returning with two pints of Guinness.

"Better?" he asked when Owen had had a taste.

"Decidedly," Owen replied with a smile.

We sat in companionable silence for some time listening to "Danny Boy" on the jukebox. McGuinn's pre-recorded music selections ran to rebel tunes and sentimental Irish or Irish-American favorites.

"I bet the music in here hasn't changed since I used to come in here with a fake ID," Bill said at last.

"It's much better than what Peggy listens to in the Honda," Owen said. He had apparently imprinted the word "Honda" as a generic term for car.

"What does she play in the car?" Bill asked.

"I think she calls it 'Rolling Stones.'"

We all laughed but Owen, who nevertheless smiled companionably.

"It's a strange idea — taking music around with you wherever you go."

"Well, don't sailors sing while they work?" Marjorie asked.

"Aye, shanties."

"Same concept."

"Does the music help you to operate the Honda?"

"No, music in the car is just for entertainment."

"Then, it really isn't the same concept. We don't sing for entertainment. Shanties help the work along. They keep the rhythm while you're doing a job."

"All work and no play makes Jack a dull boy," Bill said.

"It *is* a lot of work, but you can't really understand what it was like."

"Well, what *was* it like?" Bill wanted to know. Owen shot him a glance that warned he'd brook no further tests to his goodwill.

"I'm serious. I want to know," Bill said.

At that point the next round of Guinness arrived. Bill must have told the bartender to keep them coming, because he simply nodded when the bartender brought more and then helped himself to what he needed from the pile of bills and coins near Bill's elbow.

"I grew up in a town, and I've spent time in different cities," Owen began, "so I know their everyday worries. At sea it's very different — a world all its own. The things that seem important on land, like politics or money, or even family, just don't really matter when you're out there."

"Well, don't you get homesick?" Marjorie asked.

"Aye, sometimes. I know some of the men did."

"What about you? Didn't you leave anybody behind when you'd go?" Bill asked. "A family? A wife?"

"No. No family, no wife."

"Well, where did you call home? Where would you go, say, for Christmas?"

"I was usually at sea at Christmas. After I'd

served with Frenchy on the *Topaz*, he used to have me stay with his family between trips, until he was ready to sail again. They were the closest thing to a family I had. I did have one Christmas with them. . . ."

"Them?" I asked.

"Aye. His wife and four children — three boys, one already at sea, and a little girl — Angeline. I was her godfather. I think I spent half my pay on gifts for her," he said, and smiled. "Martine, Frenchy's wife, was a wonderful cook, but with an iron will. She needed it, being married to Frenchy. He was a great big bear of a man, nearly always laughing, and he let the children take all kinds of liberties. Martine had a tongue like a sheath knife, though, and she kept us all in line."

I had never heard him speak so wistfully of his earlier life. The way he spoke of his friend's wife made me think he might have been in love with her.

"Was she beautiful?" I asked.

"No," he said with a smile, "she had a face like a toad's." He laughed and took a swig of the dark foamy stout. "But she had a heart of pure gold. She used to always make me feel welcome, like I was really a part of their family, and she never wanted to accept the gifts I'd bring. They hadn't much money, but she was proud. She used to call me *l'âme perdue*," he said with a melancholy smile. "I guess maybe she knew something I didn't."

I automatically translated the phrase in my

mind — *l'âme perdue,* the lost soul.

Owen finished his drink and took his time filling and lighting his pipe.

"If you could, would you go back?" I asked, and I wasn't sure I wanted to hear his answer.

"I like some things better now," he began, I believe in deference to my feelings.

"Such as?" Marjorie wanted to know.

"I like being clean and having good food to eat. It's very safe, too, compared to life at sea." And, giving Bill a good-natured dirty look over the top of his glasses, he added, "Most of the time."

"But . . ." I said.

"I've been at sea for most of the last thirteen years. It's not a bad life. Every man is important on a ship, useful. And the sea can be so very beautiful with all its different moods. The things I've seen, the places I've been. You can't imagine what it is to see the sky filled with a million stars, with no land in sight, or snow falling at sea . . . how peaceful it can be."

"You make it sound so romantic, but from what you told me earlier, it can be pretty brutal, too," I said.

"On a ship it's a separate world, with its own laws. It may be harsher than life on land sometimes, but without discipline you could all die."

"But your expectations are so low," I argued. "Is that the most you could hope for — getting enough to eat and getting through the day without someone beating the hell out of you?"

106

"What are you talking about, Peggy?" Marjorie asked.

Owen and I ignored her. "Maybe that is enough for the likes of me, Peggy," Owen said. "I have no schooling to speak of, no grand family, not a dime to my name."

"It's different now, Owen; you'll see," I said, and hoped I was right.

I was more than a little tipsy as we stumbled out of McGuinn's. Marjorie seemed to have paced herself, but I guessed that Bill and Owen weren't in a whole lot better shape than I was. Owen took my arm at the elbow, although it was unclear who was actually steadying whom. I'm pretty sure I was giggling, which is definitely not my wont. I do remember asking Owen to sing a sea shanty on the walk back to my house.

"Oh, it's very bad luck to sing shanties on land," he answered.

"Risk it," I demanded with mock seriousness.

"You certainly know how to live dangerously," he said.

"Aye, sailor," I replied.

"Are you making sport of me?"

"Yes, I am."

He laughed warmly.

"How about 'Blow the Man Down'?" I suggested.

"You know it?" he asked with surprise, and when I nodded he said, "I knew you were my kind of girl."

We ended up sounding like the drunken

chorus we were on the way back toward the beach, with Owen handling the verses and Bill and I, and occasionally even Marjorie, helping to belt out the refrain. I think the gist of the song was about a sailor getting scammed by a woman who takes advantage of his drunken state to get him to sign onto a ship bound for Australia. I do recall the last verse:

"I'll give you a warning before we belay,
And away, hey, blow the man down.
Don't ever take heed of what pretty girls say.
Give me some time to blow the man down."

As is typical of situations like this, it seemed very, very funny at the time. We were all of us laughing, but we stopped in unison at the end of our off-key recital when we rounded a corner and were confronted by the moon. It hung low, just clearing the rooftops — full, golden, and enormous. The as-yet unchanged leaves were silhouetted against the sky, which ranged from an unearthly paleness at the horizon, through sapphire, to a perfect velvet darkness at its zenith.

"Is that a harvest moon? Or, what's the other full moon called you see around this time of year?" Marjorie asked.

"A hunter's moon," Owen replied. "But it's too early for that. It's only just gone the equinox. This is a harvest moon."

"It's unbelievable, it's so huge," I said as we continued our walk, eyes glued to the sky — a

Maxfield Parrish sky, enameled in layers and layers of blue. We grew quiet and as contemplative, I believe, as the warm soporific comfort of alcohol would allow.

I felt as though the moon were pulling, rather than guiding, me home. I thought of the lunar nature of the female of the species as I remembered my mother telling me how she'd waited in vain for my birth for nearly two weeks after her due date, only going into labor with the onset of the full moon. It occurred to me, too, on that walk home, that to the constant moon, bringer of tides, the days of sail were only yesterday.

Back at the house, Bill and Marjorie decided to take their leave. I was awake long enough to see the moon rise and turn from gold to white as it ascended in the now-complete darkness that it penetrated with a brilliant light.

The events that followed after Bill and Marjorie left did not occur in slow motion, but that is how my mind recorded them. Owen and I sat at the window observing, and being observed by, the moon. I lay my head on his shoulder. I think I may have slept for some little time. Then, taking my hand, he led me to my bedroom where he tucked me in, softly ran the back of his hand along my cheek, and then sat, still as night, at the foot of my bed until I drifted, calmly and safely, off to sleep.

In the morning I felt much better than I expected to. After a shower and a couple of aspirins, I felt better still.

I came downstairs to find Owen bent over the coffee table on the sunporch, intent on some project, his shaggy blond mane falling forward to hide what he was doing from my eyes. Definitely time for a haircut, I thought, but I was more curious as to what he was up to on a morning I would have expected to find him hung over.

"What are you doing?" I asked in a voice I hoped wouldn't startle him.

He looked up and grinned at me. "These pens of yours, with the ink already inside, they're terrific!" he said, brandishing an inexpensive rollerball pen I'd bought recently. I still do some of my writing longhand, and I'd really hoped the novelty of a new writing instrument would get me back to work. It wrote smoothly with a fine point in pitch-black ink that could be seen through its clear barrel. I'd had some fun turning it and watching the bubble inside move back and forth, like one in a carpenter's level, but I hadn't yet produced a word of a new manuscript.

A nagging sense that I should be writing constantly hung at the back of my consciousness these days, making me wonder sometimes if the knack I'd had for creating characters, plot, and place had deserted me. In the big scheme of things, compared to death, it hadn't seemed important, but I didn't want to think that the pleasure of creating was going to be forever denied me in the future. I decided to suppress the thought for the time being; I wanted to know

110

what Owen was doing.

"What are you writing?" I asked.

"Not writing — making a picture for you. You were fresh out of whale's teeth," he added with a glowing smile. He was clearly pleased with himself.

"May I see it?" I asked.

"One more minute."

"How is it you aren't sick this morning, after last night?"

"I hope you don't mind, I had a dram of whiskey when I got up."

"Ugh. You know you could have just asked me for an aspirin."

"Aspirin?"

"Never mind. Just tell me next time you've got a headache or whatever. We've got some really great stuff now for whatever ails you."

Owen nodded. "Almost done," he said.

In a moment he handed me a piece of white paper. On it was the most exquisite little drawing, one inch by two, of a sailing ship.

"Owen," I said, "you're an artist!"

"No, it's just something Frenchy taught me, to make a little extra money," he said, but he was beaming.

He proceeded to point out to me, within the intricacies of the drawing, the various parts of the ship. The technicality of it did not intrigue me as he named the bowsprit, the foremast, the mainmast, the mizzen, but I liked the way the nautical terms rolled off his tongue. I think I spent as much time scanning the happiness in his face as I did following his lesson. Then something caught my eye. He had signed the work, in a stylized manner, with his initials. They were rendered as though made from rope, with the *O* thrown like a ring over an anchor. The *S* was reversed.

"Owen," I said, "Do you always make your *S* like this?"

"Aye, more or less. 'Course if I'm just signing shipping articles, I don't do it so fancy. Just plain letters."

"Wait here a minute," I said. I came back with a magazine where I was sure to find lots of large print in the advertisements.

"You told me you know your letters," I began.

"Mostly," he answered, looking definitely less comfortable now.

I randomly pointed to various letters and asked him to name them. He seemed to have no problems. "Now, you read some aloud to me," I said.

He did and did well, although he tended to read them off from right to left as often as he did from left to right. When he came to a lower case *d*, he stopped.

I looked at him expectantly.

"I don't know," he said.

"Guess."

"It's either a *b* or a *d*," he said. "I always guess wrong."

"Come on."

"Peggy, I'm just too dim-witted to read. I've know that since I was six or seven years old."

"I'm the one who's been dim-witted. Look at your *S*, it's backwards," I said, pointing to the picture he'd drawn. "And look at the letters you get confused — they're mirror images of each other."

He shrugged, unsure of my point.

"Owen, I think you're dyslexic."

"Is that bad?"

"It's inconvenient, to be sure, but I think you can be taught to read. Your brain just processes visual information differently than most people's. It certainly doesn't mean you're stupid. In fact, I think I remember hearing that dyslexic people tend to be more intelligent than average."

He looked skeptical.

"Trust me on this. We'll just have to have you talk to someone who's a specialist on learning disorders," I said. "What I don't understand, though, is how you can draw like that, if things get turned around inside your head."

Owen smiled. "Well, if I draw from a picture in my mind, I do all right, but if I have the ship before me, sometimes the bow ends up where I'd meant the stern to be."

I had to laugh.

"But do you really think I can be taught to read?" he asked. He sounded excited but cautious, afraid to get his hopes up.

"Yes, I really do."

"Well, when the day comes, then, that I'm able

to read, the first thing I want to read is one of your books."

It concerned me that I might no longer be considered a viable author by then, but I'd be lying if I said I wasn't touched. Owen had a way about him that constantly brought to the fore his innate decency and his uncommon goodness. If I could help him in this fundamental way, I would consider it one of my best accomplishments.

There followed after this revelation several days that were virtually indistinguishable from each other. Each morning began shrouded in fog, and the effect of the fog was such that each discernible object appeared to be painted on a separate theatrical scrim or length of silk, and this multitude of strata, placed one behind the other, stretched on and on between my eye and the far horizon. Later in the day, the mist would burn off to reveal the radiance of the autumn sky and, at last, the leaves began to change.

On one of these days we finally got around to Owen's haircut. As the competent young woman plied her trade with scissors and comb, the image of the falling hair, like so many filaments of gold, became inextricably tied in my mind with the cascading leaves outside. I had never been inordinately fond of blond hair, but I found myself feeling relieved when I saw at completion that she hadn't cut Owen's hair too short.

# CHAPTER 6

A day or so later I got a call from Marjorie, asking if I minded if she stopped by on the following Saturday with someone she wanted me — and Owen — to meet. I was a bit surprised at her formality but, of course, assented. Other than Owen, I hadn't met anyone new in quite a long time and it sounded like it might be fun — provided this didn't turn out to be along the lines of a blind date. Even so, my curiosity was aroused.

I soon put the request out of my mind, though, as Owen had finally prevailed on me to put him to work. I had a hard time coming up with a job that he was capable of doing without hours of explanation beforehand. We finally settled on painting — walls, that is, not pictures, although I planned in the near future to buy him some watercolors and acrylics to see if his abilities as a draftsman could transcend line to the use of color. Although the idea of premixed paint was new to him, he took to the job almost immediately. He was a tireless worker, and a careful one, too. He worked methodically, one room at a time, moving the furniture to the center, draping it with plastic tarpaulins, coating first the ceiling, then the walls. He wouldn't hear of my helping and, as I knew he felt he had a debt to pay, I didn't argue.

On Saturday, Marjorie arrived right on schedule, accompanied by a man I'd never seen before. She looked great. Her hair was tied back with an expensive-looking scarf, and her sweater and jeans set off her trim figure nicely. When she removed her sunglasses, I could see, too, that she'd been maybe even a little more particular than usual about her makeup. My first thought was that the effort might be for the man with her, but when I got a better look at him, I realized Bill had nothing to fear in that quarter.

It wasn't that he was unattractive — just not Marjorie's style. She introduced him as Joseph Maglia, a graduate student in American history at N.Y.U. who was interested in talking to Owen about life as a sailor in the nineteenth century. He wasn't my idea of a scholar. The hair that framed his classical features was very dark and perfectly conditioned, pulled back in a ponytail that hung like a glossy rope down his back. He had on tight blue jeans with a pink polo shirt and a variegated Harris tweed sport coat that somehow worked well with the other two colors. He also wore a lot of gold, including a Rolex wristwatch that, if it was real, was probably worth as much as my car.

He looked me very directly, very intently, in the eye as we were introduced, taking my hand as though he were going to kiss rather than shake it. With the nearly perpetual frown now gone from my face, I supposed I was going to have to get used to the inevitable flirting of insincere men again, but his smarmy charm nearly caused me to laugh out loud. I covered my amusement by calling Owen out to the kitchen to meet Mr. Maglia.

Owen entered, wiping his hands on a rag. His glasses, face, and hair were splattered with tiny dots of white paint.

"Owen," Marjorie said, by way of introduction, "this is Joseph Maglia. He'd really like to talk to you about your sailing days. He studies maritime history, and he might be able to use some of your experiences in a paper he's planning to write."

"Sure, Mr. Maglia," Owen answered, shaking his hand. "I'd be glad to help. My name's Owen Sinclair."

"Yes, Marjorie told me. Great to meet you. Call me Joe, though, would you?" He may have been cultivating smoothness in his appearance, but his voice was pure New York. "Peggy. You don't mind if I call you Peggy?"

"No."

"Peggy, is there some place Owen, here, and I can sit down to talk?"

"Of course. How about on the sunporch? Oh, wait, Owen's painting in there. The parlor, then," I said.

I seldom used the parlor. It is a traditional, formal Victorian room with a predominantly bloodred Kashan Persian rug on the floor. In one corner stands a marble-top table with an intricately carved base, in another stands my diamond disc Edison phonograph, silent now since the Christmas before Peter died. A suite of three pieces, two chairs and a settee, faces the marble mantel. Like the table's base, the wood employed was walnut, but this set is Renaissance revival in style, carved with a raised medallion in the center back of each seat above the tufted green damask upholstery. The seats are further dignified with beautifully turned, but rather short legs, and classical female heads are carved into the arm supports. On them, one sits lower than on standard modern furniture, as they were made with a woman's physical limitations while wearing a gown in mind. They are, in my opinion, extreme in their beauty, but no one would argue against their general discomfort.

The whole decor, including the fireplace and its mantel, which had cost an arm and a leg to have built and installed, had been my idea. Peter had found my taste for the past somewhat amusing, but as long as everything could be used and not just admired, he really cared little whether I bought old or new furniture, dishes, and books. I think he came to appreciate the craftsmanship of the things I'd bring home that had been handmade in some bygone era. He would sometimes even surprise me with a piece of antique jewelry or, once, with a set of porcelain figurines of the characters of *Great Expectations*, my all-time favorite book.

I caught myself studying the room as an extension of the life Peter and I had had together.

Every item — the mantel clock, the lustres, even the paisley shawl thrown over the Victrola — had come to represent the detritus of an irretrievable love. But now they produced in me a memory of comfort that hadn't been awakened for some time.

Joe's voice brought me back to the present.

"You know, you two don't have to hang out here," he suggested to Marjorie and me, and we took the hint and went back to the kitchen for some flavored coffee. I felt like we were in a commercial, enjoying our overpriced beverage, and our quality time.

"I appreciate your . . ." I began.

"What?"

"Believing him. Or pretending to."

"Well, the other night at McGuinn's . . . I just wanted someone to make some use of what he knows, you know?"

She seemed distinctly uncomfortable. She'd never in her whole life been good at admitting she was wrong, and maybe that was the problem.

"Are you sure it's OK to be telling this guy Owen's story? I mean, how did you get him to believe Owen knew anything that could be of value to him, especially firsthand?" I asked.

"Well, I had thought of making up some story about Owen getting his information about sailing handed down from his great-grandfather or something, but I didn't know how Owen would react to that."

"I don't know how he would either."

"At any rate, Joe's OK. He's my secretary Stephanie's cousin, so it'll be all right for Owen to just be himself. You remember Stephanie, don't you?" I nodded. "Anyway, Joe should get an interesting perspective on nineteenth-century sailing, even if he thinks Owen's a bit off his rocker. And he can't really use what Owen tells him, of course. I mean, Joe couldn't quote a living source on something that happened in the 1860s or something."

"1850s actually. And I guess Joe will be able to see through Owen's story if it's full of holes?"

"That wasn't the main idea, but if there *are* inaccuracies, you would want to know, wouldn't you?"

"I'm not sure. I guess so. It's a bridge we don't have to cross at this point anyway," I said, and thought to myself that I had confidence Joe wouldn't prove to be Owen's undoing.

I changed the subject then, and we chatted about Bill, the holidays on the way, about Halloween costumes we'd worn as kids, about Peter. I could talk about him now as someone whose name made me smile, not break into tears, and that at least felt good.

She asked me if I had spoken to or written various writer friends whose antics I once so enjoyed relaying to her. I felt as though I had let her down a bit when I told her I'd done neither, but she was pleased when I told her I'd seen Arlene Graber, saying she hoped I'd at least keep that connection open. She mentioned other people I hadn't thought of in months — members of Peter and Bill's softball team, a high school friend or two who still lived in the area, the local librarian I'd gotten to know well while doing book research, even Darren Hurley, the boy I'd known since our childhood days of dance lessons — and I realized that I'd certainly had a wide circle of acquaintances before Peter died. It was obvious she was hinting that I begin picking up where I'd left off, and I found that the idea no longer scared or repulsed me.

During our talk, I periodically heard a word or two from the parlor, but never enough to piece much together. I couldn't really tell who was doing most of the talking. Sometimes I'd get the impression that Joe was having to urge Owen to speak, sometimes it seemed as though Owen was willingly spilling out information. It might have been fun to see how they reacted to one another — one all style with dubious substance, the other the picture of ingenuousness.

"Marjorie," I said, "have you known this guy long? He's quite a character."

"He is, isn't he? Did you check out the boots? — ostrich hide, or something. He looks like a model, or a drug dealer."

"Do you know him well?"

"No, I only met him once before, through Stephanie. I don't know how it came up that he studied American history, especially maritime stuff, but I remembered after I'd met Owen and, well . . ."

"I really appreciate your taking an interest."

Marjorie looked embarrassed, so I changed the subject.

"Oh, I have some great news," I said.

"What?"

"I think I've figured out Owen's problem with reading. Wait a second," I said as I grabbed the drawing Owen had made for me and handed it to my sister.

"It's very nice. Did Owen make it?"

"Yes. Take a good look at how he signed it. I'm pretty sure he's dyslexic. I'm taking him next week to talk to a specialist."

"That's great, Peggy, but if you don't mind my saying so, solving all of Owen's problems could run into a lot of money."

"What do you expect me to do? Now that I think I know what's wrong, I can't just do nothing."

"Why not? He's not your responsibility."

"Maybe not legally, but I want to help him. It makes me happy. And besides, it's not like he's sponging off me. He'd do anything I asked, and he's constantly volunteering to do things I haven't asked him to do."

"OK, I won't bring it up again."

"What do you think of the drawing?" I asked.

"It's really very good. Reminds me of an etching."

"Me, too."

"I'd like to show it to Joe, if that's OK?" she asked.

"Sure."

At that point I heard Owen and Joe returning from the parlor.

"Peggy?" Owen began.

"Yes?"

"Do you still have my clothes, from when you found me? Joe seems to think it would be useful to have a look at them." His look seemed to say that he thought otherwise. "I told him they were pretty well destroyed, and that you'd probably gotten rid of them by now. . . ."

"No, I think they're still here. If I was a better housekeeper, they probably would be gone, but you know what they say, 'a clean house is the sign of a dull woman.' "

"I've never heard anyone say that," Owen said, raising his eyebrows, mischief in his eyes as he teased me for my justification of laziness.

"Oh, shut up. I'll go find your old clothes," I said, and I felt like laughing because I was so comfortable now with Owen in the house. It was getting harder and harder to remember how empty and painful a place it had been.

Owen's clothes were hanging in the laundry room, where I'd left them draped across the utility sink. Both the shirt and the trousers were stiff but not mildewed, and I shoved them in a bag as I headed down the stairs.

"Can I call you or stop by if I have any more questions?" Joe was asking Owen.

"If it's all right with Peggy."

"Sure," I answered as I entered, handing Joe the bag. "I don't know if these will be much help, but you're welcome to them. They aren't much use anymore for their original purpose."

"Thanks," Joe said.

"Oh," Marjorie began, "don't forget, I want to show Joe the drawing Owen made for you. And then maybe can I borrow it just until I can make a photocopy of it for Joe to keep?"

"I guess so. I do want it back, though."

"You'll get it back. I promise."

I handed the drawing to Joe who scanned it with a studied look, as though he were doing his best to imitate an eminent scholar so that we would be sure to take him seriously. It was, to me, the equivalent attitude of a painter affecting a Left-Bank appearance with a beret and smock to show that he was the genuine article. The effect, of course, was just the opposite, and I enjoyed a little inner laugh at the slick Mr. Maglia's expense.

"This is really very interesting" was all he said, and restated Marjorie's request to let her borrow it for reproducing. I assented, feeling that it couldn't hurt, as long as I was promised its safe return.

There was really nothing more to say as, for Joe, this had been a strictly business kind of visit, and I had no real desire to try to pursue something personal with him. Owen and I stood on the stoop and watched them drive away.

The wind had picked up, and I imagined the polychromatic leaves that would be traveling around town, blowing in concentric circles close to the ground or taking flight above the corridors made by the streets. The change in seasons here on the edge of the continent made itself felt more through the lowering clouds and shortening days, subtleties compared to the motley show going on just a block or two inland.

It was really autumn now, and Owen and I fell into our own rhythms and routines. I was taking notes again, my first step toward beginning another book, which made my agent and editor extremely happy. I found myself full of ideas, some conflicting, and knew that before long I'd have enough material to start plotting out at least two distinct stories. I was toying with the idea of a Victorian mystery, having a live-in expert on the time period as I did. I even used this possibility as an excuse to get out my old one-speed bicycle, strap on a backpack, and take a ride over to the local library to do a little preliminary outside research. The friendly greeting I received from Theresa, my librarian friend who had given me such unstinting assistance in the past, made me all the more pleased that I'd made the trip. The truth was that I had ample books at home to get me started in almost any field, but I wanted to be out in the fresh sea air, and walking just wasn't fast enough. I wanted to fly, and cycling was close enough to do the trick for me.

While Owen was otherwise occupied, I also made a few trips over to the stables where my mother boarded her horse, named Cuchulainn after the legendary Irish hero, thereby keeping a promise I'd made to do my bit to keep him in shape until my parents returned from a trip overseas. Marjorie had taken on the bulk of the work in this regard, but, with her schedule, it was a bit much to ask that she exercise the big brute every day. What had only recently been a chore grudgingly done, I now found rather invigorating. After a particularly good workout with the stubborn animal, I stopped by the hardware store to pick up some ranunculus bulbs, flowers that had always defeated my gardening skills in the past. Maybe this would be the spring I'd manage to get them to bloom. On the way to the car, I eyed the window displays of one of Slea Head's antique stores and planned to pay another visit there to check out some intriguing English pottery, when I wasn't dressed for the barn.

I was also pondering the fates of my fictional detectives, John and Rebecca Garrett, the protagonists of my five novels to date. I would need to decide whether it was thumbs-up or down for John Garrett, who had been murdered in my last, as-yet-unpublished book, his poor grieving widow solving the crime in the end. The Garretts had been my goose that lays the golden egg, and the debate over John's demise wasn't an easy one. The manuscript, still in the hands of my agent, was not typical of the glibness of my other work, but in some ways the reality of its subject matter to me had made it my best. In any case, it was sure to displease a good number of my readers.

Owen and I had gotten gradually less inseparable, and I think the independence was good for both of us. A reading specialist had confirmed my amateur diagnosis that Owen was, in fact, dyslexic, and he had begun having tutoring sessions several days a week. His teacher, Mrs. Morlock, was a spare, sweet woman in her sixties, happily retired from teaching recalcitrant public school students whose learning disabilities had been nearly impossible to overcome, coupled as they were with disruptive home situations. Now, out of the city, working primarily with rich kids and adults like Owen, her patience and capability could really shine.

Besides exploring the world of the written word, Owen seemed to be enjoying the freedom to investigate his new life in other ways as well. He would occasionally wander into town on his own, and he had gotten to know several of my neighbors fairly well. He was especially helpful to the elderly couple next door, Tom and Martha Dorrity, giving them a hand at pruning, grocery-carrying, lightbulb-changing. One day I came out to find him on their roof, patching a leak. He waved and smiled, obviously completely at ease. I guess with all that climbing in a ship's rigging, he had no fear of heights.

I don't know if it was the image of him up on that roof or my own Catholic childhood coming to the fore, but I decided I wanted very much to get him a religious medal to wear at all times. All the Bresnahan men, from my grandfather to my brother Ryan, had, to my knowledge, always worn them. I vividly remember playing with my father's medal as I'd sit in his roomy lap, rolling it from one part of the chain to another. To make matters more complicated, I got it in my mind that the saint should be Elmo, the patron saint of sailors, not exactly a medal to be found at every jeweler's. I ended up calling around to dealers of religious mementos in New York, where I was finally able to locate what I sought. As a bonus, the reverse side of the medal pictured Saint Christopher, protector of travelers. Very appropriate, I thought and ordered it immediately over the phone. I had only just hung up when Owen came in from outside, his cheeks showing pink from the stiff breeze.

"I need to get some more paint," he said.

"OK. I'll drive you into town."

"No, thank you. The walk will do me good."

"But the paint will be heavy to carry back."

"I could always 'join a gym' instead," he said with a grin. This concept was one that he had found hilarious: people did so little physical labor, they actually paid money to be forced to move around and to lift heavy things. It had become a bit of a running joke around the house. He may have found the runs I now took on the beach four or five mornings a week just as inane, but he had so far refrained from teasing me about them.

"OK," I laughed, "but take the label from the last can. I always save it, since it's hard to tell the difference between bone-white, antique-white, eggshell, and I don't know how many others. I put it over next to the phone in the kitchen."

Owen retrieved it and headed out the door.

I sat down on the sunporch with a magazine to enjoy the lazy sunny afternoon. I guess I fell asleep because I was very startled when the phone began to ring.

"Hello," I said, hoping I sounded more alert than I felt.

"Peggy Millwright?" The voice was a woman's, competent and efficient sounding.

"Yes?"

"I'm calling from Slaney's Hardware. There's a man down here trying to use your credit card."

"What?"

"Mr. Slaney has called the police, but the man claims you gave him the card. He gave me your phone number to call to confirm that."

"Owen. Oh, shit," I muttered. I had had him memorize my address and phone number like an elementary schoolkid in case he got lost. "Is he blond? Late twenties?"

"Yes."

"It's OK. Please tell the police it's all right, that he's not a thief."

"I still can't let him sign the receipt."

"Of course not. I'll be right down."

As I grabbed my pocketbook, I remembered that I had left the card by the phone — on top of the paint label. I guess it wasn't such a stretch that Owen had assumed he was to take it to pay for the paint. How was he to know that only I could use it? I was angry at myself for not realizing he had no money, so of course he'd jumped to the wrong conclusion when he'd seen the credit card and I hadn't offered any cash. I pictured him waiting for me with the police, maybe in handcuffs, and I was even more ticked off at my sloppiness. Sometimes I just forgot how like a child he was in some ways.

I arrived at Slaney's after a drive characterized by a great deal of impatience and agitation. When I saw Owen, I realized I had overreacted. He was fine. The officer who had answered the call was calm, polite, and willing or hoping to believe that everything was a mere misunderstanding. Owen looked at me with a half smile.

"Just when I think I've got things figured out . . ." he said with a shrug. He apologized to me, and I think he was embarrassed. Not worried or afraid, but as though this incident was just another one of the inconveniences of life, rather than an overreaction on the part of the store's owner. He certainly wasn't indignant, as I felt I would have been in his place.

Mr. Slaney apologized as well, stating that he had known my husband and was only trying to look out for my interests. I thanked him and the officer for their courtesy, signed the receipt, and left with Owen at my side.

It was my turn to apologize, and with good reason. I told him that I would be happy to pay him for the painting he'd done, but he staunchly refused, saying that that was just to earn his keep and to try to pay me back for all the things I'd bought for him already. I then told him in no uncertain terms that I would leave some cash at all times in my right-hand desk drawer that he was to use whenever he needed it. I'd been such a fool not to realize how impossible it was to function in the society of my time without at least *some* money. I was pretty sure the same could be said of his era, with the exception of the times he was at sea. There, I guess, cash would have been of little value.

"You took that very calmly," I said as I started the car to drive home.

"What else could I do?"

"What if I hadn't been home? They could have put you in jail!"

"Aye."

"Well, weren't you scared or angry or . . ."

"I wasn't pleased, if that's what you mean, but I wasn't about to get into an argument with those people or a fight with the policeman. They know your rules far better than I do, so I figured if they said I was in the wrong, then I was."

"Sometimes you have to stand up to people, Owen. I didn't mean you should get into a fight, but didn't it bother you, being treated like a common thief?"

"Of course it did, but the whole situation was out of my control. I was pretty sure that if you came, it would be all right."

"And if I didn't?"

"Sometimes things just happen, Peggy. They don't seem fair, but what's the use of asking 'why me?' when that's not going to change anything. I'd like to know why I'm here, why certain things have happened for me the way they have, why I am the way I am, but we're not meant to have all the answers, and no one has ever promised, as far as I know, that things were always going to be pleasant, that the rewards in life would be just."

"Sometimes I just don't understand you. There's nothing wrong with fighting for what you want in this life. You only live once."

"You don't really believe that, do you?" he asked, and I could feel his eyes searching my face as I watched the road.

"No," I said softly, and I could see the relief he felt expressed in his posture. Had he feared he was living among heathens, or was this more concerning his own fate? Was he wondering if he would ever find himself where he thought he was meant to be? In any case, it was clearly important to him that I share in his profound unshakable faith.

# CHAPTER 7

The phone rang. It was my mother.

"Hi, honey. I just wanted to let you know we'd gotten back from Ireland in one piece. The flight was so rough at times, I wasn't sure we'd make it back at all," she laughed in that fluty voice of hers.

"Oh, Mom, I'm sorry. I should have called you when you got in last night."

"Nonsense. We were so tired. The ride back from JFK was a mess, and the limo driver had put my bag with my antacid in it in the trunk. . . . Well, anyway, it's just as well you didn't call."

It was nice of her to let me avoid making excuses. She would never have let me off the hook so easily before Peter died.

"Did you have a nice time?" I asked.

"Oh, yes, and luckily we didn't get as much rain as last time. We were able to either golf or ride nearly every day. Eamonn and Anne are well, and their latest yearling promises to be the fastest of the line. Thanks, by the way, to both you and Marjorie for looking after Cuchulainn for me. He looks to be as fit as ever, and it would seem that you two girls have finally figured out one end of a hoof pick from the other. The job you did was certainly more conscientious than the way you tended your own horses when you rode," she said, and I could picture the accompanying indulgent smile.

She then went on at some length about the status of the Connemara ponies belonging to the Riordans, with whom my parents had spent the last eight weeks. My mother practically lived for riding and, although he was a fine horseman, my father, at sixty-four, preferred a daily game of golf. When he did ride with the Riordans, he and Eamonn, with their long legs, would opt for one of the Riordan's Connemara-Thoroughbred crossbreeds. The ponies themselves were lovely animals I had often ridden in my several stays with the Riordan clan. I never failed to appreciate their courage and love of jumping. I had learned to jump one summer in Ireland on a Connemara, and, though I have never been nor aspired to be the equestrian my mother is, I felt I could fly while seated on the back of that pony. In my mind, Pegasus must have been at least part Connemara.

We were somehow distantly related to the Riordans through Anne's side and my mother's, and our families had exchanged visits many times over the last twenty years or so. I could picture their farm in every detail as my mother spoke, but I know I was seeing the seven Riordan children in my mind as they had each appeared at our last meetings, some as many as ten years ago. I was unsure that if I saw them now I would even recognize them, whether they would be so altered by experiences that I had in no way shared with them that they would have, for all intents and purposes, become different people. I wondered, too, if *I* looked the same, if having gone through fire, I had changed hue or become tempered into something harder and, eventually, colder.

"If it's all right, Peggy, I'd like to stop by with a few things I picked up for you while we were over there," my mother said.

"Sure," I said, "but you shouldn't have. Really."

"Nonsense. It's just a couple of sweaters and some of that perfume you like so well."

"Thanks, Mom. Stop by whenever you want."

My parents had invited me to come with them on this most recent trip across the sea. I was, at the time, too numb to appreciate the gesture. Neither did I note the inherent parent-child relationship of the arrangement. Now, I thought back to how my parents had used a previous trip abroad to wean my sister Marjorie from an unsuitable boyfriend here at home. They had just assumed that a summer among the youth of the old country would cure her infatuation for an inappropriate American boy, and I had to admit that it had worked in Marjorie's case. She'd had a brief fling over there with one of the local Kerry boys, a Gaelic football player, if I recall correctly, whom she'd easily forgotten after returning to college that fall. Then she'd met Bill — fun-loving, acceptable, Hibernian Bill — and my parents had been able to breathe a sigh of relief at their job well done.

Peter had, of course, been a different story, but everyone loved Peter from the start. It's not that my parents ever insisted that their children marry others of Irish descent, but we were expected to marry well, and Peter certainly fit that bill. He had beautiful manners that were so much a part of his breeding that he never said a word that didn't feel sincere. He was also so damnably good-looking. He'd been a gifted athlete, a wonderful lover, a considerate friend.

The first time I ever saw Peter, it had been purely by accident that we'd both ended up in the same place at the same time. Even our introduction had been, at least on my part, by chance and not design. I had gone to a party with a group of friends that was hosted by some fellow coeds I didn't know particularly well. It was really just an excuse to laugh and talk and probably drink a bit too much with my own select group, and I hadn't really looked on it as an opportunity to enlarge my sphere of acquaintances. I wasn't actually averse to the idea of being at least nominally friendly to outsiders, but I had specifically decided that I was *not* looking to meet men that evening. Meaningless flirtation, I felt, would only spoil the hoped-for satisfying conversation, and there wasn't even any need to try to get someone to buy drinks for me. There was a cover charge at the door that was good for endless glasses of beer from kegs that rested, surrounded by ice, in both bathtubs in the house.

I was in my halfhearted angry-at-the-world

phase at that time, which ran to general criticisms of the state of the arts in America and a somber wardrobe of black tights, miniskirts, and turtlenecks that I felt made me look half Bohemian, half beatnik. I pretended to admire apocalyptic poetry, though I understood less than half of it and was offended by the violence of the rest. I had just written and seen performed on campus a one-act play called *The Cynic and the Empty Stage*, and I was rather pleased with myself, affecting the air of a misunderstood intellectual. Never mind that the audience for the performance had been small; I preferred to think of it as select and discriminating. In short, I was a typically silly college student, exploring different possibilities as to who I wanted to be for the rest of my life.

I saw Peter that evening, as it were, across a crowded room. He was handsome, sure, but the last thing I needed in my life right then was a steady boyfriend. He had hair like deeply stained wood — a rich dark brown that matched the color of his eyes. He was tall, obviously well-built, and he carried himself well, with confidence but not cockiness. And when I happened to catch him reacting to someone's attempt at humor, I could see that his smile was downright radiant. He was physically everything a woman could ask for, and at that moment he was headed over to where I stood.

"Hi," he said, as though that were enough.

"Hi," I answered, noncommittally, and was inwardly miffed to see my friends desert me, believing that I wanted to be alone with my good fortune. They, of course, couldn't have been further from the truth. I had, after all, come to share their company and not that of some unknown, albeit very good-looking, stranger. But no, I was on my own.

"Kathy tells me you're a playwright," he said.

"Kathy?"

"She's one of the girls who lives here. Her brother is one of my housemates."

"Oh, yeah, Kathy."

"So, are you?" he asked.

"What?"

"A playwright?"

"If you can call someone who's only written one short play a playwright. . . ."

"I think that's great, you know, that you're willing to go out on a limb and let people see a little of what's inside you."

"What makes you think my play is in any way autobiographical?" I asked, thinking that my diminutive and sarcastic story that explored ambition and unspoken unrequited love had at least *felt* autobiographical, if the characters' lives didn't exactly echo my own.

"Um, well, I have a confession to make."

"Yes?" I asked, allowing the warmth in his eyes and smile to melt some of my reserve.

"I saw it — your play, and I thought it was good, really good, and thought-provoking. Not at all what I would have expected from something produced by undergraduates. I think you're really going somewhere with your writing."

Boy, had he ever hit the nail on the head if he wanted to get to me through flattery, but gorgeous guys like him, I thought, don't need lines like this.

"Thanks, that's nice of you, but I'm surprised you saw it. It wasn't exactly the hot ticket on campus."

"Um, well . . ."

"Another confession?"

"Yeah, another confession. By the way, can I get you another beer?"

"No thanks. The confession?"

"I've been asking around about you."

"You have?" I didn't know whether to be pleased or feel as though my privacy had been invaded. The scales tipped in favor of pleased when his dark eyes met mine. "Why would you do that?"

"I am . . . devastated by you."

"Meaning?"

"Laid low, reduced to helplessness, overwhelmed. I can hardly think of anything else."

"You've got to be kidding," I said, hoping against hope that he wasn't. "I don't even know you, and you certainly don't know me."

"My name's Peter Millwright. And I know you're Peggy Bresnahan."

"That's me, all right," I answered, wondering if the real me wasn't going to be an amazing disappointment to him.

"Can we sit down and talk? I'd like to get to know you better, if that's OK," he said.

There was a cajoling little grin playing at the corners of his mouth, and I nodded and followed him to an unoccupied corner where we were able to sit on the faded olive-green sculptured carpet.

I found myself telling him about my classes in English literature, my friends, my family, Slea Head, and a little of my partially formed dreams for the future. He listened attentively and then related to me funny stories about the guys he shared quarters with, his family in North Jersey, his likes and dislikes, his professional plans, and his infatuation with me. He said he felt ridiculous, having a schoolboy crush at his age, but he simply knew that we would hit it off if he could just engineer a first meeting between us. He had been right.

We dated until we had both finished our studies, trying without much patience to make the time go faster until we could settle down together for good. We kept our separate residences, primarily for the sake of our parents, but I was a frequent overnight guest at his off-campus house, as he was at mine.

We had the usual fairy-tale wedding, or at least the more realistic version of one that went smoothly other than a slight spat between myself and my mother and a little bitchiness between the bridesmaids. All was forgiven over champagne at the reception, though, and there were moments that seemed truly magical to me, inebriated as I was with happiness. I would never forget the feeling that evening when we shared the traditional first dance together — a waltz, at Peter's request. I wasn't lying when I'd told Owen that I hated to dance, but just this once I felt as though I was the spirit of gracefulness as Peter guided me around the floor to the music of Strauss. I didn't think I had it in me, and perhaps it was his Anglo-Saxon genes that helped Celtic me to pull off such a feat of orderly Teutonic coordination, but for those few particular moments we were united in dignified timeless elegance. At least that's the way I remember it.

The remainder of the reception was spent mostly in fulfilling obligations — posing for photos, visiting each table, doing all the usual, wonderfully inane things like feeding each other cake and throwing the bouquet and garter — and afterward Peter and I headed off for the airport and Bermuda in high spirits.

The honeymoon was pretty much a waste of money as we rarely saw the outside of our rented cottage, but we were extremely happy in each other's company. We wandered out for meals at the nearby restaurant and took a rare walk around Hamilton, the capital city, but other than that we pretty much avoided anyone else's company.

About a year after we were married, Peter came home with a surprise for me that would lead to a special high point in a generally already stellar relationship.

"I think it's time we took another trip," he said.

"OK," I answered eagerly. "Where do you want to go?"

"Now, please, don't be mad. I already bought the tickets," he confessed. "I wanted to surprise you, and. . . ."

"And?"

"And I was afraid you'd think I was nuts," he admitted with a smile.

"Where are we going? Siberia? Some jungle infested with poisonous snakes and giant beetles?"

"No, actually, we're going to Prague."

"Prague? As in *Eastern Europe?*"

"Yeah. This patient of mine was going on and on about how beautiful it is, that it's Europe unspoiled by fast-food chains and modern architecture."

"It sounds nice, I guess."

"The other reason I liked the idea of going there is that you and I have done a fair bit of traveling in our lives, and I wanted us to go somewhere that neither of us had ever been before so that it would be *our* place, that we wouldn't associate anything there with other people. Do you know what I mean?"

I threw my arms around him.

"I'm sure it will be wonderful," I said.

When we arrived in Prague, Peter and I were both tired from the flight and afraid there might be a lot of red tape at customs, but we got the idea immediately that the Czechs were a very welcoming people and encountered no serious problems or delays. Peter, intrepid traveler that he was, had rented a car called a Škoda, which turned out to be pretty basic transportation, but it managed to get us where we were going.

The streets were wholly unfamiliar to us, the road signs indecipherable. I was a bit uneasy at first at our having to do so much guesswork in threading our way through town to our hotel.

"What do you think that sign said, Peter? Do you think we should have turned?" I asked.

"As long as it didn't say 'Bridge Out Ahead,' I guess we're all right," he answered with his easy smile that alleviated the tension that had been building inside me. After all, what's the worst that could happen? I'd be lost in a beautiful city with my best friend in the world.

And beautiful it was. Prague lived up to Peter's expectations and far surpassed mine, which I had intentionally kept low, even after looking through travel guides that highlighted some rather remarkable architecture. The spring sun was shining, the Communists had been sent packing, and Prague was smiling. At least, that's how it seemed to me in those halcyon days. Besides, I thought, a country that would elect a writer for its first president couldn't be all bad.

We managed to reach our hotel and check in without causing any international incidents, and my unaccustomed ears began to like the sound of the Czech language that was being spoken around us.

We went upstairs to our room to freshen up after the long flight before going out to see the city. As always when I found myself abroad, I was excited at the idea of being so far from home in a foreign land, doubly so because I'd be experiencing its sights and flavors this time with Peter.

He came up behind me and nuzzled my neck as I removed our hanging clothes from their garment bag and placed them in the room's big armoire.

"Mmm. Girls smell so nice," he murmured.

"Been smelling a lot of girls lately, have you?" I teased.

"Only the best one in the world."

"And she would be. . . ."

"My soon-to-be famous author wife."

"Mmm. You say the sweetest things, but let's get out on the town before my body realizes I missed an entire night's sleep."

"*You're* all business."

"I didn't say we couldn't turn in early tonight."

"Deal. Now, what do you want to see first?"

"Anything at all. Grab the tour book and the map, and let's just start exploring."

"You got it."

We walked the city for hours, enjoying the broad handsome faces of the people with their fair skin and prominent cheekbones beneath their rosy cheeks. They were a lovely people generally and, though I'd been raised not to stereotype, I couldn't help but think of them collectively as being more attractive than the average. Most were blue-eyed, although I saw perhaps as many brunettes as blonds. In keeping with my preconceived notions of Europeans, the women seemed more fashion conscious and aware of the power of their own sexuality than the American women I had known at home, especially those outside of Manhattan. We Americans were still reeling under the influence of those repressive Puritans, I guess.

Everywhere in the city, it seemed, there were peonies in bloom, huge tousled heads of white, pale pink, or deepest magenta. Old women wearing black kerchiefs held large bundles of the blooms for sale in the subway, and Peter bought me a bouquet so overwhelmingly large that I laughed as I tried carrying it down a busy sidewalk. We ended up placing it on the tomb of the astronomer Tycho Brahe, inside Týn Church, simply because we were tired of carrying it. We both got a kick out of what an absurd gesture it must have seemed to both the city residents and other tourists alike, as though we had come all the way from America on a pilgrimage to do just that and were finally relieved of this pious but weighty responsibility in laying our floral burden down on the floor of this magnificent Gothic church.

Peter asked my opinion of just about everything, and I his. I had more grounding in the arts, but he had an eye for symmetry and detail that could have belonged to an architect rather than a dentist. Even after a year or so of marriage, we were truly interested in each other's thoughts and experiences, and I don't think a morning went by without Peter asking me if I'd slept well or an evening without our sharing a recap of how each of us had spent our hours apart. Now on vacation and living the same adventures, it was evident that our mutual fascination was no less strong.

In my happy state, I imagined that all of Prague was in love, too, and I smiled at everyone and laughed at the many little things that later became our private jokes back home. I especially enjoyed how the Czechs took their dogs with them almost everywhere, even on the trolleys and subway, the preferred breed being the dachshund. Forever afterward I would think of it as a city of dog walkers, a stylish people with an abiding love of their pets.

"We should get a dog," Peter suggested enthusiastically, "something that will eat us out of house and home, like a St. Bernard or a Newfoundland. We could take him for romps on the beach, and then when we start to fill the house with kids, they'd have him to play with."

"Maybe the dog would baby-sit, like Nana in *Peter Pan*."

Peter laughed, his dark eyes sparkling.

"But don't those dogs always want to go in the water? Sounds like a mess," I said.

"OK, so maybe I haven't completely thought it through yet, but we'll eventually need a dog if we're going to have kids. Every kid should have a pet, don't you think?"

"Definitely, but I don't know about filling the house with kids. How about one kid and a spaniel?"

"Two kids and a retriever."

"Sounds perfect," I said with a laugh, feeling as though planning the future were really so easy.

We continued on our way, reveling in the Art Nouveau buildings as well as the far older Gothic ones. I found I was falling in love with the city. It was all that it had been cracked up to be and more.

Dark and gloomy Týn Church, a focal point of the city with its Gothic facade of sharp, foreboding towers, was only one of the images that Peter and I treasured in this great city's Old Town. Luckily Prague had escaped the major damage inflicted on other European capitals in the two world wars, and the architecture that surrounded the Old Town Square was impressive. The buildings were, for the most part, tall and narrow, five or six stories high in cream or pastel shades of peach and yellow. Above the windows impressive detailing looked like it was made of sugar icing. The roofs behind the mansard windows and decorative pediments, some of which were painted with beautiful figural scenes, were a uniform orange-red tile. In most of them the ground floor was occupied by a shop or café behind an arcade of arches that seemed to run cohesively from one building to the next.

147

In the center of the large square, various stands sold local products, from Bohemian crystal and garnet jewelry to hundreds upon hundreds of puppets. These were my particular favorite folk art of the Czech people, ranging from frightening monsters, princesses, and silly jesters to the less universal stock character of the Good Soldier Švejk, a sort of antihero dear to the hearts of the Czech population. Needless to say, I bought some puppets for various family members and a military-uniformed, stubble-chinned, beer-drinking Švejk for myself to hang by my desk as a sort of writing mascot.

There were more vendors attesting to Prague's new free enterprise state on the Charles Bridge, as well as suspicious-looking gypsies wanting to change our U.S. dollars for the now-useless extinct currency of the recent past when Prague was just another city behind the Iron Curtain. We politely declined the deal, the experience of the attempted scam just another part of the exoticism of the place, though I did appreciate the subtle way in which gallant Peter placed himself protectively between me and the vaguely threatening gypsy con artists.

The Charles Bridge, a pedestrian-only span over the Vltava River, is an impressive fourteenth-century marvel with dark and solid square towers at either end and light posts and statues of saints at regular intervals along its length. There are no fewer than thirty-one of these statues either censoring or blessing passersby. At the time I tended to think they were giving us benediction rather than the opposite.

On our hand-in-hand walk across the cobbled surface of the bridge, we watched the swans on the river below, the waters golden in the setting sun. On the bridge itself, musicians and salesmen were hard at work, trying to get a few Czech crowns thrown into an open accordion case or crossing the palm of a fledgling entrepreneur. At the far end Peter and I stopped to listen to a group of musicians and had to struggle not to laugh out loud. This band, it seemed, had followed us around the world, from New Jersey, where we'd first seen them or a reasonable facsimile, to Bermuda and beyond here in Eastern Europe. They were Peruvian, I think, complete with woven ponchos and pan flutes. Perhaps they were not the same men that we had seen on the two earlier occasions, perhaps they were. Their music was pleasant, but out of place, and its absurdity, given our location, only added to the spirit of the day.

"I'm going to buy their tape," I told Peter.

"No, don't. I swear I'll lose it if you do."

"I insist," I said, and picked up a cassette, leaving behind the stated number of Czech crowns. I could see the corners of Peter's mouth creeping up as he tried to look as though he were a connoisseur of Latin American Indian music. Once out of earshot, though, we both doubled over in helpless laughter at the reappearance of this band or one very like it in Prague, of all places, and added the experience to a growing store of private treasured moments of intense bliss.

I held out the tape like a trophy once we'd recovered enough to speak.

"Now, honey, I'm sure one of the numbers on here will forever be 'our song,' don't you think?" I asked.

"I thought that Barry White album I used to play for you when we were dating had our special song on it."

"Get real, Peter. I never liked Barry White."

"Come on, it's the ultimate romantic mood music. It can't miss. All women melt when they hear it."

"I promise you, it wasn't the Barry White music I fell for at your apartment," I said with a laugh. Peter put his arm around me and, as I pocketed our musical souvenir, we walked on, building memories one by one.

During our stay in the city, we were charmed and awed by the numerous churches, grand views, and other landmarks that distinguished Prague as the world capital that it is. We visited the diminutive Jewish Town section, with its heavily roofed yet austere-looking synagogue and its sadly impressive cemetery. Thousands of Jews had had to be buried within its limited confines because they were not permitted to be interred outside what were once the neighborhood gates that restrained them within their ghetto. Prague has matured over the centuries, and the

Jewish Town is now recommended with pride to tourists of all faiths. Still, the burial ground, with its headstones on top of headstones, was a grim reminder of the ignorance of the past.

We took a long steep walk up to white-trimmed, almond-colored Prague Castle, more of an impressive and formal palace, actually, than what I thought of as a castle, and we, as Americans, enjoyed the graffiti we encountered on a wall along the way: *"KOMUNISMUS-FAŠISMUS."* It needed no translation.

At the palace we watched the changing of the guard behind an ornate and imposing iron gate, admired the stone tracery on St. Vitus's Cathedral that looked like soot-stained lace, as well as the rest of its Gothic overabundance, including some spectacular gargoyles. Alas, its interior was closed for "technical reasons," although what technology was really necessary for a building erected so many years ago, Peter and I couldn't imagine.

Within the castle grounds we saw the charming little residences that comprise Golden Lane. Peter took my picture in front of the tiny homes that once billeted the castle guards. These castle protectors must not have been too fear-inspiring, though, as the ceilings inside these blue, brick-red, and half-timbered structures were only a yard high.

We paused while on the hill that is graced by the castle to admire the spectacular panorama of the rest of the city below us. It was like a sea of

151

orange-red tile, with the roofs all seeming to intersect each other at crazy angles. To me, coming from the other side of the Atlantic, this was quintessential Europe. Peter and I shared a grin at our joy and surprise, as though we alone had taken in this wonderful picture, and we pointed out various roofs and windows, pretending to choose a vacation home for ourselves that we could return to over and over. I knew, though, that though this was a mere flight of fancy, we would take a little piece of Prague home in our hearts.

"This is forever," I'd said to him then, as we took in the spectacular view, not referring to anything of tile or stone, but of the feeling we were sharing at that one moment.

"Yes" was his reply, and in my ignorance I'd believed him.

Later that day we visited the modest-looking Church of Our Lady Victorious to make a sort of pilgrimage to see the original Infant of Prague figure that had been reproduced so many times to grace bureaus and television sets back home. I lit a candle for the rest of the world as our happiness was testimony enough that we need not bother a higher authority to intervene on *our* behalf.

On Peter's suggestion we bought religious mementos for my grandmother. Though he wasn't Catholic, I think Peter enjoyed the unrestrained hopefulness exhibited by some members of my family as far as the powers they thought they could exert through prayer and good deeds. The candles inscribed with the Infant of Prague would be appreciated by my grandmother, and I knew sooner or later they'd be lit on someone else's behalf.

On one of our last nights we decided to visit a special restaurant called U Kalicha or The Chalice, made famous as a watering hole of the author of *The Good Soldier Švejk*, and paying homage to that dubious literary hero. The walls were covered with irreverent drawings and quotations (in Czech, of course), and everything from the matchbooks to the china illustrated the little man Švejk in his overly-large green uniform and matching outsized books. He was at once ridiculous and endearing, and Peter and I spent a wonderful evening in his spiritual midst. It didn't hurt that the Czech food and beer were delicious or that the music was entertaining. First, the proprietor wound a large music box, in a small armoire-like cabinet, that played lovely folk tunes probably known to every schoolchild in Prague, yet unfamiliar to us. Then, as the evening progressed, we were all serenaded by two musicians, dressed like our little friend Švejk, playing the accordion and the tuba with surprisingly pleasant results.

We couldn't help but notice a misty-eyed older gentleman at the next table who was singled out for special musical numbers and seemed to receive complimentary beers from all over the room. It turned out that years before he had defected to America to play professional hockey and was home for the funeral of his dear mother. He spoke decent enough English and, before the night was over, he had invited us to join him to lift his spirits by being able to observe young love in action. We were more than willing to give him a hand with all the free beers, too. He had been a hero of the local premiere hockey league team called *Sparta Praha* ("Praha" being the name of the city in Czech), and the drinks were testimony to the gratitude of the fans who remained loyal to the memory of his great playing days both at home and in faraway Chicago.

In talking to our new acquaintance, whose name was Slava, Peter was relaxed and comfortable, asking a slew of questions about the older man's days as a professional athlete. Peter was a big fan of sports in general and wanted to know which well-known players had been teammates of Slava's and which were particularly nasty opponents. Slava's very blue eyes beamed, and his pale mustache twitched with glee as he related stories of his early days as a defector in the United States, particularly in the context of his sport. I let the conversation drift by me, drowsy with a bit too much beer and content in the knowledge that Peter was enjoying himself, too, though in a more active manner. I perked up when the conversation changed from sport to more general talk about Prague. I enjoyed Slava's bravado as he hinted at romantic exploits along the banks of the Vltava and in various women's flats around the city. At that point the waiter came by to see if we needed anything, and Slava had us laughing when he began to talk to the waiter in English, then got turned around again and addressed Peter and me in Czech.

"What's the story with this little soldier character?" Peter asked, seizing the opportunity to get a little more of an explanation.

Slava told us all about the origins of the Švejk character — a fictional World War I soldier who managed to circumvent orders and regulations by pretending to be an imbecile — and some of his silly exploits in foiling the German army.

"I like to think that I, too, am a Švejk," Slava said with a wink, "that maybe I am not quite the simple retired hockey player people think I am. I think it is good to fool people sometimes. If they are thinking I am too stupid or too old to do something, then I will be able to choose not to do that thing if that's what I want. I still play hockey at least three times a week back home in the States, but if someone decides I am feeble, it can work to my advantage, don't you see? The army thought Švejk was stupid and lazy, and he went through the war without having to do much that he did not choose to do. We should all be a little bit like Švejk sometimes." I laughed, thinking that maybe we are all of us more than what we let the world see.

We ended the night with a last swallow of beer and a promise that Slava would visit us in New Jersey if he ever got the chance. I still think of him sometimes when I look at the puppet that hangs next to my computer, though we never did see him again after that wonderful evening.

On our last day in the city, I insisted that we revisit the famous Astronomical Clock that had so captivated me earlier in our walks around town. On the hour, figures of the apostles parade past two open windows high up on the clock, while down below figures, two of which represent the human vices of greed (holding a money bag) and vanity (holding a mirror), shake their heads "no" to mortality. Meanwhile Death, in the guise of a skeleton, says "yes" with the ringing of a bell, whose finality contradicts their self-deception. Little did I know at the time as I stood there holding hands with Peter that he was ringing that damned bell for us.

It was time to stop the flood of memories, to stem the tide of sorrow and panic that threatened to send me backward into a hole of sorrow. Owen was with me now, and I needed to remind myself that I was, for the first time in ever so long, not alone.

I wandered out to the sunporch to put on some music. Owen had found most of my musical tastes odd at best, but I'd found an old tape of mine of Gaelic music played on the hammered dulcimer, among other instruments, and he liked that. It was already in the tape player, so that was what I put on after the conversation with my mother. Owen wandered in a short time later, but sensing my nostalgic mood, I guess, he turned to leave.

"Wait. Don't go," I said.

"It's all right if you want to be alone, Peggy."

"No, I don't think I do," I said. "This is the tape you said you liked," I offered by way of starting a conversation that wouldn't involve my reminiscences. The notes insinuated themselves in and around us, like the music of angels. It probably wasn't the best choice to break my mood or its inherent regrets.

"I suppose you like bagpipes, too," I said with what I hoped was a gentle smile.

"Aye, but they always put me in mind of weddings and funerals. We had an Irishman on the *Elizabeth York* who played something called Uilleann pipes, and they were grand to listen to."

"They are," I agreed quietly.

"Skye Boat Song" began to play, its haunting melody carried by plaintive strings, underlining a state of mind I did not wish to be in. Nothing else can mourn like a cello, I thought.

"You're not happy," Owen said.

"It'll pass."

"What was he like?"

He knew that I knew whom he'd meant.

"I don't know if anything I could say would give you a good idea of what Peter was like," I said, seeing him in my mind's eye once again, laughing and toasting our new friend at The Chalice in Prague, "but I can show you a picture of him."

I reached down into the built-in bookshelves on the sunporch and came up with my wedding

157

album. I smiled at what I knew I would find in-side — flattering portraits of two people who would now seem very young and unrealistically, giddily joyous at the prospect of a lifetime to-gether. I hadn't looked at it for quite some time.

"Sit down," I said, motioning to the spot next to me.

I opened the photograph album across our knees so that its spine rested in the space be-tween us. I felt his nearness to me and, glancing at his downturned eyes, I thought how he literally paled in comparison to my late hus-band, his fair hair a stark contrast to Peter's al-most mahogany-brown. I could see, though, that in his own unassuming way Owen could be con-sidered quite appealing, that more than one woman would consider herself lucky to have such a partner. The idea of his finding happiness elsewhere, I found, was strangely disconcerting. I guess I was starting to like being able to assume that I'd have company when I came downstairs in the morning and at night just before I decided to call it a day. The thought of going back to where I'd been before I met Owen was not a happy one.

A picture of Peter and me on the dance floor caught my eye. He was so gallant in his black tie and tails, so tall and straight and true. He and Owen were as different as they could be, I thought. Peter was nothing if not clear as to who he was and confident that he was a good man, or at least as good a man as any. He was used to refinements in his life, but he was never fussy, not a victim of what I called the "Shaken, Not Stirred Syndrome." Owen had had no such advantages and was, therefore, more willing to accept whatever fate brought his way. Whether all his claims were true or not, I could well believe that he had faced hard times Peter and I could only imagine. He was a walking Horatio Alger hero who'd never quite been able to pull himself up by his own bootstraps.

As Owen studied the photos, I continued to try to read his face. He was earnestly poring over each picture, not the way he did when he tried to decipher words, but as though he were a little disturbed by what he saw. Possibly the changes in styles from his own time to now were unsettling, or the very color and quality of the modern photographs themselves were a bit of a shock to him. There was a trace of stubble on his cheeks, and I remembered all at once how I used to like to run my hand against the grain of Peter's day-old beard on weekends and how I used to like to watch him without his knowing it as he pulled off his shirt at the end of the day. I wasn't even sure that Peter had realized how much he still affected me when I looked at him. Owen glanced up at me and asked me if I was all right. I guess thoughts of Peter had made me forget where I was, and I may have been staring. It had been a very long time since there had been a man living in the house, and I was unused to it. Owen and I were sitting so close that I could sense his warmth beside me, and his forearm came into contact with mine when he moved from one page to the next. I could actually feel the plentiful blond hairs on his arm tickling me, and I moved back a bit to be sure he had room to turn the pages when he so chose.

Indicating a formally posed shot of Peter and myself at the altar of our little local church, Owen said, "I wondered how you would have looked . . . in my time."

"You mean in a gown?" I asked.

He nodded.

"And?"

"Beautiful. You look beautiful. And your husband . . . he was a very handsome man. You both look so happy."

"Well, you know how it is when you're in love."

"No, not really."

"Weren't you ever in love?"

"No, I never was. There was never really time."

"Haven't you ever been with a woman?"

He looked at me for clarification. I guess he figured out what I meant from my expression. Predictably, he blushed.

"I've never 'been with' a woman who wasn't a . . ."

"A what? A prostitute?"

He nodded, ashamed. "You don't think that's why I'm here, do you?" he asked.

"You mean why you're not in heaven? Are you really so anxious to die? It isn't that bad here once you get used to it. Maybe your being here is a reward, or the correction of a mistake. Maybe you weren't supposed to go overboard in the first place."

I really wanted to hear what he'd say to that, but a persistent knocking interrupted.

"That'll be my mother," I explained.

"Would you like me to go out for a while?"

"I'm not ashamed of you, Owen. Come on, we might as well get this over with."

I guess those weren't exactly words of inspiration, but Owen dutifully followed me to the kitchen door. My mother's first impression wasn't going to be the best, as the kitchen was the room currently in disarray, midway through its paint job.

I opened the door, and my mother and I embraced, the kiss she'd aimed at my cheek terminating somewhere in the air near my right ear.

"Oh, I see you've hired a painter," she began.

"Mom, this is Owen Sinclair. Owen, this is my mother, Catherine Bresnahan. Mom, Owen is my houseguest. He also happens to be doing me a big favor by doing some work around here that's long overdue."

"Well, that's nice, dear. I know Peter never had a lot of time for manual labor. It's good you aren't letting the house go downhill."

"It's nice to meet you," Owen offered with an awkward smile.

I changed the subject to one that I thought would be pleasant to all. "Well, tell me all about your trip!" I prompted. "How is everybody? Were any of the kids there?"

"Everyone and everything is fine with Eamonn and Anne. We managed to see quite a bit of Breda, her husband, and their four children, too." Breda was the Riordans' daughter closest to my own age, a fiery redhead with whom I'd always gotten on well. "Very little changes over there, you know," my mother added, but I couldn't tell if she'd meant the comment wistfully or with regret.

"Did you manage to get down to the local?" I asked, meaning the nearest pub to the Riordans' farm. I clearly recalled going there one evening for some good "crack" (the general Irish term for fun) and authentic Irish music, only to be serenaded by an area band playing nothing but American country-western tunes.

"We stopped in for a light meal once or twice. We seemed to be continually crossing paths with that scruffy-looking old man that used to do odd jobs around the farm — Pádraig, I think it was — and he was there both of the times we stopped in at the pub."

"You mean that old thatcher from up the road? Maybe he lives there — at the pub, I mean," I said with a laugh.

"It wouldn't surprise me," my mother replied with a disapproving look for both disheveled old Pádraig and my own glib attitude.

I shot her a grin and she weakly returned the gesture, the smile never reaching her pronounced cheekbones or her eyes.

"Well, let me show you what I've brought," she said.

She opened a large colorful shopping bag and drew out a beautiful sweater with interlacing Celtic designs in shades of green, my favorite color. The second was knit in soft natural shades, rendered in a complicated arrangement of stitches. She also handed me a bottle of my signature perfume, an Irish product that I could readily buy at both the import shops in town. I was, nevertheless, grateful for her thoughtfulness and generosity.

"Did you buy that skirt while you were there this time?" I asked, referring to her subtle predominantly grey plaid kilted skirt. Her black turtleneck and red blazer picked up on the secondary colors that threaded through the tartan.

"Why, yes, I did. Do you like it?"

What's not to like? I thought. It wasn't exactly a risky fashion statement.

"It's very nice," I said. "And thank you for the gifts. The sweaters are beautiful, and I was almost out of perfume, so I really appreciate this," I added, holding up the scent in its elegant box.

"Peter used to buy you such nice things. You must miss all those little surprises he was always bringing you."

"Yes, he was full of surprises," I said, knowing it was true, but reluctant to stress Peter's perfections too much in Owen's presence.

"Now, why don't you go put those sweaters away, Peggy, before they end up full of paint."

I knew enough not to argue. "Sure. I'll be right back," I said.

When I returned, the kitchen was quiet, and I wondered if my mother and Owen had stood in silence the entire time I was gone.

"I'd better be going," my mother said when she saw that I'd returned. "Next time your father and I go over, why don't you think of going with us? I think in the long run, it would be better for you."

I felt like heaving a sigh of relief when she'd gone, even though the visit had been better than I'd had a right to expect.

Owen was quiet after we were once again alone, almost sullen, which was anything but characteristic of him. He never seemed to resent anything or feel like ranting and raving at the world as I too often did. I asked him if he wanted to work on his reading, and I was surprised when he said no. He was usually very excited to do whatever lesson he'd been assigned by Mrs. Morlock, his reading specialist. He had grown very attached to her, and that was part of the reason he worked so hard at his assignments. I suspected that in other aspects of his life, he had been motivated, and perhaps still was, less by a desire to please than by a fear of displeasing, but this did not seem to be the case with Owen and Mrs. Morlock. He evinced a great deal of affection for her and gratitude, too, as he seemed to think she was slowly performing some kind of miracle in teaching him to read. That was why I was more than a little taken aback when he told me he wanted to go for a walk rather than do his homework.

I didn't feel that I could take for granted that he'd want me to accompany him, but when I asked if I could join him, he didn't object.

We meandered silently up the sand, letting the surf do all the talking. The waves made such a lonely sound, I wanted to break the silence between us. Instead I waited, watching him smoke his pipe, hoping he'd feel he could tell me what was bothering him.

We walked a long way, not talking. When I asked him if he'd like to continue out to the lighthouse, a walk of nearly two miles, he nodded. I was hoping that he would open up to me, as his behavior was clearly not what I had come to expect from him, but we got all the way out to Slea Head Point without his unburdening his mind to me.

I managed to encourage a little small talk, though I got the feeling that he answered me out of good manners, nothing more. He certainly lacked the enthusiasm that might easily have accompanied the information he imparted if his mood had been lighter.

"I guess the lighthouses were all occupied back when you sailed," I said, hoping to start a string of memories flooding his mind and, therefore, giving him a topic to at least begin talking to me, but he merely nodded in reply.

"I can't imagine what it must have been like to live in a lighthouse. Were you ever inside one?"

"No. I was once one of a party chosen to row supplies out to one, south of here, off the Carolinas. We'd all heard that the keeper had a beautiful daughter, so it was hotly disputed as to who'd be lucky enough to get chosen to go. But the keeper was intelligent enough to keep her far out of our sight, and we never could tell if she was as pretty as her reputation would have it."

I would have expected a smile with such a tale, but the disappointment all those years ago was just a reflection of the way Owen seemed to be viewing his new circumstances now. I hadn't managed to get through in spite of my best efforts by the time we reached our journey's end.

The lighthouse stood, as it had for over two hundred years, in elegant simplicity. Its tall octagonal base had recently been repainted a clean bright white, and the metalwork surrounding its lens was a faded red.

"Well, here it is," I said unnecessarily, thinking this little bit of humor would start him, if not laughing, at least smiling. "I'll bet you never thought you'd see it from this side. The land side, I mean."

"It looks like there is no other side!" he exclaimed at last, when he'd finally left his thoughts behind enough to take in his surroundings. "What happened?"

"What do you mean?"

"It's all silted in. There are trees growing all around it. Didn't anyone keep up with the dredging and the clearing? It's all gone to ruin!"

"I wouldn't exactly say that, but it's true that it's not in use anymore. I mean, the light hasn't been lit in I don't know how long. It's just a historic site now. It's one of the oldest lighthouses in the country."

"How can you call it a lighthouse if it has no light?" he asked incredulously. It seemed to really agitate him that it was now much farther inland than in his time, and that it was no longer functional. I guess it somehow reinforced for him the changes that had taken place in a way that all our new technology hadn't been able to do. I also figured that whatever he had been mulling over on our walk had left him in a heightened state emotionally, and it needn't have been anything this dramatic to have unsettled him further. He kept silent for a while as we tacitly decided to begin our walk home and then surprised me by taking a new tack, changing the subject without elucidating what was really on his mind.

"Did your TV tell you there's a big storm coming?" he asked quietly at last.

"No, I haven't watched it today. How can you tell?"

"The sky, the wind, I don't know, really. It should be a good one, though, bigger even than the storm the night I ended up here."

"That's not what's bothering you."

167

He looked at me and smiled, a melancholy kind of smile, full of unspoken regrets, but as though he'd come to an important decision.

"You're not leaving?" I asked, trying to keep the panic I felt from my voice.

"I don't know what to do, Peggy."

"Oh, God, my mother. What did she say while I was upstairs?"

"She asked me if we were living in sin. Of course I told her we weren't."

"And?"

"Nothing. I suppose she thinks it looks bad, my staying here with you. She's probably right."

"Owen, things change a lot faster now than they did when you were, well, you know, before you came here. What was unacceptable for my mother's generation is sometimes perfectly all right for me. There's nothing wrong with your being here with me, and if a few tongues wag, I couldn't care less."

"She said I should talk to your priest."

"That's her answer to most of life's little problems. Please don't let her make you feel like you should go. I want you to stay, Owen."

"I don't want people to treat you badly because of me."

"They don't. Now, why don't we go back, and I'll help you with your studies."

Owen shrugged, and I couldn't help but wonder if my mother hadn't had more to say than he'd told me.

"If you want to be able to read, it's going to

take a lot of hard work. It's too early to give up now."

"All right," he agreed, but without the expected enthusiasm.

"If you'd like, I can read something to you. What kind of book would you like me to read?"

"I don't know. I see all those books in the house, and I wonder what could possibly be in them. Are they stories or histories? I don't have any idea."

"Well, haven't you ever been read to? You know, when you were a boy?"

"No."

"Not even in school?"

"We had primers, not storybooks. And I couldn't make heads or tails of them anyway. I guess books are pretty much of a mystery to me, but I know they're important to educated people. I just don't know what they're about."

"Oh, Owen, this is going to be fun! You're going to love Dumas, Dickens, Robert Louis Stevenson, Sir Walter Scott. . . ."

"Who are they?"

"Wonderful writers, you'll see. I feel like a kid in a candy store. I want to share them with you. When I was younger, they were like my best friends. Later I loved other writers — Joyce, Faulkner, Salinger, Fitzgerald. But you'll get to them when you're ready. Come on!" I shouted and took off at a run back across the beach. I guess my excitement was contagious because Owen joined me, then passed by and ahead of where I ran. I'm a pretty good runner, but there was no way I could keep up. I watched him beat me to the house, running straight as an arrow to my door. He was waiting for me when, out of breath, I reached him. We broke into spontaneous, joyous laughter as children do at meaningless play, laughing simply because it feels good.

When the sun had begun to set and the wind outside to pick up, we lit a fire in the parlor fireplace, or rather Owen did, as that was a chore that had hardly changed at all in the years of either of our lifetimes. We got comfortable on the floor with pillows, and I began to read to him from *Kidnapped*.

Other than the coincidence of its having a character named Campbell like his stepfather, which prompted a decided frown on Owen's part, he was enthralled by the story. For someone who had never seen a film or a play and had never been read to, other than from the Bible, it must have been an eye-opening experience. Several times he begged me not to stop.

When we got to the first illustration, he looked long and hard at it, as though using it to correct the image in his mind's eye. After the fourth chapter, I left him in suspense to make a pot of tea. I drink a lot of coffee, but in front of a roaring fire, for some reason, I always prefer tea.

The wind had begun to howl, which seemed quite wonderful in the warmth of the house, and rain started to fall in greater and greater volume until it didn't seem possible for it to come down any faster.

I read two more chapters, passing another of Wyeth's wonderful illustrations on the way, and although I knew I was leaving Owen figuratively on the edge of his seat, my voice needed a rest.

"Now, that's why you'll want to do your assignments for Mrs. Morlock from now on — so you'll be able to do that for yourself, and no one will be able to leave you hanging there wondering what happens next," I said, and took a sip of my tea.

"Couldn't you read just a bit more?"

"Not another word. I know it's obnoxious of me, but I'm tired."

"I'm sorry, I wasn't thinking. It's a very exciting story, though, isn't it? And you know how it ends?"

I nodded to both questions, but the noise of the gale interrupted my thoughts, and I went to the window to look out at the storm. I couldn't see much, but I could hear the rain slamming against the glass.

"A good night to be inside," Owen said.

"What's it like on a ship on a night like this?"

"Wet."

We started to laugh, and I put my arm around him as he stood next to me at the window. He had come to mean so much to me, but when he returned the gesture I pulled away, though I'm not sure why.

"I have a surprise for you," I said. "Wait here."

While I was upstairs, the power went out. It was far darker than I would have expected, but I was reasonably sure I could find my way around the house with my eyes closed. I used to do that for fun when I was a child living at home with my parents or when I'd stay at my grandmother's house. I only stubbed my toe once on my way to the closet, where I kept a flashlight.

"Are you all right?" Owen called up the stairs.

"I'm fine. I've got the flashlight now."

"The what? What happened to the lights?"

"The storm must have knocked the power out. It's no big deal," I answered as I grabbed a small box from one of my bureau drawers.

When I got back downstairs, Owen was sitting cross-legged in front of the fire. I stood for a moment, unseen, watching Owen watching the fire. The light reflected off his glasses and, behind them, his eyes. The blaze of the fire seemed to set his fair hair aglow in shades from gold to deepest red. He looked as though he really belonged in that room with all my old treasures.

I know I had many times studied Peter's face — in admiration, for pure pleasure, as an act of love. I don't remember spending a lot of time looking at his features as if to figure him out, but then Peter had never been an enigma to me.

I realized that the pummeling of the rain wouldn't cover my presence forever. I wished I could know what Owen had been so quietly contemplating at my hearth, but it was time I gave him his gift.

"I'm back," I announced as I crossed through the arch that separated the parlor from the dining room. I turned off the flashlight, which was superfluous once I got close enough to the flames. I sat down next to Owen and handed him the wine-colored gift box I had retrieved from upstairs.

He removed the lid, looking to me for explanation more than watching what his hands were doing. Inside, under a layer of cotton, was the medal I had ordered for him. It sparkled gold in the available light as he drew it out from the box. It dangled from his fingers, then he palmed the medal to study its inscription or rather the representations of the saints pictured there in relief rather than the words, which he couldn't decipher. I watched as he turned it over and smiled.

"It's Saint Elmo," I said, "and Saint Christopher on the other side. I don't know if it really keeps you safe, but I'd feel better if you'd wear it."

"It must have cost you a fortune, Peggy. It's gold, isn't it?"

"Well, if it wasn't, you couldn't wear it all the time, and I don't want you to ever take it off."

"I won't, ever," he said, and undid the clasp and put it around his neck. "I feel safer already." He gave me a shy smile, more unsure than I'd seen him in some time. "Thank you. It's the best present I've ever had." As he expressed his gratitude, he held the medal between his fingers and I could almost feel the cold metal warming to his touch.

"I have something for you, too," he said, "but not nearly as nice as this."

He rose, and I turned on the flashlight and handed it to him. I listened as he made his way to the sunporch and back, carrying a thick piece of paper into the parlor. He placed it in my hands, and it was, as I had hoped, another work of art for me, this time in color.

"I didn't know you'd used your new paints already," I said. "This is great! It looks like you've been painting all your life."

"I had a little paint box with my things on board the *Elizabeth York*. I didn't get too many chances to use it, but it was fun, and I made a picture of the *Glen Rover* for the inside of my sea chest. Just being sentimental, I guess, her being my first ship and all."

The painting he had done for me was primitive in the sense that he'd had no formal training, but it appeared to me to rank with the best folk art of the last century. It was well executed, the ship's lines true to formula but individual, I had no doubt, to the characteristics of the particular vessel. The sea and sky, without the constraints of a ship's precise dimensions, were fanciful but eminently believable. The germ of an idea — that his work would be marketable and might even provide him a means of supporting himself — popped into my head.

"This is the best present *I've* ever gotten, Owen. If you'll let me, I'd like to show it to the owner of a gallery I know in Cape May," I said, thinking of good old Darren from my step-dancing days. "I think you may have found your true calling."

I could tell he was pleased, if a little embarrassed, but he told me I was being silly if I meant people would buy pictures like the one I had in my hand.

"Then, give me a chance to make a fool of myself, OK?"

"OK," he agreed.

"Let me put this somewhere safe," I said, and as I rose to leave the room the lights came back on, flooding the room with what appeared now to be overly garish light.

Whatever spell had characterized the stormy evening was broken, and when I suggested we call it a night, Owen had no objections.

# CHAPTER 8

The last day of October arrived, All Hallow's Eve, and I tried to explain the tradition of trick-or-treating to Owen, to prepare him for the young visitors we'd soon be receiving. I know I was excited as I told him about the costumes, the candy, and what a highlight the evening was for children who had only fairly recently returned to the discipline of school schedules and homework and who had little else to look forward to before Christmas. I hadn't even turned on my porch light the previous year, making sure that it was clear to the world that I was exempt from merry-making of any kind. It was a kind of sweetness to find myself involved once again in one of the small rituals that make up a typical American year.

As the sun began to set, we were ready for the children that would surely arrive if word hadn't carried over from the recent past that my house was off limits as a nonparticipant. I didn't expect any such scenario as I had virtually every down-stairs light lit to demonstrate my willingness to be a part of the day, and Owen and I had had fun the day before carving several jack-o'-lanterns with ghoulish faces, his creation reflecting a real ability to turn even a silly project like this into a small-scale work of art. I was sure they'd be frightening-looking enough for even the older treat- and thrill-seekers we'd see later that evening in the second wave of kids, after the youngest ones were safe at home again.

The doorbell rang, revealing three costumed elementary-school girls. One was dressed as a witch, one a ballerina, and one a princess. Their grins were nearly as wide as their open bags that were already partly filled with candy bars and lollipops. At least, I thought, no one gives out apples anymore. We, as children, had always considered them poor excuses for treats.

Looking at this group and those that followed, the thrill came back to me of my sister Marjorie, my brother Ryan, and me cutting through yards across rime-encrusted grass, the frost making each blade a stiff spike that crackled beneath our feet. Since I'd grown too old for beggar's night activities, I'd often wondered why daylight savings time wasn't extended just a bit to keep children in safer, brighter conditions as they made their Halloween pilgrimage from house to house, but as a child I'd considered the eerie darkness an essential element in turning familiar territory into ghostly terrain in my mind. By the dim light of a flashlight, it wasn't hard to make believe that unthinkable creatures lurked just out of sight and that the very trees, a deeper black against an already dark sky, were capable of intelligent movement with unpleasant intent.

In spite of our childish desire to let our imaginations run a bit wild as we negotiated Slea

Head's residential streets, the three of us had still kept a strategy in mind to get our goody bags as full as possible by the time the curfew our parents had set arrived. We knew which houses were those of year-rounders and which to avoid — those of the seasonal people who would have been long gone by the end of October. It was also best, we knew, to stay away from those families our parents knew well, where we would be questioned as to our identities and even asked to come in and show off our costumes in better light. As far as we were concerned, this was time ill spent on such an important evening.

The next visitors Owen and I greeted were a boy and girl with their parents in tow. The boy was a cowboy for the occasion and the girl an angel. The next ring of the doorbell that almost immediately followed brought a ghost and a pirate. I remembered being dressed as Minnie Mouse, Dorothy from the *Wizard of Oz*, and, one year, when Marjorie and I couldn't decide what to wear, we'd donned our step-dancing costumes. This compromise was certainly more pleasing to Marjorie than it had been to me. Even though we had together taken classes in this very Irish style of dance for a number of years and faced the inevitable recitals that followed, this discipline that most people found utterly charming just wasn't for me. I hated going to our lessons, hated practicing, and truly detested performing for the whole clan, whether on a stage or in my grandparents' living room. It may have been that experience that led me to dislike dancing in my later years. I know it didn't scar Marjorie at all, and I had to admit that there might not have been much future for me in that art whether I'd ever been coerced into learning Irish step-dancing or not as a child. The only part I'd actually relished had been the pizza dinners after lessons with our old family friends, the Hurleys. Remembering how silly I'd felt getting ready to go out for Halloween in my kelly-green dress with its Celtic tracery (Marjorie had gotten the dark forest-green color that I would have preferred), I smiled and my smile widened as I recalled my glee when it started to rain and I got to cover my dress and its short flared skirt with a coat before we made our rounds.

I looked over at Owen as he delivered candy bars to a dalmation and a harem girl. His own smile was pretty bashful as they thanked him and ran out to their next stop. I could tell that he liked children, but it was equally apparent that he wasn't too used to their company. The little ones didn't care; they wanted their chocolate and to be able to move on to the next house, nothing more.

The costumes delighted Owen. Even the serial killer with goalie mask and bloody blade seemed to tickle his fancy, and he grinned at some of the sillier impersonations. There was a black-and-yellow-striped bee, about age nine, with wiggly antennae, and a brother and sister act, each dressed in half of a big appliance box painted yellow with black polka dots that he seemed to enjoy in particular. In response to Owen's questioning gaze, I asked the kids what they were supposed to be, only to be told matter-of-factly that they were, of course, pieces of Swiss cheese.

"Anything goes," I said with a shrug, and noted an increased alacrity in Owen's movements as he went to answer the door to see what would turn up next. The nonsense and pageantry of the day made at least as much sense to him as it did to me — a ritual that seemed to satisfy something primal — a need to confront evil things that go bump in the night head-on with ridicule and disdain. The biggest discovery of the day for me was something on a much smaller scale.

Of all the things that were new to Owen, I don't think any surprised me more than the fact that he had never tasted chocolate. To me it's not a luxury or a treat, but one of the staples of life and an absolute necessity in times of acute downheartedness.

Whether through timing, poverty, or the isolation of a life at sea, he had never experienced so many things that I took in my stride, but this one really blew my mind. I was mildly astonished when he'd tell me he'd tried some strange fruit or foreign dish that I considered exotic, but this wasn't so incomprehensible when I took into account that he had traveled to Java, Singapore, and other ports of call. He'd seen the world before it had begun to be homogenized with franchised hotels and restaurants, before we all watched the same film stars and drank the same soda, when each region had its own mode of dress and no beliefs or taboos were universal. Sometimes I envied him for what he'd seen, but when I thought of the conditions under which he'd traveled, I was content with what I'd been able to experience of the world from jets and cabs and clean hotels.

At any rate, we finished off the final bag of Halloween treats that were left over after the last of the bigger kids had come and gone. They were wonderful chocolates, filled with peanut butter — another first for Owen — and he seemed to enjoy them almost as much as I did.

The fire that Owen had lit earlier in the evening was dying down, but he threw another log on at my request, and we sat down for a little quiet reading in the stillness that marked the end of the holiday's rites. We had already gone over his work for Mrs. Morlock, and he'd showed me some of the clever tricks she used in her efforts to make him literate. She had had him go over with his fingers the shapes of the letters of the alphabet cut from what looked like sandpaper, to imprint them on his mind in a way that was not purely visual. She'd also taught him to make the letter *L* with the perpendicular extended thumb and forefinger of his left hand, showing him in the process that the opposite shape made with his right hand did not create that letter. This became the tool he used to remind himself to work from left to right, as this did not come naturally to him. I knew that progress was slow, but to him any improvement was almost worthy of awe.

He could now pick out a few words as I read to him, not many, but enough that I got to enjoy his delight in this discovery of his own dormant abilities. We had gotten to the part of *Kidnapped* when poor David Balfour is swept off the brig in which he was being transported to America. I had not thought of the similarities to Owen's life when I'd picked up the book. In fact, my recollections of the specifics of the story were actually few. I had only thought to read an adventure story that was unsophisticated enough for a novice to comprehend, one that I hoped would hold Owen's attention. I stopped when I finished the chapter, leaving the hero alive but alone on the islet of Earraid.

"I forget how lucky I am sometimes," Owen said. "When I think of where I might have cast up. . . . I must seem ungrateful at times."

"Not at all. I think you're doing great, considering all the changes you've had to make."

"It *is* bewildering at times. Well, most of the time, really. I sometimes still wonder if I'm not dreaming."

I smiled. "You've got to admit it's better in some ways." I guess I wanted him to have a marked preference for life here in Slea Head in my time rather than in his own, but his ability to see the good, even in times of duress, was one of his more endearing qualities.

He smiled, too, but more to himself than to me. "In some ways it's grand," he said. "There was a lot that was grand for me, too, before I came here."

"Such as?"

"I did like being a sailor. It was the first thing I'd ever been really good at, I mean other than cleaning stalls and grooming horses, and there's not much pride to be had in that."

"But the work does sound like such drudgery — when it wasn't downright dangerous," I said, still not prepared, I guess, to believe that his life shortly before we'd met was any better than mine had been.

"Oh, it could be both, but it had its nobler side as well."

I waited for him to elaborate, and after a minute he quoted, " 'They that go down to the sea in ships, that do business in great waters; These see the works of the Lord and his wonders in the deep.' "

"And have you seen wonders?"

"Aye. Waterspouts and Saint Elmo's fire, flying fish and whales and ships in full sail, native people so beautiful you almost can't believe they're alive. . . ."

"New Jersey must seem pretty tame after all that," I said, impressed with the images he'd conjured up in my mind.

"I don't mind that. It's wonderful to sleep for eight hours at a stretch and not eat the same thing every day and to have you to talk to."

I had started to forget his shyness until I saw how he avoided my eyes as he said it.

"Well, you've told me how bad the food is," I said to change the subject back to something safe and relatively impersonal. "What's such a big deal about a full night's sleep?"

"We work in four-hour watches — four on deck, four below, and so on. Then, there are the dogwatches from four to six and six to eight in the evening. They're only two hours each to ensure that whatever schedule of watches you had one day, you'll have the opposite during the next twenty-four hours. I'm not sure if I explained that well enough, and I don't know if it makes any sense, but it seems to me like it would be better to always have the same schedule of watches so as to get used to it."

"It makes perfect sense, actually. Constantly changing from one to the other upsets your circadian rhythms."

"Your what?"

"I just mean your body was constantly adjusting to the different hours spent awake and asleep, so you couldn't just get acclimated to one or the other way of living. There are plenty of people who work at night, but their bodies have to get accustomed to being opposite to what they're used to, and switching back to a more 'normal' schedule is another big adjustment for them.

"Anyway, why don't you tell me what some of your duties were."

184

"Of course it depends a bit on your watch, again, as some duties are part of the morning watch at sunup, for example, and some duties require all hands."

"OK."

"Well, let me see . . . we wash down the decks, coil rope, scrape rust, repair and adjust the rigging, tar, paint, grease, set sail, reef sail, furl sail. Then there's the night watch and a million other duties. There wasn't a lot of free time and plenty of hours are spent aloft, but once you get used to the swaying, it's a grand way to see the world." He looked down at his hands and added, "I think I'm starting to lose all my calluses, though, that I worked so hard to get, but I suppose that won't matter much now."

"Where were you going — on the *Elizabeth York*, was it? — when you ended up on the beach here?"

"We were headed back from Hong Kong. Before that we were in San Francisco."

"Oh, San Francisco is such a wonderful city!"

"Are you daft? I mean . . ."

"No, I'm not 'daft.' I was there a few years ago, and I had a great time. I'd like to go back sometime."

"Well, it must have changed since I was there."

"What was it like then?"

"To begin with, the prices there were almost as bad as they are here."

"For example?"

"I don't know. A meal cost five dollars, a pair

of shoes forty or fifty. And it was a wild, lawless place. It was the worst place for getting waylaid; you didn't dare go about on your own. I surely was relieved when we finally left there. Still, there were plenty of men who wanted to stay. We took a crew double what we needed because the captain knew half the men would jump ship when we got there."

"Whatever for, if it was as bad as you say?"

"To look for gold, of course."

"Oh, the forty-niners. I forgot. Why didn't you stay to hunt for gold?"

"Didn't feel lucky, I guess," he said with a shrug and a smile.

"Maybe one day you could go back and see San Francisco as it is now. Parts of the city are really beautiful."

"As long as I wouldn't have to sail around Cape Horn again, I guess that would be all right."

"What's so bad about Cape Horn?"

"Well, on the way west the wind is nearly always against you. You can be stuck there for weeks, and it storms nearly all the time. You're constantly cold and wet. The only way to get dry is to sleep in your clothes, if all hands aren't needed and you can actually get some sleep. The deck would be under water and the rigging full of ice. . . ."

"It sounds awful."

"And all that for twelve dollars a month!"

"My God! Why would anyone be a sailor?" I

asked, hoping my exclamation hadn't been too harsh. I really did want to give him an opportunity to convince me it wasn't so bad, to get him to show me his past through his own eyes and words.

"A good question, I suppose, but it isn't as if I could decide to go off to some university and study law like your sister and her husband, or write books like you."

"Why not?" I demanded.

"You know why not. I can't read, I have no money. I haven't the brains for it, but I'm a hard worker like my father was before me."

"I thought you never knew him."

"I don't remember him, really, but my mother told me about him, and people were always saying how very like him I was."

"What did he do?"

"He was only a common laborer. He took whatever work he could find. I know he'd worked at the nail factory in Yarmouth for a time, but I think he was a road mender when he died. His people had been crofters in Scotland, but they were forced off their land and came to Nova Scotia to start over."

"How did he die? He couldn't have been very old."

"I think he was twenty-seven, younger than I am now."

"Did he die in some sort of accident?"

"No, he died of a fever. My mother said he went very quickly."

"I know how that is. It must have been very hard for you and your mother. I'm sorry."

"I'm sorry as well. I would have liked to have known him."

"And your stepfather? What did he do?"

"He was the sexton at his church."

"What does a sexton do?"

"He tends the church building and grounds, but he also buries people."

"How gruesome."

"It suited him," Owen said with an unaccustomed ounce of bitterness.

"Was he really so awful? Why did your mother marry him?"

"He was very good to her, really. It's hard to believe how different he was with her. And she didn't have to work any more after she married him, which was a relief to me, since I thought she would work herself into an early grave as well."

"Was she happy with him?"

"I don't know. I think maybe," he said as though it was the first time he'd really thought it through, "when I wasn't around."

"Why not then?"

"He used to tan me good sometimes, and it made her cry to see it. Maybe he thought I'd come between them."

"So you went to sea."

"Aye. I expected someday to be buried at sea as well. It's amazing how everything has changed," he said quietly. "Now, tell me about your father. What does he do?"

"He just retired, actually, but he was a vice president at a bank in New York before that."

"He must be an important man."

"I guess so. To a kid, though, he's just your dad. He wasn't home as much as I'd have liked."

"What does he do now that he's not a banker anymore?"

"Plays golf, mostly. He and my mother are very social, always going to parties and fund-raisers. They both like the theater, my mother is active in her garden club, and, of course, she spends a lot of time riding."

"Will I ever meet your father?"

"Sure. On Thanksgiving, if not sooner."

"Thanksgiving?"

"It's a holiday," I said, and looked question-ingly at him to see if he knew what I meant. "You'll see when it gets here. In the meantime I'll see about getting a kids' book from the li-brary about the Pilgrims and all that, and I can read it to you. OK?"

"Whatever you say," he answered good-humoredly.

"Well," I said, "I think I'll put *Kidnapped* away for the night. I think you're enjoying the fact that the Campbells are the bad guys."

"I can't deny that," he said with a grin, and I kept a picture of his smile in my head as we said our good nights.

Later that night, I think thoughts of his smile must have stayed with me in some small capacity in the back of my mind, only to come back to me later in a dream I had, altered by my subconscious into another's.

I woke in the darkness around two o'clock in the morning. My comforter was on the floor, and I was cold. I rearranged it and threw a blanket on top, but by then I was too alert to go right back to sleep. I was afraid that my old cycle of lousy sleep patterns might be returning. It seemed that the rest I'd been getting of late was almost too good to be true.

I got up, had a drink of water and, on a whim, padded softly down the hall to Owen's room. I cautiously, soundlessly opened his door, telling myself that this was not an invasion of privacy but rather the act of a good Samaritan. Justification was easy as I saw that he, too, was not adequately covered for such a cold night. His clothes of the day before were carefully folded and placed on the bureau next to the bed. He wore dark flannel pajamas that I guess Mr. Murray had picked out for him the day we shopped for clothes in town. In the dim light I could only guess that they were probably navy blue.

I was almost overwhelmed by the tenderness I felt as I gazed at his sleeping form. The pale moonlight that filtered in from the clear cold night picked out the golden chain around his neck. Its being there made me unexpectedly happy. I smiled, at his faith in the power of its protection, at his tousled hair, his bare feet, his rough sailor's hands loosely clutching the pillow. I guess even a woman like me was capable of maternal instincts. I think I had always expected one day to be somebody's mother; I had hoped to show I could shine in the role. This was, of course, not to be, and I had made peace with its impossibility. Though I'd made periodic attempts to get close to the children in my own family — nieces, nephews, the offspring of cousins — it felt like mere playacting, as though even these little boys and girls could see through me, that I wasn't *real* mother material. My serious attempts at surrogate parenting ended there, and when Peter died so suddenly, I found myself regretting the fact that I hadn't even been able to take care of him through a fatal illness, that once again my natural desire to succor another was without an outlet.

I straightened the comforter that Owen had kicked to the bottom of the bed, draping it gently across him. For good measure I added a heavy trapper blanket on top of that. Satisfied, I went back to my own room, and after a reasonable time I fell contentedly back to sleep.

I awoke again later after a particularly vivid dream. In it, I rolled over in bed and opened my eyes to see Peter beside me. His face was only inches from my own, his eyes glistening, his smile warm, and he looked at me as though he'd been studying my features for some time while I slept. I awoke with a start, both surprised and not surprised simultaneously to find him not there in his accustomed spot at my side. I don't know if it was noble or pointless of me to still miss him so. We'd been a perfect fit, and I some-times wondered that if I was destined to only have such a small piece of paradise, if it might not have been better if I'd waited until later in life to find it. I was nowhere near tears as I lay in bed. The sun had begun to take its time light-ening the morning sky, and my room was still nearly dark even though it was almost my usual time to rise. I was through grieving for Peter and for what might have been, but sometimes the fu-ture loomed very large and empty for me. There was just so much time to fill and all to the tune of the relentless Atlantic. At least with Owen here I wasn't so lonely anymore.

Remembering my dream, I had a sudden feeling that Peter had come to me in that way, not to deepen my regret, but as though he were giving me approval for some reason, and with his tacit encouragement to continue on, I got out of bed to begin another day.

When I got downstairs, I found that No-vember had brought the first frost. I was invigo-rated by its appearance and longed for a stroll on the beach, which I knew would now be virtually all mine. Even the Dorritys next door would be in Florida by now, I thought, and I remembered that this was why Peter and I had bought this house — to be able to be part of the shore long after its holiday visitors had gone. I had grown up here in Slea Head, not many blocks from the ocean, but I had never been a summer person. I avoid crowds whenever I can, and I sunburn easily. But it was more than that. I never fully appreciated the sea, or nature in general, unless it was at its moodiest. The picture-postcard kind of days that most tourists long for hold less attraction for me than a grey lowering sky or a windowpane pelted with rain. I reveled in the thought of the coming decay of the leaves and the purity of the first snow of the season.

# CHAPTER 9

Marjorie and I sat at the kitchen table, watching a few fat flakes of snow dance outside the window, knowing they'd never amount to anything. Owen was in the parlor with Joe Maglia, who apparently needed some more information for his thesis or dissertation, or whatever.

"Have you started your Christmas shopping?" Marjorie asked.

"No. It's not even Thanksgiving yet. When it gets a little closer to Christmas, I may go into the city and get a lot of it done then."

"It'll be pretty crowded if you wait that long."

"That's half the fun."

Marjorie shook her head.

"I'll bet you're halfway done at least by now," I accused.

"You know, being organized isn't a bad thing, Peggy," she said, and shot a meaningful glance at the pile of mail on the counter I hadn't yet dealt with.

"I've tried. It just isn't possible."

"Peggy! Come here!" Owen called cheerily from the other room. "You've got a visitor."

"Jesus, get it out of here," Joe complained as Marjorie and I entered the parlor in time to see a dark-colored bird fly from the shade of my cloissoné lamp to the top of my green moiré drapes. It seemed only a matter of time before it knocked something over.

"Damn," I said, but without anger. I rolled my eyes at my own carelessness. "I must have left the flue open again."

"Does this happen all the time?" Marjorie asked.

"No, this is only the third time," I said, and realized how silly that sounded. I laughed, and Owen joined me. Marjorie and Joe seemed unamused, which made it even funnier.

"What is it, a seabird or something?" Joe asked, clearly disgusted with the idea of nature invading the human domain.

"No, it's just a starling," I replied.

"Hey. I'm from New York. I only know it's not a pigeon," he said.

"Well, how do you usually get rid of them?" Marjorie asked. "Open a window?"

"That can't hurt," I said. "But so far I've always had to catch them and then let them go. I'll go get a laundry basket. That's what I used the last time."

"I'll go and fetch it for you," Owen offered, and after I'd thanked him I could hear him taking the stairs two at a time up to the laundry room. He returned with a round blue plastic basket that was flexible enough to fit the bill. He handed it to me, and we chased the bird with it from one side of the room to the other, but without success. I started to laugh again at our own ridiculousness.

"*Whist,* Peggy. You're scaring the poor thing," Owen said, but I could tell that it wouldn't take much to start him laughing, too.

Marjorie stood off to the side, her arms crossed, her expression one of tolerance, in a martyr-like sort of way. Finally the bird seemed to settle, on top of the drapes again, and Owen silently pulled the arrow-back chair out from my plantation desk and moved it over in front of the window. He somehow managed not to spook the bird as he climbed up onto the chair to reach it where it had perched. Before I knew it, he had the starling gently cupped in his hands, held in such a way that it was unable to reach his hands with its sharp dark beak, which was parted in either anger or in fear.

Owen stepped down, and I studied the starling's iridescent plumage and shining black eyes.

"Well, you're a little bit lost, aren't you?" I said.

"What did you say he was called?" Owen asked.

"A starling."

"I know a lot of birds, but I don't recognize this little fellow."

"You're kidding. They're everywhere. They're really a bit of a nuisance — they chase off other birds. They also fall down chimneys periodically," I added wryly.

"Well, what do you say we take him outside?"

Marjorie and Joe opted to stay in as it was still cold in spite of the fact that the snow had stopped. From the porch, Owen and I watched the bird take off as soon as he opened his hands. We stood and followed its path with our eyes, away from the house and the sea, until it was lost from view. We smiled at each other, knowing we had done something intrinsically good.

Back inside, I took the unused basket back upstairs and grabbed a book from my well-stocked library before returning downstairs to the kitchen. Owen was making a pot of coffee, but I thought he was being optimistic if he was expecting Marjorie and Joe to stay to enjoy it. He'd gotten quite good at a lot of the necessities of modern life, and to Owen and me coffee definitely fell into that category.

I sat down at the table, thumbing through the index of the field guide I'd retrieved from upstairs.

"See, here he is," I said, pointing to a photograph of a starling. "Don't tell me you haven't seen these guys before."

"I don't think so," Owen insisted.

I flipped to the descriptive pages and found the entry I wanted. I pointed to the map of North America with the areas highlighted where starlings can be expected to be found.

"See," I said, "they're all over the whole country and up by Nova Scotia, too."

Owen shrugged. "In that case, I don't know how I could have missed them."

I skimmed over the paragraphs on physical characteristics and habitat until I came across a piece of information that surprised me. I read out loud, " 'Habitat: introduced. One hundred starlings were released in Central Park in 1890. The species has since spread over most of the continent.'

"Son of a gun," I muttered. "You couldn't have known that."

"What?"

"Nothing. But you're right. There weren't any starlings here in the 1850s. You learn something new every day, I guess."

"The coffee's ready," Owen said, and from his facial expression I got the feeling he was uncomfortable with the hint of doubt I'd betrayed.

As I'd expected, Marjorie and Joe excused themselves, and I felt a pang of regret as I watched Marjorie put on her coat. I wondered briefly if she and I had ever had as close a relationship as I'd once thought we'd had, or whether it had always been this superficial, with our differences making closeness impossible, and I just hadn't been able to see it. All I knew was that we couldn't seem to get past meaningless small talk lately and that she sometimes seemed like a stranger to me. Nevertheless, I gave her and Joe a warm send-off, hollow though I knew it to be.

"Peggy," Owen began that evening as we sat by the fire. We had come to spend a lot of our time in the parlor, and I rarely watched television in the evening anymore. I didn't even mind that I hardly kept track of what was happening in the news.

"Hm?"

"I haven't been to church since I came here. Do people still do that?"

"Of course. I just haven't been very good about going lately. I used to go almost every week. I'm not sure why I stopped. Would you like to go tomorrow?"

"Yes."

So, the next morning after a light breakfast, Owen and I got ready to go to my local church of St. Michael's. He was surprised when I told him that it wasn't necessary to wear his new suit, that something a bit dressier than jeans was all that was required these days. I put on dark corduroys and a nice sweater and, with Owen similarly attired, we headed out into the crisp coolness of the overcast morning.

The last of the cars was leaving from the earlier Mass when we reached the church, but we were plenty early for the eleven o'clock service, as Owen had insisted on going to confession beforehand. I would have loved to have been a fly on the wall for that. I usually didn't bother with that formality, though I knew I should have, but I decided it couldn't hurt. I confessed the usual bad thoughts that had never made it into deeds, and felt lightened by the experience.

I could tell that Owen was disappointed by St. Michael's. Although the outside is quaint, traditional, and of stone, the inside had gone through the same modernization or streamlining that had bared many American Catholic churches of their statuary and mystical qualities.

There was a comforting familiarity to me in being back at the church I'd attended all my life, but the experience was coupled, too, with memories of great sadness. I'd witnessed the Sacraments of Baptism, Confirmation, and Matrimony within those walls, sharing joy with those around me. But I'd seen too many funeral Masses performed there to be without sorrow now, from my dear grandfather's to the one that had confirmed to the world my status as a widow.

I was never particularly active in church functions outside of the Mass; I had never been much of a joiner. I always preferred keeping church time as private time for contemplation, rather than make associations in my mind with endless committee meetings and fund-raising efforts. It wasn't stinginess, as I'd never begrudged the giving of money where needed; I just didn't want the *politics* of the thing to interfere with its spirituality for me. Still, a person can't belong to the same parish in her hometown community all her life without knowing the majority of her fellow worshipers, and when we made the Sign of Peace, I shook hands with old neighbors and acquaintances, accepting the good wishes and smiles they directed at Owen and myself. Even Father Zelinski had given me a nod before Mass began when he recognized me among the congregants.

Owen was silent throughout the service, but afterward he expressed his dismay at the disappearance of Latin, among other things. To him, most of what had set his Church apart was gone. Still, he told me, he was glad he had come, and that if it were all right with me, he would like to start going regularly. I certainly had no objection, and I was sure this would earn him a few points with my family as well.

On the drive back home I shoved a new cassette into the tape player. It was a recording of folk music traditional enough to have been around in Owen's day. They were mostly selections that I knew well and enjoyed listening to. "The Water is Wide" was the first melody to play, and I was more than pleased when Owen said he was familiar with it. My father had always told me that it was a traditional Irish song, but according to the printed material that came with the tape, it was an old English ballad. I preferred to go with the Bresnahan revised history.

I sang along softly, feeling sort of shy about being heard, but finding it impossible not to accompany the lyrics of the song. It had been a long time since anyone had heard my singing. There had been a time when I had thought that it might be something I'd want to pursue, perhaps even in a professional capacity, but, then, I'd wanted at various times to be a movie star, a knight of the Round Table, and a renowned surgeon. I still preferred singing to dance, but my career ambition finally lay in a more private and anonymous direction than publicly performing songs.

"You have a fine voice," Owen said.

"Thanks. It's been a long time, but I used to sing in the choir. I liked to daydream about doing guitar Masses when I was little. Hippies were pretty romantic figures back then."

"Hippies?"

"Never mind. I'll explain that another time. Do you mind if I drive around a bit? The leaves are still so pretty, and I don't really feel like getting home just yet."

"I don't mind."

The next song was the sad and beautiful ballad "Barbara Allen."

"I've not heard this in a long time," Owen said with a gentle smile. "My mother used to sing it, but not in English. She always sang it in the Gaelic." He used the Scottish pronunciation of "Gah-lic."

"Did your mother speak Gaelic?"

"She used to say she'd mostly forgotten it, but she always understood the old people when they'd be speaking it. And, before you ask, Peggy, I haven't any Gaelic at all. Just the bit of French I learned from Martine and Frenchy."

"Am I that nosy? I don't mean to interrogate, but you're interesting."

"Only because I'm in the wrong time. I'm like a curiosity, that's all. If you were from my time, you wouldn't find me so interesting."

"Don't be so sure of that. I think you're a lot of

fun. In fact, you're the best friend I have in the world right now, Owen." I felt sort of dewy-eyed and stupid saying it, but I meant it very much.

"I'd return the compliment, but as you're my *only* friend, it might not mean as much."

I glanced away from the road to enjoy his smile. I never got tired of watching his emotions transform his countenance. He could be painfully shy one moment and mischievously playful the next.

We were driving through a volley of leaves blowing straight at us as we headed vaguely in the direction of home. There was still plenty of foliage on the trees, backlit by the sun. It was an enchanting scene.

In the days that followed, the weather was without pattern, going from balmy to bitter and back all in the same week. Then there were days that were in themselves a microcosm of the season, containing a bit of just about every kind of weather condition. Such is autumn.

My days seemed fuller than they had in months, and indeed they were. I was formulating more and more scenic descriptions and plot twists in my mind for possible later use, finding that I had to go back to my former practice of keeping index cards practically everywhere to jot ideas down before they were lost forever. I'd also started haunting the area antique shops again, getting the owners to keep their eyes open for various objects I sought, just as they had in the days before Peter's death. I was also beginning to make pictures in my mind of next year's garden. The bulbs had already gone in the ground and I was eagerly anticipating the arrival of the annual seed catalogs, those early harbingers of spring brought by the postal service.

Before I knew it Thanksgiving had arrived, and I found myself nervous as a schoolgirl with a new boyfriend at the prospect of taking Owen to meet my family en masse.

In the morning we had coffee before heading to my grandmother's to spend the day. Owen wore his new suit for the first time. He looked wonderful; there wouldn't be any reason for disapproval by my family on that score. More often than not, other than on Sunday mornings, of course, he came downstairs looking like he had toweled his hair dry, run his fingers through it, and let it go at that. Now it was clear that he'd given some effort to combing his hair carefully, though one fair lock spilled over an eyebrow, giving his face an unintended rakishness that was countered by his underlying nervousness at meeting my relatives. In his jittery condition it looked as though he couldn't decide whether to expand or dismiss the beginnings of a smile that I noted at the corners of his mouth.

"Relax," I said, noting how he appeared both the same and different to me in his new clothes. "Everything will be fine. Really."

As with most men who are lean but not too thin, he wore clothes well, the fabric hanging nicely from his shoulders and hips. The grey-blue wool of his suit looked particularly nice with his fair complexion and light eyes, and his crisp white cotton dress shirt belied his humble origins. There was only one thing missing, and I soon remedied that by handing him a tie I'd bought for the occasion. After a couple of false starts, I even managed to help him tie it.

Owen stood before the mirror. When he saw I'd caught him looking at himself, he favored me with a bashful smile. "I look like a real gentleman," he said, both shy and pleased at the same time.

"It's the Sinclair tartan," I said, indicating the predominantly red plaid tie.

"Thank you, Peggy. You're always so thoughtful."

"I've got to go change," I said, and left Owen to admire his reflection while I went upstairs.

I'd had coffee in my sweats, but I figured I couldn't put off the rest of the day any longer. I put on a dress I hadn't worn in a couple of years, and even then I'd had it on only once, for a Christmas party. It was on the formal side, but at my grandmother's house we dressed for Thanksgiving dinner. It seemed funny to get attired more formally for my grandmother than I had for church, but then she'd changed less over the years. I had to admit I didn't look too bad in the deep green velvet dress. I threw on black pumps and a choker of pearls, then took my time getting my face and hair in order. When I was satisfied, I went downstairs to get Owen to make the seven-minute drive to the other world that was my grandmother's.

"You're beautiful!" Owen said by way of greeting, and I can't deny that hearing it felt good. I smiled, but I guess Owen sensed that I was ill at ease.

"What's wrong? Would you rather I stayed here?"

"No, not at all. It's just my grandmother. She makes me nervous sometimes."

"Is she all that bad?"

"No, actually I'm extremely fond of her, and there's no denying that I'm her favorite, because I am. Maybe it's because I'm her namesake, maybe it's because I'm almost as feisty as she is."

"Then, why are you so ill at ease about seeing her? Is it me?"

"No. It's hard to explain. She's hard to please, but I respect her opinion. She's just, well, you'll see, I guess. We might as well get going."

I'd only succeeded in making Owen as nervous as I was. Not a very auspicious start to the day, I thought.

"Oh, and bring a change of clothes. We're expected to dress for dinner, but afterward the guys usually throw a football around and you might want to join them."

We drove over in silence. I didn't even feel like listening to music. Owen looked at me, obviously surprised by what he saw when I pulled into the

206

drive and the house came into view. It was a magnificent red brick slate-roofed Georgian Colonial, but I had grown up seeing it inside and out at least once a week, and its grandness failed to move me in any profound way. Its distinctive outline was blocked from street view by a fence and careful landscaping with scrub pines that took easily to the sandy soil.

It had been a long time since I'd taken someone there for the first time, and I had forgotten how dramatic an appearance the huge stately house on its weedless lawn could make. I was surprised to see that the usually immaculate grass was covered with leaves from the several maple trees on the grounds, which a gardener, rather than my grandparents, had nurtured to maturity over the years.

Bedlam reigned inside the double front doors as sunlight filtered through the fanlight onto a scene of seventeen adult Bresnahans and O'Gallivans all greeting each other, removing their coats, and talking at the same time. I guess we were right on time.

Minnie took my coat and gave me a big, sincere hug. She had been in my grandparents' employ long enough to remember my mother as a child. She had never married, and not long after my grandfather died, my grandmother had designated a room as hers and she had been a full-time member of the household ever since. I remember coming home from college for my grandfather's funeral, my grandmother holding her head high, refusing to make her grief public, and it was Minnie's well-padded frame to which I'd run for shelter and warmth. Her iron-grey hair had thinned some since then, and her back was more rounded, but her simple good nature animated her, giving her the appearance of a much younger woman.

My grandmother did not meet us at the door, nor did I expect her to. In many ways she was extremely formal, sticking to rules of protocol and good form even when they were not necessarily convenient. We would see her at the dinner table, but probably not before. For the moment, Minnie was the woman of the house, an apron her only concession to servitude.

"Something smells good," I told her.

"Well, you know, Mrs. O'Gallivan and I have had to have your mother and Aunt Helen give us a hand with the cooking. After all, we're not as young as we used to be, either one of us." This was something of an understatement, of course, as they were both comfortably settled into their eighties. The two of them had not prepared a Thanksgiving meal without help in five years, but I always went along with the myth that they had only just stopped handling everything on their own. I couldn't bear the thought of either one of them having to live without her independence.

"I've set a place at the table for your friend. Marjorie told me you'd be bringing someone."

"Thanks, Minnie."

I caught a glimpse of Owen in the immense gilded floor-to-ceiling mirror in the entry hall, before which I used to pose and play for hours as a child. He was noticeably uncomfortable with all the hubbub and all the strangers. Still, I felt a surge of pride at how well turned out he looked.

As a group, the clan was heading into the dining room, and I squeezed Owen's hand and murmured, "I'll introduce you to everyone in a moment."

As we were getting seated, still catching up on each other's lives, my grandmother entered from the butler's pantry, every white hair in place, standing ramrod straight as ever, refusing to make concessions to age. She was still a very handsome woman, though her skin was pale against the cranberry color of her boiled wool jacket and matching skirt. I could have told Owen that here was one New Jersey woman he'd never see in trousers. What a scary old bitch, I thought, as I had a hundred times before, followed by the inevitable refrain: but I wish I could be just like her. A chorus of greetings heralded her presence, and a somewhat cool smile was bestowed in return.

The sea made its presence felt through the bank of many-paned windows of the long dining room as we all dutifully took our seats, in our accustomed places, Owen physically filling the void Peter had left. I felt a pang of guilt at putting him in such a position, but it could hardly be helped now.

"Gram, everybody, I'd like to introduce my friend Owen Sinclair," I said, and Owen half stood, clearly at a loss as to what was expected of him. "Owen, this is my grandmother, Mary Margaret O'Gallivan."

"How do you do?" Owen offered, social discomfort written all over his face.

"I see no one had the nerve to tell me about you," my grandmother said tartly, eyeing him curiously but without apparent disfavor. "What was your name again?" The acuteness of her hearing, or lack of it, had lately become a tool she used to manipulate those around her. I had little doubt that she'd heard me the first time.

"Sinclair, ma'am. Owen Sinclair," Owen volunteered.

"Well, who are your people?" she demanded but continued without leaving him time to respond. "Sinclair? That's a Scottish name. Are you from Scotland, Mr. Sinclair?"

Now I knew she was playing games in her own inimitable way.

"No, ma'am, from Nova Scotia."

"A Canadian. How delightful! You play hockey, I suppose, or curling?"

"No, ma'am."

"Owen's quite a good sailor, though, Gram," I interposed.

"A delightful sport, Mr. Sinclair! I spent many a day in my youth sailing with my father, and later my husband. Peggy and Marjorie never learned to sail. I blame their father."

My father, Gerald Bresnahan, seated at the far end of the walnut banquet table, laughed good-naturedly. Whatever was lacking in our character or upbringing, Grandmother O'Gallivan inevitably laid at my father's door. In her mind a Bresnahan was inherently inferior in every way to an O'Gallivan.

"Mr. Sinclair," she began again, the inquisition apparently not over yet. "Are you sleeping with my granddaughter?"

Owen turned red, then redder still. In light of my grandmother's propensity for old-fashioned modes of conduct, it had been a shocking question, but in her house she made the rules.

"No, Gram," I assured her, and tried not to laugh.

"Well, why the devil not?" she asked in what appeared to be complete seriousness, and we all, with the exceptions of Owen, Marjorie, and my mother, started to laugh. My grandmother had apparently said her piece, and I quickly began introducing Owen to the rest of the assembled company.

"Owen, you know my sister, Marjorie Bresnahan, and Bill Connelly," I said, indicating my brother-in-law.

"I thought you were married," Owen said.

"We are, but I prefer to use my maiden name," Marjorie explained with less than perfect grace.

"Oh," Owen replied nervously, as if he feared he'd made a social faux pas, but I could tell that my grandmother, with her generally old-fashioned sense of proprieties, was pleased that he'd been confused by Marjorie's modern ways.

Next to Bill and Marjorie sat my brother, Ryan, and his wife, Kathleen. Ryan is the youngest of the three of us, but not by much. My brother and I are what is known as "Irish twins," that is, we were born less than a year apart. I'm sure the term was meant as an ethnic slur in the past, but I liked it. Ryan is a very reserved and formal man, and his demeanor goes well with his very expensive ultraconservative suits and job at the bank, where he'd worked with my father before his retirement. Ryan was expected to make vice president at an even younger age than my father had.

Kathleen, on the other hand, bubbled with enthusiasm, generally doing the talking for both of them. In social situations she generally knew the right things to say, but to lead her into deeper conversation was to strike bottom with a crunching blow. What she lacked in originality she more than made up for in beauty and Southern charm. She was a consummate flirt, and I could see already that she'd decided to add Owen to her list of platonic adorers. I didn't feel jealous. Why would I? I wanted everyone to like him.

Beside Kathleen sat my Uncle Aidan and Aunt Helen O'Gallivan, whose four grown sons sat across from us. Next to them sat my mother, my father anchoring the head of the table opposite my grandmother at the far end. My mother was turning into a lesser version of my grandmother — not as beautiful, nor as strong. Her features were fine, her eyes clear, her posture lovely from years of competitive riding, but she had never found a way to escape the shadow of Mary Margaret O'Gallivan's proud fierce nature. As usual, I found myself feeling a bit sorry for her in this, the one element where she would never shine.

My father on her right gave Owen a business-like smile at their introduction, obviously ready to get on with the rest of the ritual formalities of the day — probably so he could relax in front of a football game at meal's end. He was a handsome man, I thought, with his snowy-white hair and jet-black eyebrows, but I had never found him to be as approachable as I would have liked. He was more of a man's man, I guess, as Peter had gotten on famously with him almost from the start.

On his left was Minnie's seat, although she was out of it more than in. My mother and aunt had carried in most of the serving dishes and platters, whose weight would have been too much for Minnie's old hands, but there were still things forgotten, last little touches to be made, that were handled by Minnie alone. She also got up from time to time to check on the children's table, which was set up in the kitchen under the supervision of the au pair employed by one of Uncle Aidan and Aunt Helen's boys.

I continued on around the table, introducing my cousins and their wives. Sean, Michael,

Kevin, and Patrick O'Gallivan were big rugged men, looking for all the world like living incarnations of the Fianna of Irish legend. Though their ages ranged over a full ten years and Sean wore a beard, they still seemed more like different versions of one man rather than four distinct individuals. My sister and I as children had called them cookie cutter cutouts because they had all so obviously been made in the same mold. Their wives were physically unalike, but I tended to lump them together, because they seemed to do all their socializing in unison and because they all held such safe traditional women's jobs. Vicky and Karen were teachers, Sarah was a realtor, and Debbie was a nurse.

At long last it was time for the blessing. We droned in unison, "Bless us, O Lord, and these thy gifts which we are about to receive from thy bounty through Christ, our Lord. Amen."

"A toast!" Bill announced. He could always be counted on to get things rolling. I used to tell him he was a bad influence on Peter, but they really had so much fun that I didn't mind all the nonsense. Bill stood and posed with mock formality, his glass raised so that the crystal fairly sparkled in the incandescent light. "If you're lucky enough to be Irish," he said, "you're lucky enough." With that, he took a drink and smacked his lips. I could have smacked something else.

"That's so rude, Bill," I said, indicating Owen with my eyes. "If Peter was here, he'd give you hell for that."

"A thousand apologies," Bill said to Owen, who looked embarrassed about being forced into the spotlight again.

"Hibernian, Caledonian, what's the big deal? Celtic's Celtic, right?"

"Right," Owen murmured uncomfortably.

"Why don't you make the toast, Owen?" Bill prompted, obviously getting a kick out of Owen's discomfort. God, I hated the way men were always testing each other.

"No, really, I . . ."

"I insist," Bill said with exaggerated geniality, and I was pleased to see Owen shoot him a dirty look.

Nevertheless, he rose and said in his soft-spoken way, "To health and happiness. *Slàinte mhór!*" and drained his glass.

"Here, here!" Bill agreed, and exchanged a devilish grin with Owen.

Apparently the ice was now broken, and the meal proceeded smoothly. There was a lot of talk, I suppose, but I remember very little of the actual conversation that took place. We probably said essentially the same things we had every year for the last decade: "Pass the potatoes," "More wine?" "Aren't you glad to have finally made it to the grown-ups' table?" "Eat every bite; children are starving in China." I could see my grandmother observing, taking everything in, as she silently led the proceedings. I would have given a lot to know what she thought of Owen.

During the hearty feast, Bill turned to Owen and asked, "So, do you feel like you're surrounded by the I.R.A.?"

Owen shrugged and gave him a blank look in return.

"Or the Fenians?" Marjorie asked, changing the reference to one Owen might better understand, but this didn't seem to be particularly elucidating to him either.

Bill's attempt at humor had failed, but I knew, though I wasn't supposed to, that my father and uncle had both financially supported the Irish Republican Army. My grandmother had, perhaps more reasonably, poured thousands of dollars into a project that paired Irish Catholic and Protestant children in American homes for a summer of peace and learning. I respected her choice but had too much of the rebel in me to dismiss my father's solution outright. Action always seemed preferable to me to waiting, but I'd never been able to go so far as to give money for the purchase of weapons myself. My compromise between guns and God was to write long letters of encouragement, hope, and, humor to Catholic political prisoners in Her Majesty's infamous Maze and Maghaberry facilities in County Antrim. Luckily, two of my correspondents had finally been released to go home to their families, and the other two had dropped off the frequency of their letters of late, probably due to the lifelessness of my own recent missives.

"Well," Bill began again, "the really important

question is, are you going to play football or not?"

"I'm afraid I don't know how it's done," Owen replied.

Bill looked over at my cousin Kevin across the table. "He's on your team." He laughed.

"Oh, it's not as complicated as these boys make it out to be," my sister-in-law Kathleen said in her Georgian drawl. "I guess they don't play much football in Canada, huh?"

"I never had much time for games," Owen said. I guess he had discovered that telling his real story would only lead to ridicule and disbelief. Still, he'd handled the question diplomatically without lying.

The dinner finally ended, or at least went into the hiatus between the meat and vegetables and the pies and coffee yet to come. I was so full I couldn't imagine running around outside in the cold, throwing a ball back and forth, with the big holiday meal sitting heavily on the gut. Maybe the guys knew enough to stop before they overate. All I knew was I could never resist the once-a-year specialties I looked forward to having at my grandmother's Thanksgiving dinner.

The ending of the meal was the signal that we could change clothes. I quickly got into a pair of jeans and a turtleneck in time to help with the clearing of the table and the washing up that followed. At Grandma O'Gallivan's this was inevitably women's work. It would give me a chance to chat with my sister-in-law Kathleen and my cousins' wives, but I couldn't help wondering what I was missing.

Kathleen and I ended up tied to the kitchen, as she happily drew the job of washing (Grandma O'Gallivan wouldn't hear of having a dishwasher installed) and I lucked into doing the drying. My cousins' wives bustled with dishes, crystal, and silverware from the dining room table to the kitchen, packaged leftovers for the refrigerator, and returned my grandmother's china, pots, and pans back to their accustomed places. My mother and aunt had graduated from manual labor when their children had entered adulthood, and I assumed they were relaxing and talking while we paid our dues until the next generation could take over.

Kathleen tied on an apron that covered her from neck to knees and donned rubber gloves before putting her hands into hot water. It had been years since I had seen a woman so attired, and she reminded me of the women in detergent advertisements from my childhood. She certainly, at that moment, bore no resemblance to a modern liberated woman.

"I just had my nails done yesterday," she explained, pulling one hand free of the bright yellow latex to show me neat squarish nails lacquered in a barely discernible pale pink. If it wasn't for the gloss of the polish, I would have thought they were naturally very well shaped and delicately tinged. They did look nice; pretty fingernails had just never been a matter of much import with me. Kathleen, on the other hand, went on to explain just how hard it was to find someone who did a proper job and how often the process needed to be repeated to maintain the effect. I have to admit, my mind wandered as I was distracted thinking about Owen out there on his own with my family.

In a moment, though, he poked his head into the kitchen to tell me that he was going outside to smoke before attempting to play football with Bill and company. Clad now in casual clothes, he didn't look particularly nervous at the prospect. I got the feeling that he couldn't take seriously anything as frivolous as a game, or perhaps he was confident of his abilities in a physical situation among men, outside the realm of civilized society.

"By the way, your new boyfriend is adorable," Kathleen said when he had gone.

"Oh, he's not my boyfriend. Just a friend, actually."

Kathleen only smiled, and I changed the subject to ask her about a dinner she had had to put on for important people at my brother's bank. This set her off on a frivolous monologue of seating plans and menus. I lost track of all the details, and only pricked up my ears to pick up an absurdity or pettiness now and again. I didn't dislike Kathleen, but we had so little in common.

"I mean, can you believe," she asked with her lovely Southern charm to the fore, "that this woman was wearing white shoes in *October?* She apparently thinks she can ignore social conventions because her husband has more money than God. I mean, what else is polite society based on?"

Ideas, integrity, knowledge, charity, I thought, a longer list threatening to block out all attention to her arguments if I didn't nip it in the bud. I looked over at her in her twenty-year-old apron over her peach cashmere sweater and *winter white* lined wool slacks and thought again of how unimportant her trials and tribulations seemed to me. But, then again, my life before Peter died must have seemed pretty shallow and trivial to anyone who'd ever really known suffering or loss. I smiled at Kathleen, happy to know that she and my brother had the privilege of worrying over small things if they so desired.

Barely a minute or two later, my grandmother entered the kitchen, telling me that she wanted to speak to me, and would I meet her in my grandfather's study for a little talk. This was all but a command performance, but I looked forward to having some private time with her. I excused myself from Kathleen's company, getting my cousin Michael's wife to fill in for me with a fresh dry towel on my way out the door.

When I got to the study, I found that I had beat my grandmother there. Outside the French doors I could make out the trail of smoke that pinpointed Owen and his pipe. Through the glass between parted drapery, I could clearly both see and hear Bill approaching. He looked fashionably casual in long khaki shorts and a cotton roll-neck sweater.

"Aren't you a little young to be smoking a pipe?" Bill asked in his wry, charming way.

I could almost hear Owen's gentle smile at that. "Aren't you a little old to be wearing short pants?" he rejoined.

Bill laughed. The weirdest part of his constantly challenging Owen was, I was pretty sure, that meant he liked him. But in spite of growing up with Ryan and the O'Gallivan brothers, and having been married, though too briefly, I could make no claim to understanding the ways of men when in their own company.

"Come on," Bill said, "let's see what you're made of."

"All right. I'm curious to see if this easy life of yours makes a man soft or not."

I heard Owen tap the ashes out of his pipe, and then the two of them went beyond my range and I only occasionally heard the yells and grunting that could only be a bunch of guys playing football on the lawn.

Not long after, my grandmother came in, accompanied by my mother, who carried in a tray containing a creamer, sugar, and two porcelain cups and saucers full of delicious-smelling coffee. All were in my grandmother's ancient brown and white Wedgwood service that I remembered from my earliest years. My mother set the tray down on a side table and left, the look on her face suggesting that I was probably going to get a good talking to.

I made up both our drinks the way I knew we liked them and waited for my grandmother to begin. Drinking in silence for a while, I glanced around the room. My grandfather's study was an intensely masculine room, with dark green walls, hunting prints, and ominous ebony bookcases. Bits of brass here and there reflected the light, and I knew that when a fire was lit in the grate it could be a very homey place indeed.

Finally my grandmother saw fit to break the silence.

"Marjorie's been telling me about your young man."

"She thinks he's nuts. I know."

"Is it true that he claims to be a sailor from more than a century ago?"

"Yes."

"And do you believe him?"

"I know it sounds crazy, but sometimes I think I do. I mean, I didn't at first. I even took him to a doctor to see if he had a concussion. But, well, why would he make up such a story and stick to it all this time?"

"I don't know," she said, as if to say, "you tell me."

"I haven't told this to anyone else, Gram, but sometimes I think Peter sent him to me."

"Peter?"

"Well, suppose Owen had been in limbo, or whatever, all this time, somewhere between

222

heaven and earth — just lost, really. What if Peter found him? Peter, of all people, knew how much I love the past, with all my antiques and old books, and everything. And I think he knew I would take care of Owen. Why else did he turn up right where I'd find him, right when I'd be walking on the beach?"

"Are you in love with him, Peggy?"

"Oh, no, this is all a misunderstanding. We're not romantically involved."

"My mistake."

I smiled self-consciously and took a drink of coffee.

"He's a good man, Peggy. I'm an old woman, and I know these things."

"I know he is, Gram. He's had a rough time of it, but he has a good heart." It felt good to sing his praises to a receptive ear. Marjorie and Bill had been enjoyable companions of late, but I knew they didn't believe Owen, and in some small way I found that that hurt.

"I plan to go shopping in the city on Saturday," my grandmother said. "I'd like you and Owen to go with me. I've hired a car so we can go in comfort."

"I'd love to. I'm sure Owen will get a kick out of New York. I can't wait to see his face."

My grandmother smiled indulgently, and as I finished my coffee I felt I was tacitly being dismissed. Impulsively, I planted a kiss on her cheek, which smelled faintly of powder, and left the room feeling sixteen years old.

I went out onto the patio to see the guys heading back toward me.

"Halftime!" one of my cousins called; I think it was Kevin.

The gang of them bounded toward the house with the sort of towel-snapping camaraderie to which young men are prone.

As they came within range, Bill made an announcement to me in regard to Owen, who stood at his side.

"He can't throw worth shit, even for a south-paw, but, damn, this boy can run."

"I don't know how anyone can throw such a strange ball, and I still don't understand why you call it football," Owen answered with a grin.

"What happened to your jeans?" I asked, pointing to a tear across one knee.

"Told you she'd be pissed," Bill muttered in a singsong voice under his breath, but obviously intending that I should hear him.

Owen's words were penitent, but by his expression and posture I could tell he was exhilarated.

"I'm sorry, Peggy, but I *can* fix it."

"You sew?" Bill asked, pretending to be appalled.

"It's not much different than mending a sail."

I smiled, trying to be a good sport rather than some sort of kill-joy mother figure. As Owen joined me to go inside, I could see a scrape across his cheek. Absently I touched it and asked how it happened.

"It's a very strange game, Peggy," he said. "I think they invent the rules as they go along. Sometimes you run and they throw the ball to you, and sometimes they hand it to you and three guys jump on top of you. I told you I'm not much for games," he ended with a smile. Clearly, though, he had had a good time.

As it turned out, the guys never did return to their amateur game. Bill, my brother, Ryan, and my four cousins ended up in front of the television in the family room with my father and Uncle Aidan, and from the yelling that emanated from the room, I guessed they were watching a pretty exciting contest.

After dessert Owen disappeared, and it wasn't until later that I found out that my grandmother had cornered him for some private conversation as well. The upshot was that he had volunteered to return the next day to do some much needed yard work for her. Apparently she had recently dismissed her lawn service company in disgust, and Owen, ever eager to be useful, was happy to have the chance to help her.

It had been a good day, surprisingly so, and my earlier unease now seemed silly in retrospect. It was with light hearts and fond smiles that we waved good-bye and drove off down the length of Slea Head to my own little piece of the beach.

The sun had set, and Owen's pipe glowed in the darkness of the car.

"So, your name is really Mary Margaret, is it?" he asked.

"Don't tell me that's your mother's name."

"No. Her name was Charlotte."

"By the way, I thought you couldn't speak Gaelic."

"I can't."

"What about your toast?"

"Oh, I can drink in any number of languages."

A passing streetlight picked out his smile for me.

"Peggy."

"Yes?"

"Have all the Irish done this well for themselves, I mean, here in America?"

"Owen, my grandmother is unusually rich — in any century."

"Oh."

"Did you have a good time?"

"Aye. I never saw so much to eat all in one place before. I thought I was dreaming."

"Well, that's Thanksgiving for you."

"Then it's a grand holiday by me."

We reached the house, and I parked the car. Owen stopped and relit his pipe.

"Are you coming?" I asked.

"I'll be in in a minute."

I stayed with him as he stood silently gazing at the stars. There was nothing between us but the sounds of the ocean and the infinity of the sky. I wondered if he were lonely, or homesick. I knew I would be if I were in a strange place, surrounded only by people I had known for a mere matter of weeks, with no chance of ever going home. At last he spoke, but so softly that it did nothing to disturb the peacefulness of the cool evening air. He pointed out a number of constellations to me, of which I'd previously only recognized the belt of Orion. In the darkness I stood listening to this seafaring orphan, sharing one of the few constancies which tied my life to his, and I was comforted by the nearness of his voice.

"How did you get to know so much about the stars?" I asked.

"Mostly from night watches or from sleeping on deck in the doldrums when it was warm."

"I thought you slept in the forecastle."

"The fo'c'sle, aye, but it could be a bit close in hot weather, what with so many men in want of bathing. I used to try to learn things from the other men whenever I could. My mother had never learned to read, and she had very badly wanted me to learn more and do better for myself. One of the men on the *Topaz*, a Finn he was, who was on the larboard watch with me, taught me most of the constellations I know — in both hemispheres, too."

I took one last look at the crescent moon, hanging in the night like a crooked smile, and went inside. Owen joined me, and I shut out the night and the ever-present rhythm of the waves.

Without asking or being asked, Owen began to put a fire in the fireplace. I put on water for tea. When I joined him with two steaming mugs before the homey blaze, it seemed the most natural thing in the world.

"Have you got something I can patch this with?" he asked, referring to the gash in his jeans.

"I could probably find something."

"I *am* sorry, Peggy."

"I know. I just wish you wouldn't let them push you around."

"Who?"

"You know, Bill, and Ryan, and my cousins."

"I didn't."

"Well, none of them had torn clothes, or a mark on them."

"They knew how to play the game, and I didn't."

"I don't know about that. Just don't be a wimp. You don't have to take anything from them."

"What is that? A coward? Is that what you think I am?"

"No. I just think you shouldn't allow yourself to be a victim, to be constantly at the mercy of other people — waiting to see whether they'll be kind or cruel. You have to stand up for yourself."

"You're always looking for a fight, Peggy. I'm not made that way."

"I'm Irish, you're a Scot. You're Canadian, I'm American. Maybe there's just more rebellion built into my nature than yours, but that's no reason why you shouldn't fight back when you're being ill-used. To me, the biggest difference between us isn't the time we come from, it's the way we react to the world around us. I'm just no good at putting up with a lot of garbage from other people. I'd rather decide what I want and fight for it until I get it. At least that's how I used to feel before Peter died. Don't you think your life so far would have been better if you'd fought for better treatment?"

"You don't understand."

"What don't I understand?"

"It's not always possible to fight your way out of a bad situation. Sometimes you just have to bide your time until you can leave it and start over."

"You mean your leaving home?"

"Aye."

"You can't just keep running away from your problems. You should have confronted your stepfather."

"And on the *Aurora Borealis*? What should I have done there?"

"Couldn't you have stood up to this Wilkins, or whatever his name was?"

"Aye, and ended up on the seafloor with my head stove in. You don't understand, Peggy. There's no law at sea, except what the captain and mates decide there is. You can't appeal to anyone, and rebellion is one luxury you can't afford. You can't honestly believe the men would all mutiny on my behalf. I don't mean to insult you, but you've had such a soft life, I don't think you should judge me so quickly. You've probably never gone to bed hungry in your life, or worn secondhand clothes, and you've never had to marry someone you didn't care for just to see that your child didn't go hungry, like my mother did."

"You're right," I said hotly, "I haven't had to do without a lot. I've always had enough to eat, a warm, dry place to sleep. I've hardly been sick a day in my life, and I had every opportunity for a good education and career. But I wouldn't call losing your husband at twenty-seven a soft life." I could feel my throat tighten and tears well up in my eyes, though I tried to stop them. I was crying for myself, for my anger and my loss, and for Owen, too, and his sad past.

"Selfish as it may sound," I continued, "I intended to go on living the good life until I was old and grey, but it was taken from me, and I'd have gladly given up everything I owned if that would have saved Peter," I said, trying to let my anger outweigh my sadness so that I could block the flow of tears. It didn't work, though, and I stood there, red-eyed and sniffing, feeling like a lost child as the tears made their way unimpeded down my face.

"Please don't cry," Owen answered with obvious concern. "I'm sorry. Forgive me. I was only angry because I couldn't bear that you would think me a coward."

He was holding my shoulders at arm's length, earnestly entreating me, and in the flickering light his eyes looked for a moment both blue and then both green.

"I'm sorry, too," I said. "I have a bad temper, and I'm relentless when I'm trying to win an argument. I never thought you were a coward. I just want to see you get treated with the respect you deserve, that's all." I sniffed, and Owen put his arms around me. After having played half a game of pickup football, he smelled lightly of sweat through his wool pullover, and for a moment I thought of Peter when we used to come in from our morning runs and how I used to think, without ever telling him, what an underrated pheromone his perspiration was. But Peter was gone, and I needed reassurance and a real presence to give consolation, and so, as Owen held me in his arms, I didn't resist, but let the comfort of his concern surround me.

# CHAPTER 10

The next morning Owen was up early — eager, I guess, to get started on my grandmother's yard work. I didn't insist that he let me give him a ride. He needed his independence, and I knew I had a lot of loose ends to deal with before the day was through.

After a stiff cup of coffee, I decided to get through the most difficult tasks first. The little red light on my answering machine had been blinking all night, just as I knew it would be. I pressed the play-back button and heard the messages I'd known would be there — Thanksgiving greetings from Peter's sister and his parents.

"Hi, Peggy! It's me, Joanna." As though I'd need a reminder to know the voice of Peter's sweet kid sister. "Happy Thanksgiving and all that. Don't eat too much! Ha! Ha! Tom and I both wanted to say hello. When do you think you'll be up this way? I guess I'd better go or I'll use up all your tape. Oh! We got a new puppy we'd like you to meet, wouldn't we, Buster?" she said in cutesy baby talk, obviously addressing the dog. "He's so adorable, Peggy! All fluffy and cuddly! Well, see ya whenever! We love you!" Her perkiness was forced, but I appreciated the effort. She, too, had been awfully young to lose a loved one so close to her.

The next message I knew would be a bit harder for me as Peter's parents had always been very good to me, and I missed them, for all that I had avoided seeing them on all but the rarest of occasions since Peter's death.

"Hello, Peggy, we, that is, Dad and I, just wanted to call to wish you a happy Thanksgiving and to let you know we're thinking about you. Well, I guess that's all I wanted to say. Please give us a call anytime and think about coming up for a visit. We'd both like to see you. Anytime, really. Well, good-bye then. For now, that is, dear."

Her voice was so familiar and yet so strange to me now. The happiness in both her voice and her daughter's was not quite natural, but, after all, wasn't their loss at least equal to mine? And, oddly, they were now nothing to me. The ties that had led me to address them as "Mom" and "Dad" and "Sis" were irretrievably broken, and yet the affection I had held for them all, having nowhere to go, was out there somewhere, looking for a place to land. All I knew was that I could not pretend that nothing had changed. And so, our relationship had come to this — an occasional phone call on an important day — scarcely more than the annual holiday card I sent to my college roommate.

I picked up the phone to call Peter's mother back, making the connection from where I was in Monmouth County to northern Somerset County, a world away now from my life, in spite of the slight physical distance involved. Our conversation was superficial, the answers to her questions about my welfare generic, and after I hung up I felt relief, but nothing more, and my thoughts turned of their own accord to how Owen was getting on with my grandmother's chores.

That done, I called my agent and told her to go ahead and get my manuscript to the publisher. I explained to her that it was time for me, and for my character Rebecca Garrett, to move on. I knew that by putting Peter's death in the guise of a murder mystery, I'd only been trying to remove the randomness from his passing and ascribe to it a logical motive. But tossing out the manuscript was not going to bring Peter back. My life had changed in irrevocable ways since I'd written the earlier Garrett mysteries. It had altered even since I'd penned the death of John Garrett.

I realized that it was both arrogant and presumptuous of me to assume that the publisher would even still want the manuscript, as though the rest of the world had remained frozen in place waiting for my decision. I was surprised at how very much I hoped my editor would accept the work on behalf of the publisher. I was seeking closure with this particular piece of writing so that I could move on beyond it. I realized that whatever had happened, I was still a *writer*, and that any other form of labor would prove hollow to me. My relief was great, then, when my agent intimated that she was nearly certain I was still a valuable commodity to my editor's employers and that this final adventure of the detecting Garretts would almost certainly be accepted for publication.

The next call I made was to my old friend Darren Hurley at his gallery in Cape May, the artsy Victorian resort at the southern tip of New Jersey. He wasn't there, but I eventually caught up with him at his other gallery in Manhattan. I had sent him color photocopies of Owen's artwork to which I hoped to get a positive response that I could share with Owen. I guess the outstanding quality of the ink drawing and watercolor had shown through the inadequate way I'd presented them, because Darren was very interested in setting up a meeting with Owen so that he could see the work, and hopefully more, firsthand, with the possibility of exhibitions at both galleries if the actual pictures measured up to their copies, and if Owen could produce enough additional work for the shows.

When I hung up, I think I was fairly beaming with pride and self-satisfaction. At least this promised the chance that Owen would be able to earn a living doing something he obviously enjoyed. I, of all people, knew what a gratifying thing that could be. It would also be a boost to his self-esteem to no longer feel that he was in my debt.

For my final chore, I threw on a jacket and scarf, grabbed my car keys, and headed out the door. "Chore" was really too strong a word, but I did feel more obligation than desire in completing this particular errand.

Luckily, the weather was fine — cool, but clear — and there was still plenty of foliage on the trees as well as in the piles of leaves that now lined the roadway. No matter how leisurely I took the drive, it really wasn't long before I pulled through the gates of my destination. The little roadway was lined with headstones, dating back perhaps a hundred years, the newer graves along the western perimeter to which I now drove and parked. And suddenly there it was, what I'd avoided now for months, the name Peter Millwright, etched in stone, a physical and symbolic permanency. I didn't know if I had come to say hello, good-bye, happy Thanksgiving, or what. I only knew that I felt I had something to communicate to Peter, my husband, my lover, my friend.

"Hi," I began, addressing the lonely grave, for want of anywhere else to look. "You've been listening to me down here, haven't you? Maybe I only like to think you hear me. If you do, I think I owe you one. Maybe. I don't know. I wish you were with me, but I know better now than to make crazy wishes. I'm not sure why, Peter, but I feel like I'm saying good-bye for the first time, only that's all I've been doing for two years, isn't it?" I continued meandering aloud for some time in the same vein, expressing nothing so much as confusion, but I know I was better for having come. I ran my finger over the letters of his name. My name, too, really. Mrs. Peter Mill-wright. It was so strange now to carry the name of someone who no longer existed. Soon the ground would be impenetrably hard with the cold, and I was glad that I'd come soon enough to be spared seeing that. I preferred envisioning Peter here in the golden sunlight of autumn.

"I've got to go now. I know I don't need to stand here to talk to you, but I wanted to be sure you knew I was thinking about you. Good-bye," I said at last and, having in my own vague way made my peace, got back in the car and drove home.

Back at home, Owen was long in returning and, in spite of not really meaning to, I began to write, starting my now solo heroine on a new life that I intended to have reach happiness by the end of the convoluted format of the mystery. In this way time passed quickly, and I forgot to call over to my grandmother's to ask how Owen was doing. I looked up in surprise when, in the late afternoon, he walked, exhausted but happy, through the front door.

"You could have called me. I would have been happy to pick you up," I said.

"It's good to be working hard again. I wouldn't want to turn into a gentleman," he replied with a self-deprecating smile.

"So how is my grandmother today?"

"Fine, I guess. I scarcely saw her. Her friend Minnie made me a nice dinner, though."

"Did you get the yard all raked?"

Owen nodded and took a large swallow from the cup of coffee I'd handed to him. "I'd like to go back in a week or so when the rest of the leaves are down. According to Minnie, your grandmother is pretty particular about her grounds looking nice."

"So what's in there?" I asked, motioning to the paper bag he'd brought in with him. "Not leftovers from lunch?"

"I trimmed your grandmother's holly tree when I got done cleaning the gutters. . . ."

"Cleaning the gutters?"

"Aye, and I thought, maybe, if people still do that sort of thing, we could use the cuttings to decorate for Christmas."

"That's a great idea. Maybe later you can go up in the attic with me and start getting the rest of the decorations down. Then next week we can go and pick out a tree. This'll be fun. I haven't done any decorating for Christmas in the last two years. It's about time I did. That is, if you'll help me?"

"Of course."

It seemed like only minutes had passed when it was time to say our good nights. I may not have toiled all day at physical labor as Owen had, but I slept wonderfully all night as if I had.

The next morning I awoke to find my world in the process of being blanketed in snow. It had been a long time since we'd had any accumulation in November. Something about it seemed wrong, incongruous. I finally realized it was the leaves. It wasn't as odd to see the white-dusted bitter brown leaves of the tenacious oaks as it was to see the snow grace the yellow leaves of the maples that hung on their branches like so many splinters off a faded Canadian flag.

I called my grandmother, but as the storm was not expected to continue much longer, she informed me that, as far as she was concerned, the trip to New York was still on and that the limousine company she'd engaged to do the driving had better feel the same.

The limo arrived right on schedule, my grandmother royally ensconced in the back. It was just pretentious enough with its white exterior — somehow managing to gleam in the wan light in spite of the snow — and red leather interior. I sat down next to my grandmother in the large seat that faced forward, leaving Owen to face us in the seat which, in his terminology, faced aft. At least I think that was the right word.

"The driver put on a videotape for us to watch," my grandmother said, alluding to the small color television next to Owen, where the opening credits of "It's A Wonderful Life" were unfolding.

"Do you want to sit here so you can see the movie?" she asked Owen.

"To tell you the truth, I'm not much for TV, ma'am," he replied. This was something of an understatement as he really disliked watching. The blatant sexuality of some of the programs embarrassed him, and the intimate nature of some of the advertisements had made us both uncomfortable when we'd watched together. I wondered if his reactions wouldn't have been different, though, if he'd been watching with a bunch of guys instead of with me.

We left the movie running with the volume low and sat back to enjoy the ride. The snow didn't seem to have made driving dangerous, and I had to admit that, as far as getting into the city was concerned, this was a great way to go.

If looking alone were enough to make a person tired, I would have expected Owen to be exhausted by the time we got there. He took in all he could through the limousine's windows, and I guess I couldn't blame him. His experiences with me thus far had been limited to quaint little Slea Head and the nearby suburban shopping area. Heading into New York through gritty, industrial North Jersey was a whole new ball game.

"Are you enjoying the ride?" my grandmother asked, tearing Owen's gaze, for the moment, from the snow-covered urban sprawl along the highway.

"It's much more relaxing than riding with Peggy. She drives like her car is the *Marco Polo*."

"The *Marco Polo*?" I asked sarcastically, waiting for him to elaborate. At least I'd gotten him to use the generic term "car."

"It's a very fast ship," he said, "and *you* are a very fast driver."

"How would you know? Have you been checking the speedometer when I wasn't looking?"

"Even I can tell you're going faster than the rest of the cars around you."

I had to laugh, even if my grandmother was giving me one of her patented looks of disapproval.

And then we were there, in the thick of the busiest place I knew. If possible, Owen was even more attentive to the sights here than he'd been along the way. We were left off in front of Macy's, where the driver would be back to get us for the trip to our next destination. I felt some guilt at the pampering, but my grandmother was not capable of walking all over Manhattan, and Christmas shopping in New York was a tradition with her that was sacrosanct.

The sidewalks were crowded with people of all social, political, and financial backgrounds whose races and languages originally came from all points of the globe. Status and religion dictated clothing styles from Gucci dresses of wealthy New York to the flowing robes of Islam. Joggers in sleek running tights bounced in place at the corners, waiting, if not for the walking green, at least for a break in the traffic that would allow them to jaywalk at a good clip from one corner to the next. There were several daredevils on bikes and in-line skates in the street, and a few dog walkers (though not as many as in Prague) shared the pavement with the likes of Owen, my grandmother, and me. In spite of its being a busy shopping day, there were men hard at work washing glass doors at street level, as well as the windows of skyscrapers much higher up. Two men carried a long ladder past us, and the roar of casters announced the presence of a laundry cart being guided quickly down the sidewalk by two Asian men. It didn't appear to hold sheets, towels, or clothing of any kind, but to be merely the urban equivalent of a wheelbarrow transporting materials from one place to another.

Deliveries continued to be made, though it was the weekend and, to take advantage of all the pedestrian traffic, con men had set up along the sidewalk selling knockoffs of everything from designer watches to trendy sunglasses. The holiday spirit was upon me, though, so I paid them no attention and even came close to being able to visually shut out the filthy public trash cans whose overflow cascaded out onto the pavement.

A young man walked past with a boom box, but luckily the police presence was such that he didn't have the nerve to turn it on. Personally, I preferred hearing Christmas carols in my head.

There were taxis by the dozen, which I could see fascinated Owen until his attention was grabbed by some other new sight. It seemed that there were hundreds of women carrying handled shopping bags emblazoned MACY'S, BERGDORF'S, and so on, and I imagined before long my grandmother and I would fit in nicely in their company. Every fashion "do" and "don't" was represented, from elegant and politically incorrect fur coats to skintight leggings on couch potato figures. It was great fun to just be in the city at this time of year, watching the people and all the activity, and I hoped Owen would enjoy it, too.

At one point he backed into me, straining hard to see the tops of the buildings we had been walking past. I had to laugh, he looked so much like a country rube come to the big city for the first time. I was surprised to see a hurt look on his face.

"I know I must seem to you like some ignorant savage would to me, but you don't have to laugh at me."

"I'm not laughing *at* you, I'm laughing *with* you," I explained.

"Does one sound different than the other?"

"I'm sorry, OK? It's not very often I see someone really taken aback by anything."

"This place is enough to do that," he replied with a touch of disapproval in his voice.

"Come on, this is New York. It's exciting, exhilarating!"

"So are shark-infested waters."

At that comment, I caught my grandmother chuckling under her breath.

Inside the giant store, all was in readiness for the holiday. The colors, the lights, the scents . . . it was all very magical. I remembered coming here as a little girl, and the feelings engendered by the place while decked out for Christmas hadn't changed. Milling about, I eventually picked out gifts for most of my family. My grandmother, getting the kind of personal service she demanded, had also done well, and by the time we went out to catch our ride, we were pretty well laden with decorative shopping bags of our own. That is, Owen was, for he would not hear of us carrying our own packages while he stood around empty-handed. All in all, he was a very good sport, although, aside from his curiosity at the novelty of the experience, he didn't seem to enjoy department-store shopping any more than Peter or any of the other men I'd known did. I smiled to myself as I watched him patiently wait while I pondered yet another holiday purchase. Imagine, an aversion to shopping being a sex-linked trait through the ages. It was a humorous thought.

Saks, Tiffany's, the Palm Court at the Plaza, F.A.O. Schwartz — the day was a wonderful whirlwind of self-indulgence. Only once did I stop to examine our behavior objectively, when we walked past a panhandler asking for money for food.

Taking a glance at the Manhattan mendicant, it looked more likely that he wanted the cash for alcohol or maybe crack cocaine. It had been at least a week since his face had seen a razor, his eyes were dimly focused at best, and he appeared to be wearing everything he owned, though for all I knew this could have been a costume for his daily work on the streets. I had heard stories of people who were urban beggars for a living, bringing in enough tax-free income to provide for a middle-class existence. I was skeptical that this man was otherwise ineligible for humane help in acquiring food and a roof over his head, but I was softhearted enough to dismiss outright the idea that he did what he did because, in spite of being perfectly sane, he chose to do so. Still, I had been taught at an early age not to give in to the urge to hand money over to bums on the street. That's what charities were for, and they didn't get your hands dirty either.

"Come on, lady," the man persisted after I'd politely declined the opportunity to lighten my pocketbook on his behalf. "It's practically Christmas." His speech was somewhat slurred, and I kept walking, pretending not to see or hear him.

"Just a buck, man, that's all I'm askin' for."

I managed to ignore him or to at least affect indifference in spite of his audacious persistence and, luckily, he moved on to better prospects when we walked far enough away that he would have had to get up to follow our progress any farther.

At the corner Owen said in passing, "I thought, in this time, they'd gotten rid of all the poor people." He looked gratified in some way that the strata of life had remained unchanged, that the "prosperity and want" as he put it, continued side by side as they had so blatantly in his own Victorian age.

This one flash of guilt and social responsibility

didn't stop me, however, from being a good capitalist, and I even managed to divert Owen's attention a couple of times long enough for me to buy him a complicated-looking Swiss Army knife and a kit to construct a model of the *Cutty Sark*, which I thought we'd have fun putting together through the short cold days of winter to come. I could tell by the information on the kit's packaging that it was a little late for Owen's era, the ship having been built in 1869, and that it was a "lime-juicer" to boot (his derogatory way of designating a British ship), but it was the closest thing I could find to the vessels he'd known, and, anyway, my heart was in the right place.

We were all a bit mentally worn out by the time we met the limousine outside of the last store before leaving the city to go home. I heard my grandmother yell, "Stop!" and that was the first I realized that she'd been mugged; that is, a dark-haired, darkly clothed man had run off with her handbag. She was, thankfully, unhurt, and I'd only just been able to assure myself of that when I realized that Owen was off in hot pursuit down the street. Bill had certainly not exaggerated about Owen's ability to run with great speed, but I honestly didn't know if I wanted him to catch up with the thief or not. The minutes while we waited to see what would happen were anxious ones, made worse by the fact that I had almost immediately lost sight of Owen in the hordes of holiday shoppers that crowded the sidewalk.

My heart beat hard inside my chest, providing a percussive emphasis for my sense of panic. Where was he? I kept wondering and tried with all my might not to imagine the possible consequences of his chasing down the mugger. This was New York, after all, and every day someone added to the crime statistics as one more victim, just another urban casualty. Fleeting images of damaged lives and broken dreams passed through my mind. Above all, I worked to shove aside what I knew of the days and weeks and months that followed tragedy in its wake — the horror, the anger, the emptiness. Please, dear God, I thought, let him be all right.

It was with a great deal of relief that I picked out Owen's light hair in the mass of humanity pulsing its way in the direction of the car. When he came fully into view, I could make out a line of blood running crimson from his lower lip to his chin, just to the right of center, temporarily destroying the symmetry of his face. And that wasn't all. I could tell that he was in pain elsewhere, the way he held his upper right arm clamped to his side, but when he caught sight of me he held the recovered pocketbook up in triumph with his left.

He handed it to my grandmother with a shy smile that was tempered by his obvious discomfort.

"You're a regular Brendan O'Gallivan!" she exclaimed.

"My grandfather," I explained briefly. My

grandmother happened to be the only woman I ever knew whose husband was also her personal hero, so it was no scant praise she had chosen to bestow on him. I, however, was riled, and let him know it.

"What on earth were you thinking?" I demanded. "You could have been killed! That guy could have had a gun or a knife."

Owen looked crestfallen. "I don't know what you want from me," he said quietly, out of my grandmother's hearing. She was being helped into the limo by the chauffeur, who had been so useless as to be almost invisible during the robbery and ensuing chase. Owen gave me no further reply and followed her stiffly into the car.

I was chastened by his words. I had certainly been guilty of sending mixed messages, but I'd been angry just then because I was afraid. I know how it had upset him when he thought I'd considered him cowardly in the face of the aggressive male members of my family at Thanksgiving, but I hadn't meant for him to commit some senseless act of bravado just to prove he was capable of standing up for himself when bullied. A man who would grab a frail old woman's purse and bolt was no virile man to measure oneself against anyway.

And I felt justified in worrying about Owen, and not just because I knew what it was to suffer loss. It wasn't as though he'd come from the longest-lasting stock; both of his parents had died young. Still, genetics had to be somewhat in his favor, I thought. For one thing, when I'd taken him in for his dental appointment, I'd been informed that he'd never had a cavity. And Owen had told me that he'd only been seen by a doctor once (a "surgeon" was the term he used) before going to see Dr. Graber when he first came here. He could also run like a dream, as I'd so recently seen. So he had to be fairly hearty, I told myself. Jesus, Mary, and Joseph, I thought, listen to yourself — good teeth, good health, good speed — it sounded like I was buying a horse.

I guess the bottom line was that, for whatever reason, he was still here while all his contemporaries were in the grave. I should have gained confidence from that thought, but I was still anxious about his well-being. How else could I react about someone whose life was practically in my hands? I could hardly bear to see him hurt. The sight of him as he'd come up the sidewalk through the crowds had brought to mind a vision of him lying on the beach the day I'd found him, dead to the world, and of Peter and the last sight I'd had of him in the casket.

Owen wiped his split and bleeding lip with one of the cocktail napkins provided in the limousine, but I could tell there was more to his injuries than that. It was clear that breathing was painful to him as I watched him clench his teeth and occasionally close his eyes at an intake of breath.

"We need to get you to a hospital," I stated as fact, but Owen disagreed.

"I'll be fine. I could use some liniment when we get back, though, if you have any."

"Owen, I insist," I said as I lowered the window to communicate with the driver.

"Which is the nearest hospital?" I asked him, but before he could reply Owen was protesting that he didn't need to go.

"How on earth can you know that? Obviously you're in a lot of pain. Now, enough of the macho stuff — you're going to have your lip, and your side, looked at."

"If I agree to see Dr. Graber when we get back, will that satisfy you?" he countered.

My eyes met his in a battle of wills and, without being the first to blink, I demanded the cellular phone from the driver. My grandmother paid well and tipped handsomely, so I got no argument. After fumbling for a minute through my pocketbook, I got Arlene's number and, after a ring or two and a moment with her nurse, I had her on the line.

She was very understanding when I explained what had happened, and I was secretly thrilled when she told me she would have to see Owen at the hospital rather than at her office as she was due to make her rounds there almost right away. I breathed a huge sigh of relief knowing that good medical care was just around the corner.

"Just have me paged when you get there," she concluded. "I should be able to get you in and out in a reasonable period of time."

I thanked her far from adequately — I didn't

know if I could ever do that — and handed the phone back to the driver. When I informed the chauffeur of our new destination, Owen didn't look particularly pleased, but I explained that the hospital was where Dr. Graber was, and he *had,* after all, agreed to see her. It wasn't much of a victory, but in my concern for his health, I really didn't care whether he was angry with me or not.

The ride to the hospital was interminable from my point of view, and it couldn't have been any better from Owen's. At one point he closed his eyes, and I was afraid he'd passed out, but he rallied soon after that to the point where I thought maybe I had over-reacted. Even when my hopes rose enough to think that he might really be fine, I kept wondering why it was taking so long to get there. I didn't want to complain to the driver, but I felt that, in his place, I would have driven with more haste. I knew I wouldn't relax until Owen was under a doctor's care.

Finally we arrived and were taken care of like VIP's thanks to Arlene's intervention in the world of emergency room red tape. My grandmother had allowed the limousine driver to take her home after I had insisted. Perhaps she had realized, too, that we could be in for a long wait. She pressed me to call her later, to let her know how Owen was doing, and told me she felt partly responsible, since it was in retrieving her handbag that he had been injured. I agreed to call, gave her fragile old body a hug, and rejoined our impatient patient.

Owen was still insisting that he would be fine without any medical care. Under Arlene's direction, however, he was X-rayed and had four stitches put in his lower lip. I think the X ray, being an unknown, had been the more frightening of the two prospects for him.

He stewed in silence as we waited for Arlene to return with his X rays, though I knew he would be cooperative enough when she reentered the room. I could see that he was still in some discomfort, but the lack of panic in the faces of any and all medical staff involved had gone a long way toward calming my nerves and fears. Owen looked down at his hands, around the examining room, anywhere but at me. I knew he was pointedly ignoring me, resentfully blaming me for this whole situation, and letting me know it by refusing to meet my eyes. It didn't prevent me from giving him a good looking over, though, still trying to convince myself as I was that he would be perfectly all right. The pale blue hospital gown that he had on over his jeans both concealed and revealed the form beneath. I had many times tried to picture him in period clothes as I'd watch him at manual labor or at his art. I could see him in my mind's eye in the garb of a gentleman, from a time when that distinction actually mattered, perhaps in fawn-colored knee-length breeches and a white "poet's" shirt with flowing sleeves that clung to the muscles beneath much as the hospital gown did now. Admittedly,

I hadn't done my research and suspected that I might have one Victorian-era decade's fashions confused with another's, but the image was a handsome one all the same.

By the time Arlene came back in, Owen still hadn't deigned to speak to me, but he was polite enough to meet the doctor's gaze, even if he wouldn't meet mine. She asked him to remove the gown and I winced when I saw the bruise along his side, even as I admired the contours of his form, noting how much better he looked, in spite of his injury, than he'd appeared when we'd first met. The flesh still clung tightly to the bone, but I could no longer delineate each rib through the skin. In fact, he reminded me of a racehorse or other finely tuned and fit young animal, with just enough meat on him to sustain strength without large, unsightly bulging muscles.

"Well, you've filled out a bit, and your color's improved. At least you're eating better," she began, confirming my own observations. "Now, let's see," she said, referring to his chest X ray, hanging now where she could examine it.

"I'm fine," Owen said. "I'm sorry we have to waste your time like this."

"Well, you *are* lucky. Your ribs are only bruised — no fractures."

Owen shot me a look with "See? I told you so" written all over it.

"But you've had broken ribs before."

Owen nodded. "I broke three ribs at the same time that I broke my wrist. I told you about that.

253

That happened in forty-six — that is, about seven years ago."

"And the other time?" Dr. Graber asked.

I looked questioningly at him. It surprised me that he could still have secrets from me.

"When I lived at home, I guess."

"You guess?" I demanded to know.

He looked evasive, embarrassed, but he nodded.

"Didn't you see a doctor?" Arlene asked more gently.

"No."

She pursued her line of questioning. "Were you still a child?"

"Aye."

"Why didn't your mother take you to a doctor?"

"She didn't know," he replied with a hint of truculence now that his story was being drawn from him when he was obviously not pleased to be sharing it.

"Why not?" I asked.

"I didn't tell her."

"Didn't you know you had broken ribs?" I asked in disbelief.

"Of course I knew. I could practically hear them grating, couldn't I?"

"So that's why you knew they weren't broken today. But I still don't understand why you didn't see a doctor," I asked, confused by such incomprehensible behavior. "Was it the money?"

"No."

"Were you afraid to see a doctor, or what? Why didn't you just tell your mother?"

"How could I tell her that her husband had kicked my ribs in? Do you know what that would have done to her?"

"How old were you?" Arlene asked.

"Fifteen."

"Was that the first time he beat you?" she asked, sincere care and concern expressed in her face.

"No, but it was the worst."

"How long did this go on?"

"From the time they got married until I left. About a year."

"Why didn't you tell me?" I asked.

"I told you about Wilkins on the *Aurora Borealis* the first day I was here, and I never gave you the impression my stepfather had any love for me, did I?"

"No, you didn't," I admitted. "But why all these partial stories about your stepfather and what happened with Wilkins?"

"I don't want to be the object of your pity," he said with a trace of belligerence.

"After Mr. Campbell broke your ribs, is that when you went to sea?"

"Not long after that. As soon as I felt well enough to go."

"This sadistic guy Wilkins on a power trip is one thing, but your own stepfather . . ."

"With Wilkins there wasn't any reason. I was just in the wrong place at the wrong time. At least with Mr. Campbell it was personal."

"Personal? What possible reason could he have had?" I asked.

"I can be very stubborn sometimes, I know," he said. "Mr. Campbell liked to believe he was an important man because he was sexton at his church, and even though he forced my mother to attend there, I never would set foot inside after their wedding. I think it was an embarrassment to him, my willful behavior, but I continued to go to St. Ambrose, the church where I'd always gone, and I think people laughed at him because of it. It also didn't help for him to constantly hear from people how much I looked like my father and what a well-liked man he was. Anyway, it was a long time ago, Peggy, and now that he's dead, I'd rather just try to forget about it."

"All right," I agreed quietly.

"I'm going to prescribe some medication for you to relieve the pain," Arlene said, back to the business at hand.

"No. Thank you," Owen said firmly, then gave me a look that emphasized the stubbornness he'd recently admitted to.

"Oh, and you can put your shirt back on now," Arlene added, and Owen let me help him get re-dressed, hiding the ugly purple mark on his side in the process.

I thanked Arlene profusely and had to thank her again when she informed me that she'd arranged transportation for us back to the house. As it turned out, we rode back in style — nothing like the comfort of the limo, but even safer. One of Arlene's friends on the police force, at the hospital visiting his girlfriend who was an R.N., agreed to take us back to Slea Head in his cruiser as a personal favor to Arlene. Just one more reason that I owed her big.

Owen looked tired when we finally got inside and had settled ourselves on the sunporch. We faced the inactive television, drinking hot coffee. I missed our roaring fires in the parlor, but the settee in there was so stiff to sit on and I figured Owen would be too sore to take our usual spot on the floor by the hearth.

"If I give you something for the pain, will you take it?" I asked.

"I'm all right," he said, but didn't look it.

"I get the feeling you don't completely trust Dr. Graber, but surely you trust me."

"I'm not thrilled with doctors," he admitted. "I think they do as much harm as good."

"They didn't still bleed people and medieval stuff like that in your day, did they?"

"You mean they don't do that anymore?"

"Most definitely not."

"Then, how do they get out the poisons that make people sick?"

"There are better ways of getting people well, I assure you. Now, will you take something?"

"Peggy, I'm all right, really. You needn't worry."

But I did worry. He had come to mean so much to me, in a lot of different ways. It hurt me

257

to see him so obviously in discomfort.

"Please?" I asked, and his eyelids drooped enough for me to take that as a tacit assent.

I went to the kitchen for ibuprofen and a glass of water. I handed him a couple of tablets, but before I could give him the glass, he was chewing the pills. It was really my fault, since I'd gotten him chewable vitamins to encourage his taking them. I guess he figured that was the norm.

"You're supposed to swallow them," I said softly as I handed him the water.

He shrugged. "They don't have any taste, really," he offered lethargically, and I could tell he was exhausted.

"Time for bed," I said. "It's been a long day."

He didn't protest as I walked with him up the stairs and into the guest room, which was now his. He kicked off his shoes and settled himself in bed without changing out of his clothes. I arranged the bedcovers gently over him, and he closed his eyes, certain in the belief that he had found safe haven here. The protective tenderness I felt for him at that moment was like a catch in the throat — physically palpable and moving. I'd experienced just such an impression of complete safety from the world in Peter's arms, and I saw that giving it was as good as receiving. I realized, too, that Owen gave a measure of this feeling of well-being to me, too, and I smiled down at him. His eyes were still closed in what I hoped was reasonably comfortable repose, his long lashes making a soft contrast against his skin. He lay perfectly motionless but for the rise and fall of his chest — a stillness, for all he'd just been through, that was less profound and more benign than what I'd found when I'd originally seen him on the sand. I was deeply grateful that things hadn't turned out any worse after our harrowing experience in New York, and now wasn't the first time that I thanked God for Owen's rescue from the sea and his continued safe existence here among us.

I made one last check to see that he was comfortably situated and adequately covered before leaving him in peace to begin what I imagined would be a long healing sleep. He had told me once that one of a sailor's most necessary skills was being able to fall asleep or come fully awake at a moment's notice. He put that ability into practice then, as I think he was out before I left the room.

# CHAPTER 11

The next morning it was apparent that Owen was going to be fine, as I'd assured my grandmother the night before. Then I'd felt I had been making a baseless statement merely to ease her mind, but when I saw him come downstairs, clean shaven and well dressed, I felt I was letting out a breath I hadn't known I'd been holding.

He looked great, considering. More and more I had begun to appreciate his physical qualities of attractiveness rather than just those of his personality. He was, in fact, rather well made, and I'd come to view his features with more than a little pleasure.

"What's up?" I asked, indicating the off-white sweater and chocolate-brown corduroys he was wearing, in contrast to the jeans he seemed to prefer.

"It's Sunday," he said, pouring a cup of coffee from the pot.

"You're not saying you feel up to going to church, are you?"

"Of course."

"OK. I'll go change."

Needless to say, when my grandmother saw us at St. Michael's, she was pleased for more than one reason. Here was proof that Owen was both well on the road to recovery and was a good Catholic boy, to boot. It was the first time Owen and I had made it to the early Mass she and my parents preferred attending, and this time it was old Father O'Reilly, the priest who had officiated at my wedding, who nodded to me from the front of the church. There were many more familiar faces, too, among the worshipers, primarily from my parents' generation, and the atmosphere was like a homecoming — safe, familiar, and warm.

Owen and I joined my grandmother, Minnie, and my parents for the service, but declined an invitation from my grandmother (respectfully, of course) to join her for lunch later. We were much too excited to get home and start getting the house ready for the holiday season.

We retrieved the bag of greenery Owen had brought from my grandmother's and eagerly began transforming the house into a sight worthy of a Christmas card photograph. On the mantel shelf I tucked springs of holly in among the lustres and candlesticks, the berries bright against the glossy dark leaves. Next I adorned the window ledges with more of the greenery, flanking the electric candles I put there each year to send shafts of light into the yuletide darkness outside. Owen suggested that we also festoon the tops of the picture frames in the parlor with holly, a custom of his time that dressed off the room nicely. This was readily accomplished by my standing on a stepladder and accepting the cuttings he handed to me, dusting, of course, as I went.

I have always been very fond of decorating the house for Christmas and, up until the time that Peter died, I usually had a hard time making myself wait until December to bring out the various holiday adornments that I had stored in boxes up in the attic. This year I was at peace enough with myself and the world to feel up to reliving the annual joy of unwrapping each colorful decoration and welcoming the recollections it engendered.

I had also brought down the several boxes of tree ornaments that I owned, but their unveiling would have to wait until I felt Owen would be up to helping me cut down and then set up a tree. In the weeks to come I anticipated completing the job as I had in better days, with garlands of pine boughs draped above the mantel from its shelf, up to the ceiling, across in a deep swag, and back down again, and also entwined along the stairs' handrail and banisters. I planned, too, on adding more organic touches with an arrangement of pomegranates, pears, and other fruits centering a pineapple above the front door, poinsettias for the center of the table, and strings of cranberries for the tree. For now, we had to settle for longer-lasting accessories of the festive season.

With Owen's help I got everything from its protective tissue-paper wrapping and set about arranging things where they'd look best. I put my old German nutcracker in his accustomed place in the center of the mantel in front of the mahogany shelf clock, which I noticed Owen had wound and had running again. I smiled and thanked him before moving on to the next item. By the time we'd finished, scented candles in Christmas holders graced the tables, an old papier-mâché angel and an antique feather tree found homes on the top of the desk, and stiff tatted snowflakes made by my grandmother hung from the knobs of my multipaned glass-fronted kitchen cabinets. I had dug out a grape-vine wreath made for me by a grateful friend who'd spent a week visiting Peter and me here at the shore. It sported starfish, shells, a small wooden sailboat, and a replica of the Slea Head lighthouse less than half a foot in height. I hung it on the parlor's French door, where I could enjoy it without exposing it to the elements. A real pine wreath for the front door would come later.

I reached down into the large cardboard box and retrieved a smaller box that, I knew, contained a crèche. I haphazardly set the stable and figures on the cool stone of my marble-top table and asked Owen to set them up for me. I was delighted to watch him out of the corner of my eye as, like a small child, he arranged and rearranged the pieces according to what he thought logical and proper. He seemed no less pleased with doing the task than I was in observing him at it.

The last items in the box took me by surprise, and I sat quietly, Owen's project with the nativity set momentarily forgotten, as I drew out the Christmas stockings I had made for Peter and myself in the first year of our marriage. They were done in needlepoint of Persian wool, mine depicting a millefleurs design on a green background, Peter's a scene of the magi beneath a brilliant star. Just because I couldn't cook and didn't like to clean didn't mean I was wholly deficient in the "womanly arts." I vividly remembered curling up on the sofa with my canvas, needle, and wool, trying like crazy to get the two of them completed by Christmas Eve. I had succeeded, just barely, finishing them off with our names at the cuffs. I hugged Peter's to my chest for a second and then placed both back in the box for a return trip to the attic. The Christmases Peter and I had shared were gone forever.

The next day we passed into December, month of dreams, and by the end of the week I finally decided to take Owen's word that he was sufficiently recovered to go and get a tree.

"Have you ever done this before?" I asked as I handed him a coil of nylon rope to use in bringing our prize home and started the car.

"I've heard of the custom among Germans new to the continent, but I've never actually seen an evergreen inside someone's house. It seems a bit odd, I must admit."

"I suppose it would seem quirky from your point of view, but wait till you see it all decorated. It's actually pretty spectacular."

"I'll take your word for it," he said with an indulgent smile.

"Well, I know you never had a Christmas tree growing up, but what did you do to celebrate?"

"We decorated, with sprigs of holly like we did at your house, and also with evergreen cuttings. Sometimes there would be a kissing bough — a hanging ball of greenery and candles. Do you still do that?"

"Sounds like mistletoe. Do people standing under it get a free kiss?" I asked.

"That's the rule," he confirmed with raised eyebrows and a smile, "although young ladies would be careful not to get caught under it in the wrong circumstances. I think they were very clever in engineering who they found themselves next to under the bough, and some young men could wait all day and never get a free kiss."

I laughed. "Not speaking from any personal experience, I'm sure."

"Of course not," he answered quickly, shooting me a glance out of the corner of his eyes before taking a moment to get his pipe going.

"Well, what else did you do for Christmas?" I asked as we drove south on a rural four-lane highway that had been bypassed by the interstate a decade or more before.

"We went to work, unless it was a Sunday, and we went to church, regardless of the day."

"Well, what about gifts?"

"Usually my mother would knit me a new pair of stockings or a muffler, and I generally got some oranges, which were a real treat, not like now when they don't seem very hard to come by."

"No toys?"

Owen smiled, clearly remembering something pleasant. "One year — when I was only two — I got a Noah's ark that my father made for me from scraps of wood. He was quite capable with his hands and made a good job of it. It was my favorite plaything when I was very young, and I remember I had to be very good in order for my mother to bring it out for me. I think she was afraid I would break it. I suppose it meant even more to her than it did to me."

While his descriptions didn't sound exactly joyless, I looked forward to sharing our more spectacular, overdone, ostentatious version of the holiday with him.

"I think you'll like some of our newer traditions," I said. "I know it's not as religious an occasion anymore as it probably should be, but it's a lot of fun, with parties and good food. . . ."

"It sounds more like Hogmanay."

"Like what?"

"Hogmanay. New Year's Eve. That's when we would have *our* wild times — eating and drinking and making noise to drive out evil spirits and bring good luck."

"Sounds raucous, more like our Halloween, I guess. It sounds like fun, though, and I plan on taking your lead when we welcome in the new year. Tell me more about it."

"Well, it's not all fun and games. First the house must be cleaned from top to bottom."

"Ugh," I said, and saw with delight that I'd given him just the reaction he'd expected. We both laughed.

"And you have to make sure you're all up-to-date on everything. All debts should be paid, all items borrowed returned."

"That sounds all right. Better than the cleaning part."

"Then the eating begins."

"I'm with you on that. What would you have, ideally?"

"Haggis."

"Ugh."

"*Whist!* You'd like it if you tried it."

"OK, go on."

"And barley broth and smoked salmon and oatcakes and scones . . ."

"And I think *my* family's too 'old world' sometimes," I said.

"I think I'm making myself hungry."

"It does sound like quite a feast."

"Well, you did say 'ideally.' We never had all that, mind, but we did the best we could. Then at twelve we threw open the windows and doors and made as much noise as we could to drive out all that was bad of the old year and waited for the first-footer to arrive."

"What's the 'first-footer'?"

"That's the first person to enter the house after midnight."

"Were you ever a first-footer?"

"No. It's best luck when the first-footer is a

tall, dark-haired man. You'll remember I wasn't really quite grown when I left home, and you can see why else I wouldn't be much in demand for the job."

I smiled, thinking Peter would have been perfect for the role, but then it wasn't his tradition. It was Owen's.

After about a total of an hour's drive, I pulled the car onto the gravel lot of the Holly Hills Tree Farm. It wasn't especially hilly, and there was no holly in evidence, but I liked the holiday theme of the name. The sky was overcast, but I didn't think it would rain before we got the job at hand completed. I wasn't so sure how long the light would hold out, though, as we'd gotten a late start and the sun set earlier and earlier each evening. In some ways it seemed such a short time ago that the long nights of summer were upon me. But those days also seemed worlds away at times, as I had been alone for so many of those day-lit hours, and I no longer had to be unless I so chose. The very idea that I would be out searching for something to brighten the Christmas season would have been inconceivable back then, and not just because the hot days at the beach would have driven yuletide thoughts from my mind. The truth was that Owen was good for me, that I would never have reached this stage of recovery without his daily presence. But for now it was time to select a tree to lay down its life for us on the altar of beauty.

We got out of the car, Owen tapping the ashes

out of his pipe against the heel of one of his work boots before laying it on the dashboard. We both buttoned our coats tighter against the chill outside after the artificial heat inside the car and headed from the parking lot toward the working part of the tree farm.

Some snow would have been nice, I thought, to invoke the holiday mood, as we approached a man in heavy tan coveralls who seemed to be in charge. We waited a moment while he finished the transaction in progress, our feet sinking slightly in the spongy ground. I could see water-filled ruts in the main pathway leading deeper into the farm, and I was glad that I'd worn my gum boots. Owen's tan work boots were already taking on a dark outline where the moisture of the short brown grass had crept up the sides on our brief walk from the car.

The owner turned to us with a good-natured smile. He appeared to be a hale and hearty seventy years old or so, and his teeth looked like dull white planks against his wind-reddened face. Other, much younger men, were busily bailing recently purchased trees in plastic netting for transport or taking money from customers. One, not much more than a boy, was helping to lift a tree onto a waiting car roof. I guessed that they were the owner's sons, grandsons, or nephews as this looked to be a strictly family operation. Finished now with the people he'd been speaking to, the farmer quoted the prices for us for the various species of trees and handed Owen a loaner hacksaw and a piece of cardboard.

"What's this for?" I asked, indicating the torn-off piece of a corrugated box.

"That'll keep your knees clean while you're cutting. Ground's awful muddy in spots."

"Good idea. Thanks," I said.

"Now, your firs are over to this side of the main trail here, and the spruces are on the other," the old farmer continued. "If a tree's marked with a ribbon on the top, it's been spoke for. Otherwise, take your pick. When you're all set, one of the boys here will bring a wagon 'round to help you bring it back here to the baler."

"Thanks again," I said. "Ready?" I asked Owen. He nodded, and we were off.

"Well," I said as we made our way down the central path, "I think I want a spruce. Let's see what we can find over here where the guy said they were."

We entered a huge grove of evenly spaced ever-greens. At first glance, they all seemed to be completely flawless. Obviously, whoever had the chore of trimming them periodically throughout the year had a real eye for symmetry. As I looked closer, however, I saw that there were degrees to their apparent perfection.

"What about this one?" Owen asked, his arm out to a reasonably good-looking specimen.

"Too short," I said. "I'm looking for one about eight feet tall." The first floor of my house, luckily, has fairly high ceilings.

We wandered a bit farther before Owen spoke again.

"This one's nice," he offered.

"Hmm. Too bushy, I think."

"And this one?" he asked after finding the next likely subject.

I looked it over carefully. "Too fat," I said. "I want an old-fashioned-looking one. Kind of stately and thin, with room between the tiers of branches so the ornaments will really show."

Owen shook his head. "I never realized there was so much difference. I would have sworn these all looked alike."

"Each one is unique," I said, "like people. It's almost as if each one has its own personality."

"Next thing I know you'll be giving them names."

"Very funny. Imagine you were drawing them. Wouldn't they look individual if you drew each one in detail?"

"I suppose so. All right, how about Freddy here?" he said, putting his arm around the next tree we came to.

"Freddy, is it? Looks more like an Elmer to me," I said with soft sarcasm.

"Help! It's got me!" Owen joked, pushing himself back into the waiting arms of the spruce he'd named Freddy.

"Stop it!" I hissed softly, trying not to laugh and hoping we wouldn't get caught in our shenanigans by the proprietor or any of his boys. "You'll break the branches!"

"Sorry," Owen said, extricating himself and fluffing the foliage back to its original shape. We both broke out laughing.

"OK, you go that way, and I'll go this way. When you find a tree you think I'll really love, call me and I'll come look it over. We haven't got that much time left before it'll be too dark to decide."

It was, in fact, getting rapidly dimmer as the sun sank lower and lower on the horizon. A cold wind had kicked up, too, dropping the temperature by, perhaps, ten degrees in as many minutes. I did want a beautiful tree, but I was willing to compromise with one that was less than perfect in the interests of saving time and getting in out of the elements before dark.

"Peggy!" I heard Owen call.

"Owen?"

"Peggy?"

"Owen! Where are you?" I demanded with mock seriousness as I stifled a laugh at this silly game of Marco Polo we seemed to have started in the woods.

"Boo!" Owen said, jumping out from behind a large blue spruce.

"Oh, nice, Owen. I fell like I'm tree shopping with a little boy."

"Come on," he said. "She's perfect. I've named her Clara."

With the borrowed hacksaw we cut the tree down and, with a spring in our step, carried it to the roof of the car, scorning the use of the little red wagons available for transport. Owen carried his end of the tree easily, as I clumsily and half out of breath, brought up the rear. His strength was such that the work seemed to be effortless for him, but I wasn't about to take any chances that foolhardiness would bring on a relapse. Without being too obvious, I managed to engineer it so that two of the owner's younger relations did the actual lifting to the roof, as I wasn't entirely sure just how painless Owen's bruised ribs would be after such a strain. Together Owen and I then tied the tree down with a wish, a prayer, and the best of intentions. I only hoped it would make the ride back to the house in one piece. I had very little confidence in my input to the job, but Owen, as I should have expected, was a master at tying knots. When all seemed relatively secure, we headed off down the highway to the tune of the merrily pompous Christmas choral music that chanted from the tape deck. I already knew this day would become a memory I would treasure each year at this time for the rest of my life.

Back at the house, setting up our beautiful blue spruce was the usual unbalanced comedy that I had enacted with Peter each December of our marriage. "The Annual Tree Swearing" he had dubbed it, to commemorate the language that such a frustrating job produced even in the best of us. Owen didn't curse, but I could almost see the words form silently on his lips as the tree listed first one way and then the other.

"Are you sure this little thing can do the job?" Owen asked in exasperation, referring to the plastic tree stand, obviously keeping his tongue in check. "It hasn't got much weight to it."

"Well, it has a pretty big base, and it'll weigh more when we've filled it with water."

Owen mumbled something as he tried to re-adjust the screws that dug through the tree's bark and into its soft trunk.

"What did you say?" I asked, deliberately provoking him. I'd never seen him completely lose his cool, and if this wouldn't test his ability to keep his temper, I figured nothing would.

"I said that I see a big mess in your future. This whole thing is going to come down, I swear it, and if this holder or stand or whatever you call it is full of water, your rug here is going to get soaked. I don't think I need tea leaves or a crystal ball to see that," he added, wiping the perspiration off his brow with a gloved hand. The needles were prickly, and we had both kept our gloves on while we wrestled with "Clara."

"This is the third stand we've had, and it's a big improvement over the last two. The one before this one wouldn't hold a trunk big enough, and Peter always had to trim off part of it. The one before that, well, I can't remember what was that one's flaw. I do think I'm forgetting something else though."

"A miracle?"

"Wait," I said excitedly, and stepped behind

the tree to a small watercolor hanging on the wall. "Ta da!" I announced, removing the painting and revealing a hook Peter had put in the wall to which he'd unobtrusively wire the tree. "I forgot. Peter used to string a wire from the back of the tree to this hook and one to the heater down here, too," I said, indicating the baseboard radiator.

Owen sighed. "Well, I think that *will* make a difference. You do have some wire, don't you?"

"Of course I do . . . somewhere. First we'll need to find out which side is the best so we'll know which side faces front."

This turned out to a be a sort of ponderous ballet, with Owen "dancing" with the tree, turning it heavily in his arms as I stood back and rated the various views. For a while it seemed as though the density of the branches was unusually irregular, and the baldest spot would routinely turn out to be the one facing front and center. At the end, we held a sort of police lineup photo session as I commanded, "Face front," "Now to the side," and so on before the perfect angle suddenly revealed itself as though it had only just materialized. I quickly got the wire from the basement, and we completed the job of securing the tree in its final position.

So, as it had been every year that I could remember, the task had eventually been accomplished and was, as always, pronounced to be the most difficult one to date. The continuity of this was reassuring.

I sat down to rest for a moment, tired, I think, just from watching Owen maneuver our big blue spruce to its present, perfect location and angle. The effort hadn't seemed to bother him any; it had just raised the color a bit in his cheeks until they'd acquired a healthy-looking glow. Obviously, a man could keep in great shape without the use of a gym, I thought. But now it was time for the fun part.

Indulging every bit of my sentimental nature, I then unwrapped my collection of ornaments with Owen's help. They were mostly of blown glass, dating from a period that spanned the decades of the 1890s to the 1940s. I liked to think their age would make them more familiar to Owen, but they and their like had no place in his memory. Still, he took such pleasure in their colorful appearance and delicacy that the experience was in no way diminished by its being so new to him.

What delighted him most were the lights. Although he'd sit quietly in the darkened parlor admiring the glow coming from the tree we'd decorated with our own hands, I think he most enjoyed the outdoor light shows put on at various homes in town. To him they were works of amazement worthy of long looks of pure gratification that he had assumed had taken days and days to create. I was almost sorry when I corrected his inaccurate assumption, explaining to him that the lights were, in fact, strung together and had not needed to be put up individually as he'd first supposed. Even after he'd helped me drape our own strings of lights around our tree, the disillusionment was not enough to spoil the magic for him. To him, the idea that people had put up these many lights around their homes at all, with no logical reason other than to give pleasure to others and at no small expense, fit well with his idea of the spirit of the season. I found myself enjoying them all the more in his reflected delight.

In spite of all the December frivolity, I was still uneasy at times. If the last two years had taught me anything, it was to be aware that feelings of emotional safety and well-being were illusory or, at best, fleeting. I think I was waiting for something to go wrong so that I could stop being afraid that it might. It was like anticipating a phone call in the dead of night, a harbinger of doom. Participating in life was a risk, and I'd lost the knack for it. The arrival of disaster, I thought, might even prove to be a relief. The best I could do was to try to ignore the periodic flashes of panic and tell myself that I deserved this happiness, and perhaps some fluke of justice would allow it to last a bit longer.

One evening on her way home from work, Marjorie stopped in with her customary knock, and I was tickled to be able to share with her the fruits of our decorating labor. Owen and I had just finished our dinner and a good bottle of wine, and I was feeling especially mellow and sociable. The sun had gone down, and, with the

277

tree's lights lit, the house's charms were at their summit. My doubts about the future, for the time being, seemed ill-founded and far away.

I greeted my sister with a hug and a hello, her presence just another part of all the good that came with the season. "I'm glad you came by," I said. "Where's Bill?"

"He's working late tonight. I'll probably be asleep by the time he gets in."

"That's too bad, but as long as you're here you can see the tree. It took forever for us to get everything done, but I think the house looks great, if I do say so myself."

"I'm sure it does."

Marjorie seemed unusually quiet as I toured her around downstairs, pointing out the various improvements in the decor brought about by glistening balls and boughs of pine. I was a little disappointed in her lack of response, but still I was so pleased with the festive results of all our hard work that her taciturnity was not enough to get me down. I know I was positively beaming as I looked at the tree and thought of all the wonderful new holiday memories Owen and I had created putting on the candy canes and old glass ornaments.

My euphoric state rendered me oblivious, I guess, because I didn't notice how preoccupied Marjorie looked until we sat down at the kitchen table for a cup of coffee. There was clearly something on her mind that she wanted to share with me. I could only hope it wasn't bad news. Owen wandered in, and I got the distinct feeling from her facial expression that Marjorie would have preferred to talk to me alone. Now that my powers of observation were heightened at last, I chose to ignore her wishes. She seemed to be upset, and it appeared that her solicitude was directed at me. As far as I was concerned, if there was a problem, I'd rather face it with Owen than without him.

"I went to see Gram yesterday," she began.

"Great. How is she?"

"She's fine. She couldn't say enough good things about you, Owen. In fact, I listened to her extol your virtues for nearly an hour."

"I always thought she was perceptive," I said with a smile to cover Owen's embarrassment at the compliment.

"Peggy," she began softly, with a motherly look in her eye. There were times when, to belie her age, she'd just as soon have dispensed with the idea that she was the older sister. Then there were times, like now, when she played the role to the hilt. "Don't you think this has gone a bit too far?" she asked, not specifically defining what "this" was.

"What do you mean?" I asked in return, being deliberately obtuse on the off chance that I was wrong about what she meant.

"This relationship, or whatever it is you have going on between you — I don't see how it can be good for you," she said, confirming my suspicions in spades. "Or you, either," she added, turning to Owen.

I definitely did not want to get into this conversation, but it was like trying not to look at a car accident.

"Go on," I said.

"Peggy, I don't want to hurt you, but surely you can see that this . . . *situation* is not normal. It's a classic case of co-dependency. You lose your husband, you have no children, and all of a sudden you find someone that fills both your needs — a man that needs you to take care of him. And, Owen," she said, addressing him with feigned confidence and expertise, "without help you can't even survive everyday life. I don't say that to be unkind. You yourself admit that even the most mundane things seem strange and new to you. I think, with some help, you could have a much fuller and, yes, a more *normal* life. Look at yourselves! Here the two of you are just getting by when, potentially, you each could have so much more."

In spite of my earlier suspicion that I wasn't going to like what she had to say, I was stunned. I didn't know how to respond to her analysis of our lives. I was tempted to throw her out, but I couldn't leave it like this — unresolved and bitter, driving a wedge between us that could easily turn out to be permanent.

Owen looked to me — to fix the problem? To show what a fighter I had always bragged about being? I don't know, but when he saw that I hadn't an easy answer, he turned and left the room. I started after him, but Marjorie called to me to wait. Her entreaty was so kind, calm, and concerned that I turned back to hear what she had to say.

"Marjorie, let me get him back here. Anything you have to say concerns both of us anyway."

"Peggy, please, just give me a little of your time," she asked, and I wondered if I was a bit muddled from the wine, but I decided to hear her out before rejecting her arguments.

"I want you to listen to me," she began, "and use your head, your sense of logic, for a minute. I know you think you believe all these wild stories. I tried for a while to pretend I did, too — to make you happy. It's very romantic, really, and Owen is very convincing, but if you think rationally, you know there are more plausible reasons for Owen's being here."

My first reaction was to tell her she was wrong. She didn't know him the way I did. He'd never lie, and he knew so much about the sea, and his paintings were so well-done that Darren Hurley was thinking of showing them at both his galleries. . . . Then there were all the little things — the way he talked, the marks on his back. Hell, he even smoked a pipe, which was certainly odd for a man in my day.

I knew, too, that Owen had been good for me, that he'd helped me to become part of the world around me again. But I was equally aware that I'd never be able to put that thought into words quickly enough, perfectly enough, to convince her.

"If you really knew him, Marjorie . . ." I began inadequately.

"What? I'd start believing in time-travel just because he's a nice guy? That's not the point, Peggy, and I think you know it. I'm not arguing that he isn't a decent person, just that he isn't quite the person you believe him to be."

"But all the things he knows . . ."

"Yes, that is impressive. Even Joe Maglia said he didn't see any holes in his nautical knowledge, but that doesn't preclude the fact that he could have studied maritime history at some time in his life. But we're straying from the point."

"Which is?" I asked, definitely feeling the effects of the wine as my mind seemed to have slowed to a pace that couldn't keep up with Marjorie's.

"All right, be patient with me. Let's walk through this, OK? You find some man on the beach one morning, unconscious. How did he get there?"

"He fell off a ship."

"Or?"

"I don't know. He fell off a ship," I insisted stubbornly.

"Or maybe he passed out after a night drinking at the shore with his buddies, or maybe he was fishing and his boat capsized. . . . There could be any number of reasons. Am I right?"

"He fell off a ship," I repeated, but with less

conviction. Looking at it the way Marjorie had put it, that it was just "some man" found on the beach and not the one of which I'd grown increasingly fond, it seemed preposterous to believe anything extraordinary could follow in the wake of his arrival.

"But let's say he tells you that he fell off a sailing ship from the last century or a space ship, for that matter. Do you automatically believe him?"

"No," I replied truculently. "I'm not an idiot. For weeks I thought he was full of it. It wasn't until I got to know him better that I . . ."

"What? Got sucked in? Believed that he came from the past?"

"You're making it sound like he's some kind of con artist!"

"Now that you say it, that *is* the first possibility."

"He's not lying!"

"OK, although, to be objective, you have to admit that he's found a pretty cozy spot here with you. No need to get a job, plenty of food, a nice place to stay, an attractive widow who may make herself available at any given time."

"Marjorie! Stop it! It's nothing like that!"

"In what way?"

"He doesn't ask for anything, and he works hard around the house. I'm the one that's kept him from going out to look for a job!"

"So much the better."

"Marjorie, I refuse to believe that Owen is trying to take advantage of me, that he showed up on the beach, half drowned, just to get me to offer him a middle-class existence."

"OK, OK, even I'm willing to admit that he doesn't particularly come across as a schemer. But that leaves only two other possibilities that I can see."

"Which are?"

"Well, let's start with the first one. Clearly there's a possibility that he's delusional, in which case he needs help that you know you're not qualified to give."

"But I can," I interrupted, hoping it didn't sound like I was admitting that he had serious emotional problems, only that I thought I was good for him, just as he had indisputably been for me.

"I thought you cared about him."

"I do!"

"Then, why do you want to keep him here living like this? Let him get help and get on with his life."

"I can get him help — *if* he needs it — *and* he can stay here."

"You're part of the delusion, Peggy. You have to let him go. Don't be selfish simply because you enjoy his company."

I thought back to when Owen had been injured in New York. How bitterly and, yes, how selfishly I'd wondered if another of life's little vagaries would leave me alone again. The thought still frightened me, but was I only thinking of myself?

"From what you've told me — and this much I believe — he's been a victim much of his life, unable to look beyond simple survival. I know you want to help him, but it's really only his vulnerability that appeals to you, because in it you see yourself. You've been unable to move beyond grief, to be anything but passive about the rest of your life. Look at yourself and be honest. You've allowed one thing that's happened to you — and I admit it's a really terrible thing — to make a victim out of you. It's made you incapable of living a normal, full life."

I felt tears of self-pity come to my eyes. I had had a right to grieve for Peter, for as long as it took.

"Peggy, it's like you're waiting for the next bad thing to happen. Prevent it. Be proactive in your life."

"But nothing's going badly now," I sniffed. "I'm happy for the first time in two years."

"Look at the situation you've created here. You have a man in your life again, but you've found one with a problem, and his problem allows you to have a platonic, nonthreatening relationship that avoids the whole issue of commitment. With Owen, you don't have to feel you're betraying Peter's memory, do you? It's nice and safe. You never have to worry about losing Owen, either, because you're just friends, right? Is that it? You look out for him, you *like* him, but you don't ever have to get any deeper than that because you know he's delusional. It's like he isn't real because his stories are patently unbelievable."

"I don't believe he *is* delusional," I said, but there was less force behind my words than I'd have liked.

"There *is* another possibility, Peggy."

"What?" I asked, blowing my nose, determined to be finished crying once and for all.

"What if he's only lost his memory, and his mind has for some reason constructed this whole confabulation of being some long-lost sailor. Again, if that's the case, he needs professional help. Are you going to deny him that?"

"I'm not denying him anything!" I said as the tears came again. "You're just trying to mix me up. He doesn't act at all crazy, and he seems to remember things just fine. It's just that his memories are of a different time, that's all."

"He may have had a head injury or experienced some emotional trauma and just can't recall anything about his life before that point. Think about it, Peggy. If he has some kind of amnesia, he has a *whole other life!* Do you understand that if that's true, then sooner or later someone's going to come along and claim him? He may be married, for all you know. What are you going to do if a woman shows up claiming to be his wife?"

I was going to argue that Dr. Graber had more or less dismissed the possibility that he was suffering from a concussion when I was nearly overpowered by the upshot of her argument — that I could be setting myself up for another huge personal loss that I wasn't sure I could handle. This thought had not occurred to me, and the idea of losing my best friend again was a horror that all but stopped my heart cold. Her words were confusing me. I thought I was sure that Owen had all along been telling me the truth and now, through Marjorie, logic was once again rearing its ugly head. I knew how afraid I'd been of losing him over a few stitches and a bruise. Hadn't I already been burned once before, and badly? Just the thought of Owen now going away forever was devastating.

"Whatever his life was before, this one is better!" I cried in a last-ditch effort to brush aside any thoughts of reason.

"So now you're God? You're to decide what's best? Come on, Peggy, you know what you have to do. Before this goes on any longer, you've got to end it."

I blew my nose again and wiped my eyes — an automaton trying to get presentable. I was emotionally wiped out, drained of will and passion. The words "someone's going to come along and claim him" repeated in my head, a perverse litany that could only bring grief. I couldn't let fate take my happiness again. I didn't think I could have borne that.

I told myself that, of course, Marjorie was right. I had only been thinking of myself, and it was time to think of what was best for all concerned. I was too numb to fight reason anymore.

Clearly, I had been too close to the situation to see the error of my ways. Fear was a great motivator, too, and I *was* afraid, afraid of having to face all-too-familiar pain again.

Like someone in a dreamlike state, I found myself making my way out to the sunporch, where I found Owen sitting mutely, as though awaiting a verdict. He'd neglected to turn on a light, and I felt the half darkness hiding his dear and reassuringly familiar features from me would make what I had to say easier. At first I stumbled a bit over what to say, as though the wine had reasserted a haze of fogginess over my brain, but then the words came with less effort, and I felt a burden suddenly lifting from me. I would no longer be vulnerable to whatever the future could hurl at me. Perhaps it had not been what Marjorie had had in mind, but I felt as though alone I could steel myself to a veritable state of invincibility, that if I cared for no one in particular, I could never again be faced with a profound loss.

"I won't leave you high and dry," I concluded to Owen, inadvertently using a term of the sea. "I told you I'd help you get an apartment of your own, and I meant it. I'll take care of the rent until you're able to support yourself, and I'll set you up with a doctor to help you . . . cope with this situation you're in. OK?"

I barely perceived his nod.

"It's been like some magical game, Owen, but I can see now why it has to end," I said, and walked from the room. I thought I heard Owen's soft voice behind me, *It wasn't a game to me,* but I kept walking because I wanted to maintain my new self-image as Owen's savior by this granting of his freedom and not the one of betrayer that lingered beneath.

I was still on the same plateau of numbness as I walked with Marjorie to the door. At her car she embraced me with the words "I'm sure you've done the right thing," and I watched her drive away until her taillights disappeared in the dark.

It was quite cold outside, but a fresh, moist breeze that was warmer than the air around it fanned against my cheek. A change in the weather, I thought, and that, together with the sounds of the waves rolling, ever rolling, on the shore so close at hand reminded me of all the walks I'd taken along the strand with Owen and the evenings we'd shared in front of the fire. Oddly enough, when I saw myself now in the quietly euphoric state of my ideal dream world, it was Owen's face I peered into with his light eyes and pale hair and not Peter's.

When I got back inside the house, it was like a spell had broken. While I had listened to Marjorie, I'd been incapable of thinking for myself. Now my thoughts came in gasps, but at least my mind seemed to be starting to function again. I realized that what I had said to Owen had only been an echo of what Marjorie had spoken; I had not been relaying to him my own thoughts and feelings. What I'd said, I thought in horror, actually ran counter to everything I knew to be right for me. I had done something monumentally stupid and morally, ethically, and self-destructively wrong! This couldn't be happening, I thought. Had I actually sabotaged my own last chance at happiness? I knew I had been afraid — of loss, of trusting to fate again. But life was a risk and only a fool would try to outwit what it had in store by creating an existence without any warmth or caring at all. Hot tears fell down my face, and they seemed to wake my heart more fully yet from whatever had held it enthralled. *What was I thinking?* I wanted to scream. Owen was nothing more and nothing less than exactly what he claimed to be. I had to find him and tell him that I believed him, that I couldn't bear for him to go, that I'd been an idiot and hoped he could forgive me. I was frantic to repair the damage I had wrought before it was too late.

All these thoughts zoomed through my head in a matter of moments as I stood in panicked remorse just inside the door. I took a deep breath and prayed that Owen would be near so that I could explain my idiocy. I called to him, convinced now more than ever that I wanted him in my life, for the rest of my life. I couldn't imagine what had caused me to parrot Marjorie's words to him, but now I only needed to see Owen's face to know that I had another shot at happiness, that twice-in-a-lifetime did exist.

Getting no response, I ran to the sunporch,

then from room to room, calling his name. I wanted to explain, to apologize, to put right before it was too late the special happiness we had found together. He wasn't upstairs packing. Nor was he brooding in the parlor or out on the sunporch. I knew then that there could only be one place he would be. The sea, I thought, and fled in panic from the house.

Outside, the waves steadily mocked my alarm. The weather had well and truly changed with the moist breeze I had felt earlier, and flakes of snow eddied, dipped, and whirled as I continued to call Owen's name. I knew I was screaming then as my throat felt like I'd swallowed broken glass.

At last, as the nearly full moon slipped from behind a bank of clouds, I caught sight of him in the water. The sea had swallowed him to the shoulders, and I feared he would never hear me above the incessant pushing and pulling of the surf. Icy green water veined white with foam lapped at my ankles as I called his name again and yet again, and finally fell sobbing to my knees. My histrionics were not without effect, and I looked up to find him at my side.

"Please. Get inside," he said, disheartenment in every feature of his face.

"Come with me. I didn't mean what I said."

"I have to go back. I shouldn't be here. My being here is either a mistake or a punishment. If it's a mistake, I've got to try to get back where I belong."

"You'll freeze to death."

He didn't answer, but only looked at me in abject misery.

"You can't swim."

"That's the idea."

"You'll drown!"

"Maybe that's what I have to do."

"What's so terrible about staying here *now?*"

"If I can't be here with you . . . I have to go. Please, can't you see that?"

"Why?"

"Because we never should have met."

"Why, Owen? Please tell me why."

"Because I love you."

I caught my breath as a million half-formed thoughts fell into place in my mind. I was stunned, yet immensely pleased. All my hopes for the future were renewed. I knew now that I had wanted to hear *these* words from *this* man for weeks. If only I could make him forget what I'd said inside.

Looking into the eyes of this strange wayfarer, I thought how brave and steadfast he was to have competed all this time with a ghost. I was humbled by his constancy and devotion. My own wavering and denial in comparison seemed weak, but now was my chance to prove myself.

"Why didn't you tell me how you felt?" I asked, feeling warmth at his words but knowing full well that it was me and me alone that had kept him out and prevented his telling me before this.

"Didn't you ever see some grand house or

luxury and say to yourself, that's not for me, then? You're a lady. You have all these fine things, your own home; you've studied at a university. . . ."

"Then, I'm smart enough to know when I'm in love, aren't I?" The words came out naturally, though I'd never so much as allowed them to form in my mind before, but they felt absolutely right.

I expected him to beam with pleasure, but he only smiled gently and said, "It could never last, Peggy. Your family . . ."

"Come on, Owen. Fight for what you want!"

"I can't, Peggy. Your own mother, that day she came to the house, said to look at what you were used to and to think about what I had to offer you. I have nothing, Peggy."

"You're wrong."

"She said that while I'm around I could be scaring off someone who'd be good for you."

"And I sent *you* away because I was afraid I'd lose you. Marjorie said you'd only lost your memory and that someone would eventually find you, and you'd go back to another life — maybe with someone else."

"You mean you don't believe . . . ?"

"That's the funny part. I *do* believe you. I don't know why I listen to other people instead of my own heart. Owen, I love you. I want to be with you always, and if you leave me, I think I'll die."

He threw his arms around me, and I could feel him shivering with the cold. He was soaking wet,

but I knew we wouldn't go in until we had re-
solved this for all time.

"Oh, Peggy, if you hadn't found me . . ."

"I was meant to find you. You have redeemed
me, Owen. You've brought me back from wherever I was. So, you see, I was lost, too."

"Peggy . . ." he began, then faltered.

"Say what you want."

"I want to marry you."

"Yes."

"What?"

"Yes."

He grinned and, picking me up, whirled me
around. By then I was almost as wet as he was,
and I prevailed upon him to finally go back inside. We ran to the house, hand in hand, and I
felt giddier than I had ever felt in my life. And it
was grand.

It wasn't until we were back inside that I fully
realized just how cold we'd gotten. Owen could
hardly speak, his teeth were chattering so badly.
And, this time, a cup of coffee wasn't going to do
it. I suggested we each take a long, hot bath, and
Owen agreed. We parted on the upstairs landing
with a heady but bashful kiss before heading our
separate ways.

It was, of course, the closest physical contact
we'd ever made, and as our cold lips met, I nearly
broke into a giddy grin contemplating all the
new facets of each other we had to explore. I
hadn't thought of him before as I was thinking of

him now, and I believe the only things that prevented us from being more forward were the newness of the experience and the sure knowledge that a little patience would be amply rewarded.

When we drew apart, our eyes locked for a moment, and I imagine as much joy showed in mine as showed in his. I smiled, nearly giggling with pleasure, and all but danced down the hall, turning around several times, as though to ensure that he wasn't just a wonderful dream. I caught him glancing back as well, and if I hadn't still been shivering, I think we would have tried for a less shy demonstration of affection right then and there.

I quickly thawed in a tub of bubbles and warm water but decided to forego the decadent luxury of a prolonged soak. I was much too anxious to get back with Owen for that.

I showed up at his door in my white terry cloth robe, nervously expectant, almost drunk with the prospect of things to come. When he answered my knock, clad only in a towel, I saw in him once again the stranger I'd found on the beach, and I realized that I'd been in love with him almost from the start.

Although he'd been in my life for what seemed like ages, I now moved him into my room and my heart. At first I felt unsure; for all my bravado, Peter was the only man I'd ever been with. I could tell that he, too, was hesitant.

"A century is a long time . . . you understand

". . . to go without . . ." he said, fumbling for acceptable words, as he held me in his arms.

"So is two years," I agreed, and when we finally took each other, it really did feel as if we were meant to be together, and I thanked my lucky stars for the glitch in time that had brought him to me.

I expected a shy and gentle lover, and he was — the first time. We lay together, two latter-day descendants of kilted island warriors, cast up on America's shores, but nearly in heaven. To see us then, we might have been taken for statuary — not for our serene stillness or ideal beauty, but for the alabaster whiteness of our skin. The golden remains of the suns of more than a century ago were gradually fading from his face, torso, and arms, leaving in their place the pale translucence of the rest of his flesh. I like to think in our state of bliss that we were, for the moment, beautiful.

I had convinced myself that I could do without such intimacy — as a mark of my loyalty to Peter and as penance for having too much happiness too early in life. I knew then that I'd been wrong.

We lay side by side in a state of euphoric relaxation in what was now *our* room, and I turned to Owen and smiled. I rubbed my hand along the bristles on his face that tickled when we kissed. The scar on his lip, now painless, would begin to fade now, and the bruise along his ribs was now only a yellow reminder of the long ago before we were lovers.

We curled up as if to sleep, but the joy I felt made me feel anything but tired. I grinned like an idiot in spite of myself, then turned to Owen with mock seriousness.

"Stay on your own side and don't snore, and we'll get along fine," I warned. He threw a pillow at me and, well, one thing led to another. He certainly proved that he could overcome being bashful. Afterward, we finally slept for a time, but woke a few hours later frisky as young animals in the spring.

In the morning he held me with my head taking its natural place against his shoulder, contentment welling between us.

"Owen," I said after a moment, "I had my tubes tied — for medical reasons."

"What does that mean?"

"It means that I can't have children," I said sadly.

"My being here is miracle enough. I'm not about to ask for another. Besides, I think our having a family might upset the natural order of things too much. Our finding each other is enough."

I smiled, relieved, and nestled against his warmth.

We were happily silent for a time before he said, "I never thought I'd have a woman of my own."

"*Have?* You don't *have* me."

"I know it's not much of a bargain, but you can have me in exchange," he suggested with a smile that was almost feline.

"It's a deal."

# CHAPTER 12

It was with languid contentment that I finally rose to wash my hair and dress. I had heard Owen get up earlier, but after a kiss, was satisfied to fall back into a peaceful sleep.

When I got downstairs, Owen was standing at the kitchen counter slicing vegetables.

"What on earth are you doing?" I asked.

"Making soup. You don't want to get sick after being in the cold water last night, do you?"

"I thought we'd found an adequate way to warm up," I said with a smile as I played with his hair, comparing strands of different colors. We ended up necking like teenagers before I finally got busy helping him with the project at hand. All I had to do was look at him to elicit a ridiculous grin on his part. Then I'd start to laugh, and we'd be at it again. It wasn't until after a tumble on and off the living room sofa that we were composed enough to think about anything other than our pleasure in each other.

Back in the kitchen, I said to Owen, "You know, this is your home now. You've got to stop acting like a guest and really be part of the household."

"You have more chores for me to do?"

"No, Owen. You do more than your share."

"Then, what do you mean?"

"For example, you could let me do *all* of your laundry — not just your shirts and jeans — instead of hand washing your socks and stuff out in the sink with bar soap."

I was surprised to see that he could still be embarrassed with me.

"All right," he agreed just as the phone rang.

"And you can start right now by answering that." It would be the first time he'd done so since he'd lived under my roof. I absently listened to him talk as I stirred the soup.

"Hello," he began awkwardly, but soon seemed to forget the awkward newness of the medium. "Yes? . . . Yes, I'm still here. . . . All right . . . Of course . . . Yes . . . Good-bye."

"What was that all about?" I asked when he'd competently hung up the receiver.

"It was Marjorie. She's coming over."

"Oh. Why didn't you tell her we were busy or something?"

"Because we're not, and because she said she needed to talk to both of us, and because she's your sister, Peggy, and you have to make things right between you."

"All right, but do you know what she wants to talk about?"

"No."

We didn't have to wait long to hear Marjorie pull up beside the house. I met her, Bill, and Joe Maglia at the door. I was surprised that she hadn't come alone, and I wondered if the men were there as reinforcements, or whether she

299

didn't feel prepared to have a one-on-one with me now that I'd had time to think about her arguments of the previous night. I was cordial but still ill at ease.

"Peggy," she began, "I won't blame you if you feel like throwing me out. I'm really sorry about yesterday, about not trusting you to make your own decisions, but I have something really important to share with you." She talked rapidly, as though she knew she only had a limited amount of my time and patience immediately at her disposal. She was right.

"Owen and I have something to tell you, too," I said firmly enough that she suggested I go first. "We're going to get married," I said with a look on my face that I hoped would indicate to her that I'd brook no argument. Knowing Marjorie the way I did, I still expected something of a dispute.

Instead of the flack I had anticipated, Marjorie unexpectedly threw her arms around me, offering her congratulations. I was surprised to say the least. I heard Bill behind me give Owen a slap on the back and a hearty "you son of a gun" by way of felicitations. Joe stood off to the side, smiling, but still out of place at such a family occasion. At last, Marjorie broke away to explain his presence.

"Peggy, Owen, you've already met Joe," she said unnecessarily and a little nervously. "This is embarrassing, but I hope you'll forgive me when all is said and done."

I raised my eyebrows by way of telling her to continue.

"Well," she began uneasily, "Joe's not really a graduate student — at N.Y.U. or anywhere else. Actually, he's a detective I hired," she added, and Joe, sensing how foolish she felt, I guess, took over from there. Bill just grinned at Owen and at me as if to tell us he was in on some great secret and wouldn't we be surprised to know what it was?

"Back in September Marjorie hired me," Joe began as we all assembled comfortably in the living room. "She told me that her younger sister had taken up with some guy who had made some pretty strange claims about himself. She also said she'd like me to try to find out who he really was so that she could disprove the stories he'd been telling her sister. To put it simply, I was hired to prove you were lying to Peggy," he said to Owen, "but it turned out to be a lot more complicated than I expected."

He stood up, as if to give a presentation, and said, "I apologize if this comes off like a high school book report, but just bear with me."

My eyes darted to Owen, to Marjorie, to Bill. This was a pretty wild twist, in my opinion. Although I wrote mysteries, it never would have occurred to me, even in the beginning, to investigate Owen's claims systematically. Some detective I'd make.

"The first time I talked with Owen," Joe continued, "I hoped he'd let something slip of the real truth of his life and I'd have something to go on. I even had his fingerprints run, but they weren't on file anywhere that I could find."

"What? Did you get them off a water glass or something?" I asked sarcastically.

"No, actually, I brought an ink pad and asked him to give me a set of prints and, after I explained what I meant, he didn't mind."

I think my jaw dropped to think of all this going on without my knowledge.

"Go on," I said.

"Well, having had no luck with traditional avenues of investigation, I decided, on a whim, to see if there really had been a guy named Owen Sinclair who sailed on clipper ships."

"And?" I asked, impatient for the other shoe to drop. Owen, beside me, looked serene and unconcerned, and I gave his hand a squeeze as I tried to corral my impatience.

"Well, Owen had given me a lot of information, but I still had some more questions. That's why I came back the second time. Anyhow, I had a long talk with a nice woman at the county museum in Yarmouth, and she was able to do some research for me in their archives and in old parish records." He stopped to open his briefcase, whose presence my mind had barely registered to that point. He pulled out a sheaf of papers and, removing their paper clip, began to read. "These are photocopies of, first, the birth record of one 'Owen Robert Sinclair of Yarmouth, Nova Scotia, born January 4, 1825; parents — Murdoch Sinclair, born 1800 near John o'Groats, Caithness, Scotland, and Charlotte McLaren Sinclair, born 1806 in Yarmouth.' "

Owen's smile was bittersweet as he heard the names, but all I could think was *Robert?* — what an ordinary name. I kept forgetting that he was an ordinary man in his own time and that only chance had made an anomaly of him. He was at once common and unique, not exactly a "noble savage," but pretty basic all the same, a natural product of a man and a woman, un-altered by orthodontics or circumcision.

"There was also a marriage license for 1839 for the same Charlotte McLaren Sinclair," Joe continued, "to one Ezekiel Campbell. The last record the woman in Yarmouth could find for me up there was dated September 1853, for 'Owen Sinclair of Yarmouth, A.B., lost at sea, body not recovered.' "

"A.B.?" I asked, trying not to let the words of death affect me.

"Able-bodied seaman," Owen supplied.

Joe consulted his notes. "As opposed to 'ordinary seaman,' " he said. "It meant you knew your ass from a hole in the ground on a sailing ship."

"Please go on," Owen prompted, frowning at the language Joe had chosen to use in mixed company.

"Well, I got kind of stuck at that point. Between this woman in Canada and myself, we tried to access logs from old ships to see if we could find out anything else. No luck. I sent photos of Owen's clothes and the copy of his drawing up to Yarmouth, and it was suggested that I talk to an expert on nautical art and antiques at the maritime museum in Boston. When I sent a photocopy of Owen's drawing up there, their expert, a guy named Arnesson, was really excited to talk to me. I decided to take a drive up and, man, did I ever hit the mother lode then. Right away Dr. Arnesson recognized Owen's signature and showed me a whale's tooth carved almost identically to the drawing Owen had done for you, Peggy. The clothes, he said, were right for the time period, too, but the drawing was what really interested him. He told me the piece they had in their collection had come to the museum in 1970 from an old man who'd gotten it, together with an old sea chest with a great painting of a ship inside the lid, and its other contents, from his great-grandfather who'd also been an A.B. in the great age of sail.

"The great-grandfather's name was" — Joe consulted his notes again — "Denis-Philippe Laframboise."

"Frenchy," Owen said almost too low to hear.

"Well, this Denis-Philippe Laframboise, who, incidentally, lived to be ninety" — at this piece of information Owen genuinely smiled — "gave this sea chest to his great-grandson Charles Laframboise with the following letter, dated 1906."

Joe then read the letter to us, which was moving in spite of his New York accent.

Dear Charles,

You have asked me of my days at sea, and I have told you what I know. I am an old man now and pray to soon join your great-grandmother in heaven. I have nothing much to leave to you or your brothers, but you are my dearest living relation and I want to give something to you that I have kept for many years.

This sea chest belonged to a shipmate of mine, Owen Sinclair, a resident now of Fiddler's Green. In case you don't know, Charlie boy, that's heaven to the likes of me and other sailors.

Fifty years and more have passed since poor Owen, not much older than yourself, was swept into the sea off the coast of Slea Head Point. He was a good friend to me and an able seaman.

After Owen was gone, members of our crew got it in mind to divide his property among them. Under the threat of my knife, it was conceded that Owen's belongings should come to me, who knew him best, Owen having no family.

Perhaps I will be seeing my dear young friend again soon. I believe the angels are caring for him now as they never did in life.

Take care of these things I have kept so long.

Your loving great-grandfather,
Denis-Philippe Laframboise

305

I felt tears glisten in my eyes as Owen heard the words of his companion of so long ago, perhaps the only communication from the past he'd ever have.

"But that's not all," Joe said with a touch of pride. I guess giving someone back his past was more gratifying than proving the adulterous behavior of errant spouses. He handed Owen a photograph, an eight-by-ten black-and-white reproduction of a daguerreotype. Owen said nothing, but when he finally passed it to me, I could see a tear rolling down its glossy surface.

I knew at once who the couple had to be — his mother and her husband, Mr. Campbell. His mother was light-eyed and fair like her son, apple-cheeked, of good peasant stock, and absolutely lovely. She looked as though she would have liked to laugh, if only once life had given her a reason. Ezekiel Campbell towered over his seated wife, all sideburns and self-righteousness. He certainly looked large enough to scare the fifteen-year-old Owen had been half to death if he'd wanted.

"May I keep this?" Owen asked.

"Sure, if it's OK with Marjorie. She paid for everything," Joe answered.

"Of course, Owen," Marjorie volunteered, obviously touched now that she believed in Owen and his losses.

Without a word, Joe passed his last paper to Owen and me. I caught my breath and covered my mouth with my hand as if to stifle my jubilant surprise as I saw in the old daguerreotype the face of my love.

There he was, staring ahead through pale eyes behind his glasses, that in black and white might even have matched. He wore a white shirt with long collar points overlapping a short dark jacket, a scarf at his throat, leather boots to the knee, and white trousers that buttoned like, well, like a sailor's. On his head he wore a black leather hat — flat-topped and broad-brimmed, with two ribbons hanging down the back.

"You look like a real sailor," I said with all the pride and affection I felt.

"Not as much as I wanted to," Owen said. "When I joined the crew of the *Glen Rover*, the first thing I did was get my ear pierced, but it got so sore I took the ring out and then I lost it. I think there's still a scar." There were scars, I knew, both inside and out. And, in my heart, my mind, or my soul, I, too, bore the marks of the jagged edges that had so recently mended together, but we were going to be all right. I knew this as surely as I'd ever known anything.

"I wanted to get tattooed, too, like my idea of a real sailor, but Mrs. Arniston begged me to promise I wouldn't, so I never did."

"Is that her?" I asked, pointing to the seated woman in the photograph.

"Aye, and that's Captain Arniston," he said, indicating the man standing beside him in the daguerreotype. Both Arnistons were well-fed, upstanding citizens in late middle age, dressed in black, the very picture of prosperity and propriety.

"How old were you when this was taken?" I asked.

"Eighteen. We'd just returned to Yarmouth, and Captain Arniston took me to get this made as a gift for me. I'd planned to give it to my mother. I never expected to see it again."

"Oh, one more thing that might interest you," Joe said, "the maritime museum runs month-long voyages on an old restored clipper in the summer. You can pay to sign on as part of the crew, or, with your experience, you could probably land a job as an instructor."

"That sounds great, doesn't it?" I asked enthusiastically.

"Aye," Owen answered with a pleased smile.

"Full-time, though, it looks as though Owen may be trading one kind of canvas for another," I announced. "Darren Hurley's interested in showing his work at both his galleries."

"That's great," Bill said.

"Peggy, Owen," Marjorie began, "I just want you to know how sorry I am for, well, you know. . . . But if I hadn't been so skeptical, we never would have found all this great old stuff," she added in her own defense. "Anyway, I want you to know that I'll help you in any way I can, as your sister," she said, looking at both of us, and I think it warmed Owen's heart to feel that he had a family again at last, "but also as your lawyer. It won't be easy getting a marriage license without a birth certificate, and you can't use this one," she said, gesturing to Joe's pile of documentary evidence. "Surely you can see that. Maybe we can get Arlene to fib a little and certify that Owen has lost his memory or something. At any rate, Bill and I will help you get this straightened out, one way or another. I promise."

I hugged her, then she and Owen tentatively put their arms around each other in an embrace that was so awkward and chaste as to be almost funny. Bill and Owen shook hands, and we all thanked Joe for his labors.

"What smells so good?" Marjorie finally asked, breaking up the maudlin scene while I still had my composure intact.

"Owen and I are making soup," I said. "Well, Owen is mostly," I corrected. "Vegetable, I think. Why don't you stay for lunch?"

All agreed, and we sat contentedly, talking of things to come, but I scarcely listened, my joy in living was so loud in my ears. I'd never thought I'd be capable of loving again, and if, by some miracle I was, it would have to be someone so special as to make me stop seeing Peter every-where I looked. Owen was such a man — sin-gular in many ways. But, I couldn't help but feel proud, too, of the resiliency of the human heart, of my own heart.

It had started with being needed, a call I would rise to even in grief. I then had found I could handle more, in fact, wanted more. I felt grateful to Peter for showing me from the very first what love was supposed to be, so that I had no bad habits to unlearn. Our love had been so strong that even when I thought I would be crushed by the weight of Peter's death, my heart could not really be broken. My ability to love had been dormant, maybe, but not destroyed. I thanked Peter, too, for the part I liked to think he played in bringing Owen and me together.

It was funny really, I thought, looking out on the snow that rimed the beach, that the colder it had gotten, the more I had thawed toward Owen and everything else in general, and I looked forward now to the winter that was nearly here and to many springs, summers, and autumns beyond.

I'd learned no large truths about life, death, or timelessness, only that I could love again. And, as the dear prattle went on about me, I heard in my head the lyrics I'd once sung to my love before I knew enough to admit that that was what he was.

> The water is wide, I can't cross o'er,
> And neither have I wings to fly,
> Build me a boat that can carry two,
> And both shall row, my love and I.

It was time to grab an oar.